A
fallen
STAR

A. M. KUSI

Published by A. M. Kusi 2020

amkusinovels@gmail.com

Visit our website at www.amkusi.com

Editor: Anna Bishop of CREATING ink

Sensitivity Edit: Renita McKinney of A Book A Day

Proofreader: Judy's Proofreading

Cover Design: Regina Wamba of ReginaWamba.com

ISBN: 978-1-949781-15-1

OTHER BOOKS BY A. M. KUSI

Glass Secrets

(Shattered Cove Series Book 2)

Defying Gravity

(Shattered Cove Series Book 3)

The Lighthouse Inn

(Shattered Cove Series Book 4)

His True North

(Shattered Cove Series Book 5)

The Orchard Inn (FREE on all retailers)

(Book 1 in The Orchard Inn Romance Series)

Conflict of Interest

(Book 2 in The Orchard Inn Romance Series)

Her Perfect Storm

(Book 3 in The Orchard Inn Romance Series)

For a complete list of all our books, visit:

WWW.AMKUSI.COM/BOOKS

"No healthy relationship will ever require us to sacrifice our core values or become needless to make it work. A true partnership is life-giving, not draining. It is a reflection of two people committed to honesty, authenticity and truth. That doesn't mean there will never be conflict, but even when times are hard, both people will have space to be seen, heard, valued, loved and respected."

– Woman Rising

"Family dysfunction rolls down from generation to generation, like a fire in the woods, taking down everything in its path until one person in one generation has the courage to turn and face the flames. That person brings peace to their ancestors and spares the children that follow."

– Terry Real

GET A FREE SHORT NOVEL

Join our newsletter to get a FREE short novel that's not available on any retailer. Plus updates about new releases, giveaways, pre-orders, sneak peeks, and more.

Visit the website below to join now.

WWW.AMKUSI.COM/NEWSLETTER

TABLE OF CONTENTS

1

REMY

Remy shut the door to her friend's Jeep as she adjusted the skintight jeans over her hips.

"Come on, Remy. Don't look so nervous. They'll think your ID is a fake," Emma said, giving her a once-over.

"I've never done anything like this before," Remy admitted, squeezing her clammy hands into fists at her side.

"It's a bar, babe. You're acting like you're the one who's going to be performing." Her friend shook her head.

"Well, I . . . I . . ." Remy tried to come up with some excuse other than she had never scribbled outside the lines before. Nothing about their night would be illegal.

"Come on, Remy. Summer is here. We survived high school, graduated—despite my odds." She laughed, hands reaching wide as she gestured to the busy parking lot. "The world is our oyster. Let's just celebrate life. Remy Stone, Miss Goody Two-shoes, you need to learn how to loosen up and have fun."

"Are you done teasing me?" Remy crossed her arms.

"You're gonna be the hottest thing in there." Emma winked. She saw through Remy like no one else did.

Emma was the total opposite of Remy in every way. Where Emma was an outgoing performer, Remy preferred books and conversation. Emma had a fair complexion with blond hair and blue eyes, compared to Remy's midnight tone and brown eyes.

"Do you need some liquid courage before we go in there?" Emma asked, slipping a flask from her purse.

"No, thanks," Remy answered as her best friend took a long sip before returning the container to her bag.

"Okay, let's do this!" Emma grabbed her hand and led her towards the neon lights of The Shipwreck.

Perhaps it was an omen—the name of the bar, mixed with the nervous butterflies filling her tummy. The hair on the back of her arms stood on end, an awareness tickling her spine. Her belly twisted into knots as she wiped her sweaty hands on her pants. She drew a deep breath.

The bouncer outside asked to see their IDs. He was a big, muscular man, covered in tattoos, with a shaved head. "How old are you?" he asked, scrutinizing her face and the plastic card.

"Eigh-eighteen," she managed. A part of her wanted him to turn her away.

After another minute of his hard stare, he gave back her card and stamped her flesh with a large black X. "Be safe," he said, nodding towards the door.

Remy's mouth opened in surprise as they entered. She wasn't sure what she had expected the bar to look like, but this surely wasn't it. Overhead lights pointed towards the stage where Emma's bandmates were already setting up a drum kit. Backlit fish tanks were positioned in the walls, illuminating the room in a blue glow. A skeleton with a pirate's hat sat in one of the chairs at a table. The walls were distressed to look like they were really inside the belly of a ship.

"I'm gonna go get ready with the guys," Emma said. "You okay here?"

"Yes. I'll go sit at the bar." This wasn't as scary as she'd thought. Maybe some of her friend's confidence was rubbing off on her.

"Look at you, being all brave." Emma poked her shoulder playfully.

"Must be something about this place. It's cooler than I'd expected it would be." Remy smiled genuinely as her shoulders relaxed.

"Well, at least you won't be alone over there. Don't look now, but the man you have been crushing on since I've known you is having a drink."

Remy's stomach flipped and twisted with giant butterflies clamoring to get out. "Mikel is here?" She whispered his name like it was something sacred.

"Yes."

"He probably won't even notice me."

"I think it's a little late for that. He hasn't taken his eyes off you since you walked in. And trust me, babe, that look in his brown eyes tells me he's definitely noticing you."

"God, I hope so." *Oops. Did I say that out loud?*

Emma smirked. "Go on. Go get your drink. I'll see you after the show." She kissed her on the cheek and left.

Remy turned towards the bar, glancing at the handsome man she'd grown up with. Their eyes met for a brief moment as an electric current wound around her. She quickly focused her attention on the empty stool on the opposite end of the bar to Mikel. On wobbly legs, she managed to make it to the seat.

"What can I get ya, hon?" the bartender asked. She wiped

a cloth over the bar, the white tattoos weaving around her arm like delicate lacework as she moved. She tucked one of the loose raven-black tendrils of hair behind her ear as she looked expectantly towards Remy.

"Just a Pepsi, please."

As the pretty woman filled her glass, an invisible blaze burned in Remy's body. She tilted her head in search of a heating vent. *Nothing.* As her eyes swept the room, she met Mikel's dark pools again and she was sucked in. Lost were the sounds of the mic checks and the bartender leaving her soda in front of her. Everything was a buzz in the background as she studied his handsome tanned face as he walked up to her. Rough stubble peppered his strong jaw. Mikel Evans stood in front of her—six feet of broody man towering over her. He moved one of his muscular arms onto the bar, half caging her in. Heat and yearning like she had never known overtook her body. She clenched her thighs together, embarrassed by her sudden lust. One look and this man had the power to rule her . . . or destroy her.

"Does your brother know you're here?" he asked in his sexy gravelly voice.

She hoped to god he couldn't hear the thundering beat in her chest. She inhaled a deep breath and channeled her best Emma. "Andre isn't my keeper."

His eyes flashed and the corner of his mouth turned up. She'd surprised him. She was usually the quiet shy kid who tagged along with him and their brothers, Andre and Bently. "So, if I called him right now and told him where you were . . ."

"I'm a grown woman, Mikel. I haven't broken any laws to get in here. I came to support my friend and watch her sing her heart out. I'm not a little girl who needs you to keep an eye on her." She wasn't sure where her courage was coming from.

"You certainly have grown up. When did that happen?" he asked, his scorching gaze raking over her body. Was he finally noticing her as someone other than the little sister to his business partner?

Before she could give a response, he turned and walked back to his spot at the other end of the bar. Deflated, she focused on her drink and took a sip. The bubbles tickled her throat as she tried to regain control of herself. Disappointment weighed heavily on her.

"Three dollars, honey."

Remy dug in her pocket for a five and handed it to her. "Keep the change."

"Thanks."

The lights dimmed. The drum kit crashed as Emma's band began to play. Remy turned to watch the show, trying to ignore the firestorm blazing in her body. Her friend's voice was sweet and light and full of emotion, melding with the rock music.

After several songs, the bar became packed. The dance floor was filled with bodies seductively writhing together. A flush of heat rose to Remy's cheeks. This was her first time out by herself this late at night. The first time she had lied by omission to her parents who thought their daughter was sleeping over at Emma's with no extracurricular activities.

"Care to dance?" A deep voice came from her side. The guy was cute. He had that boy-next-door vibe going for him.

She glanced over his shoulder. Mikel was talking to a woman in a red dress. Jealousy boiled her insides. She was only gonna live once, right? Maybe she needed to heed Emma's advice and take some chances. Besides, this could be her opportunity to show Mikel just how grown up she was.

"Sure," she agreed.

"I'm Brad."

"Remy," she answered his unspoken question.

He smirked and took her hand, leading her to the center of the crowd.

Feeling unsure, she found Emma's eyes. Her friend shot her an encouraging wink.

Brad grabbed her hips and pulled her closer to him. She rested her palms on his shoulders, stiffly. He led her as they swayed, his body getting closer inch by inch. She glanced over his shoulder. Mikel stared at her again.

Brad turned her around so that her back was facing him as he ground himself against her butt. She wasn't sure what to do. *Should I move with him? Oh god! Is that his penis?*

She was used to school dances with friends; Emma had been her date to the prom. Besides a few middle school boys who'd stood a foot from her, with their hands on her hips, this was the extent of her experience dancing with the male species.

His growing hardness against her backside was getting awkward fast. She tried to turn around, but his hands held her hips in place. She searched the room, nervous and anxious, no longer able to see Mikel or Emma in the wall of people surrounding them. This had definitely been a bad idea. She should just wait until the song ended and then make her escape. He had asked for a dance and she had said yes; it was too late to stop now. Wasn't it? She didn't want to make a scene.

His palms moved over her belly towards her breasts. She panicked—the word "Stop" stuck in her throat. She'd gotten in over her head. It was getting harder to breathe. "Stop," finally spilled out of her mouth, swallowed by the loud music.

He released her suddenly and she turned around to apologize.

Brad was in a pile on the floor holding his face. As he lifted his palm, the blue lights illuminated smears of blood pouring from his nose, which appeared purple.

What happened?

Her arm was grabbed by a blistering force that pulled her from the crowd, towards the exit. She should have been terrified, being dragged out of the bar by Mikel—The truth was, it gave her an entirely different sensation.

The cold metal of his truck met with her back as she was pressed against it. His possessiveness only added to the growing heat between her thighs. She should have feared the way his brown eyes turned black as he stared at her. She didn't, because he was Mikel Evans—her dark angel.

She had never seen him this upset before, nor his eyes so wild. He leaned towards her, the light from the bar casting him in shadows. His mouth moved only an inch from hers, the smell of hard liquor on his breath. This was the moment she had dreamed about since she was old enough to have a crush. She wanted this kiss from him. Craved it.

He seemed to hesitate. His exhales tickled and teased her. She sensed the war going on inside him. The pained expression on his face. He wanted to kiss her, but something held him back.

Fear.

Remy could be brave for him. She wanted to be everything for him. If only he would let her.

She leaned in the rest of the way.

The moment their lips met, an explosion of sensations erupted between them. Hot and cold. Dark and light. Right and wrong. He took control, sliding his tongue into her mouth. She opened for him, as if she had any choice. Her body heated with lust as his rough, calloused hands cupped her face. She wrapped her arms around him, praying this moment would never end, trapped in a vortex of fantasies come to life. This was the first kiss of the century. Fireworks of their passion sparked to life from their lips meeting.

A tiny moan escaped as she pulled him closer, hanging on to his shirt for dear life.

He jolted away suddenly, stumbling back, breaking the kiss. His chest heaved as he looked at her, shaking his head. "Fuck." He ran his hand over his face in frustration and tugged at his black hair. "I'm sorry. I didn't mean to . . . Remy, I'm drunk."

She swallowed. He'd wanted this. She'd seen it in his eyes. Hadn't she?

The rejection stung. Daddy had always told her that alcohol brought out the deepest truths of a person, both the good and the bad.

"I need you to drive," he commanded, his face becoming an emotionless mask. All signs of vulnerability were gone.

She climbed into the driver's side without hesitation. After pulling her phone from her pocket, she texted Emma while he walked around to the passenger side. Adrenaline and excitement quaked through her body. Her hands shook as she spelled out the words.

Remy: *Just want you to know I'm safe. Got a ride home with Mikel. See you when you get back.*

He got in and shut the door. "Let's go."

2

———

MIKEL

Mikel woke with a pounding headache. Unfortunately, he hadn't drunk enough to forget that incredible forbidden kiss. Remy Stone had matured into a heart-stopping woman. The moment she'd walked into that bar he had been drawn to her like a magnet. He hadn't recognized her at first as he'd admired her curvy figure from afar. He'd noticed Emma and his heart had sunk at the realization that the sexy dark seductress was the one woman more off-limits to him than any other. His best friend and business partner Andre's little sister.

Of course, he had to go and kiss her and fuck everything up. Remy was a good girl. She would never be the one-and-done type—not that he would even entertain that idea with her. Remy was a dove. Pure and innocent. Not someone he should have put his filthy hands on. Everything he touched was soiled by his past. He couldn't do that to his dove. *His*. As if he actually had a claim to her.

He'd sobered up enough to drive by the time they got to her house. Those brown eyes had timidly looked over at him

9

with caution before he'd wordlessly sent her inside where she'd be safe. *From me.*

Grabbing the half-empty bottle of Jack Daniel's, he pulled the little baggy from his pants pocket lying on the floor. He swallowed two oxy—just enough to take the edge off.

He could lie to himself and say his actions last night were the cocktail of adrenaline and vodka—and whatever else was in those blue pills June had passed him—but the truth was, he wanted Remy. He'd had a taste of her, and that was enough to make him rock-hard this morning. Her skin had been buttery soft and she'd smelled like pure heaven. That little moan she'd let out—so sweet and innocent. She had no idea of the terribly bad things he wanted to do to her.

A knock startled Mikel out of his thoughts.

"Yeah?"

"You decent?" Bently called through the door.

Mikel slipped the pills under his mattress before he answered, "Yup."

Bently walked in. "You almost ready?" his older brother asked, studying his messy room. He frowned when his eyes narrowed in on the bottle of whiskey. *Always the cop.*

"For what?" Mikel asked, his brain fuzzy, though the headache was beginning to dull.

"The barbecue at the beach with Andre. Jasmine's been all set for an hour."

"Give me ten minutes," Mikel said as he rubbed the sleep from his eyes.

"Sure. Meet you there." Bently hesitated as if he wanted to say something else, but nodded and left, closing the door behind him.

Mikel jumped in his truck fifteen minutes later with a cup of coffee in hand. Jasmine opened the passenger side and climbed in.

"Thought you would have left with Bent."

She buckled herself in and placed her bag on her lap with the ever-present cell phone on top. "No one wants to hang out with the deputy's sister. The last thing I need is to show up in his truck marked 'Deputy of Shattered Cove.' Might as well say, 'Fun police.'" Jasmine brushed the black hair from her face, showing off her beautiful green eyes.

Before their mother had decided life wasn't worth living, she'd had an affair with a man from Korea—nine months before Jasmine was born. One more reason Jasmine had been a target of his father's brutal abuse.

"If your friends are that shallow, you shouldn't be hanging out with them anyways," he said, sternly.

"You sound like Bently." She smirked.

"Take it back." He laughed, lightening the mood.

Her fingers moved across her keyboard at lightning speed as he drove towards Shattered Cove's secret beach, hidden from tourists.

"Who are you texting?" he asked.

"Remy."

The name shot iced water through his veins. Had Remy told his sister about last night?

He cleared his throat. "She gonna be there?"

"Duh."

He wasn't going to get any more details from her without making it awkward and obvious, so he remained silent for the rest of the drive.

* * *

In the parking lot, Jasmine took off without a second's hesitation towards the beach that was already filing up with locals. Mikel followed her through the hot sand. Jasmine ran right up to Remy, standing at the edge of the group near the rock wall that disappeared into the ocean.

He had always admired how Remy seemed to sense a need in Jasmine for connection with an older female. He was pretty sure Remy had been the one to talk Jasmine through the whole period thing. The girls had always hung out when he, Bently, and Andre got together. Today would be like any other day with the group of friends. He just had to keep his eyes off that sweet little body in that tiny white bikini.

Who am I kidding?

He was fucked.

She waved towards him, a shy smile curving the lips he'd tasted only hours ago. Mikel turned to the picnic table. Ignoring her, like he usually did, was best.

"Guess sleeping beauty is finally awake," Andre teased, handing him a beer. No fists had been swung, so he was sure Remy hadn't said a word to him. Mikel scanned the beach already half full. A few surfers were on the water, paddling out farther.

His eyes found hers again and she waved *again,* exaggerating her arms in a bigger gesture. *She must have thought I didn't see her the first time.* He turned back towards Andre. "That's why I'm so good-looking. Don't be jealous."

Andre smirked and took a sip of his own drink. "Jealous of you? Now that's what I call a joke."

"You're both pretty. Now do you feel better?" Bently chuckled.

Andre set his beer on the picnic table. "Should we kick his ass now or later?"

Mikel put his drink next to his friend's and pulled off his shirt, leaving it in a pile on the table. "No time like the present."

Bently's eyes grew wide with shock before he started

running. Andre and Mikel chased after him and tackled him to the ground. They wrestled in a ball of sand and grit, dragging Bently towards the water as he fought against their hold. Pain erupted in Mikel's foot as Bently stomped down on it.

"Son of a bitch!" Mikel crashed on top of his brother, pulling Andre with him as a wave washed over them. They all ended up a salty sandy wet mess.

"Fuckers. I have sand in my ass crack," Bently sputtered, as they came up breathless.

Mikel and Andre laughed at him.

"'Bout time someone brought you down from your high horse," Andre teased.

Mikel walked farther out into the cool ocean waves. He swam to the first buoy. Holding his breath, he floated under the water, enjoying the cold silence that mirrored his insides. He hadn't experienced anything but pain and hollow numbness for as long as he could remember, unless it was in drug- or sex-induced stolen moments that slipped through his fingers faster than quicksand. *Except for Remy's kiss.*

His lungs burned. Relief and comfort temporarily flooded over him at the ache—at the fact that he could control this pain. *What if I just stayed down here?* Drowning seemed like a peaceful way to go.

The image of his mother's lifeless body hanging in the basement came to his mind. *I couldn't do that to Jasmine and Bently.*

Mikel relished the agony in his lungs for a few seconds longer before swimming to the surface. Remy came into view the moment he glanced at the beach. Her gaze followed him as he swam back to the shore. She was probably wondering why he was ignoring her after last night. It was for her own safety. He was dangerous. She had no idea of the beast that lived within him. The sinister wickedness lurking in the hidden recesses of his black soul.

The monster that would kill his own flesh and blood.

The rest of the afternoon passed in a dull haze. Sunshine, salt, beer, and good food. Friends and family he didn't deserve. He put on his mask, and played the happy friend and brother, joking along with them and smiling at all the right times. His mind wandered every now and then, distracted by that tiny white bikini and those dark brown curves. But he controlled it. And forced himself to look anywhere but at her.

As the day wore on, his skin began to itch. His mouth was as dry as cotton. He needed a little help to get him through. Keeping up the circus act was draining.

Mikel walked to his truck and opened the door. Patting under his seat, he found the small baggy. He washed two pills down with his beer. He stuffed the bag back under the seat and closed the door behind him.

"Whoa!" He jumped back, slapping a hand over his racing heart. Startled to see that bikini he had been ogling all day up close—those exposed dark brown legs that went on for days that he wanted to wrap around his waist. Mikel would defile her in the best of ways. "Shit, Remy. You scared me."

She was leaning against the front side of his truck with her arms crossed, pushing up those round gorgeous breasts. She had no idea what power she held. So innocent. *Dove.*

"Sorry." She looked at her feet sheepishly.

"What are you doing over here?" he asked. Had she seen him take the oxys?

"I wanted to talk about last night," she said, glancing at his face for only a moment before she looked away shyly.

His relief at not being caught mixed with anxiety. "I'm sorry about that. It was a mistake. I shouldn't have kissed you. Won't happen again."

Hurt flashed in her eyes and his chest tightened. She nodded and took a deep breath before walking towards him. Gazing up at him, she said, "The thing is, Mikel, *I* kissed *you*." Her beautiful round face showed nothing but vulnerability. She was the epitome of light and goodness. Purity and light.

Last night was fuzzy, but he was sure he'd remember if she'd been the one to kiss him. Wouldn't he?

"I could tell you wanted to kiss me, but you stopped yourself. I've thought about kissing you for as long as I can remember." Her confession was like a punch to his gut: sweet agony. Guilt slithered up his spine, twisting around his rib cage and squeezing, suffocating the sliver of hope that had blossomed from her words. He beat it down until there was no trace, like he always did. Good things were never real. They never lasted.

You filthy animal.

You disgust me.

You ruin everything you touch with your dirty hands.

He bit his lip until he tasted blood. "I'm no good for you, Remy. You should stay away from me. Besides, your brother would kill me if he found out I touched you. People like you don't belong with guys like me."

She stepped closer, erasing the distance between them. Anticipation wound thick with her nearness, making it hard to draw in a breath. Warmth radiated from her. Sunshine and light. She laid her hand over his still-racing heart. Her touch ignited a full-body blaze as she poured some of that goodness directly into his black hollow soul. Pinpricks of light scorched the hidden recesses deep within him.

Her hand trembled as she stated, "You might just be the best thing that ever happened to me."

"Hurry up, bro! Volleyball game is starting. Fifty bucks each if we win!" Andre called.

Mikel's heart throbbed as he denied himself yet again. "We're friends, Remy, and that's all we'll ever be."

He didn't bother to watch her face that would surely fall with disappointment as he walked past her. Nor did his gaze wander to hers the rest of the afternoon, but his skin tingled in awareness as her eyes bored into him.

Remy was better off without him. He'd do what was right for her and stay clear of any further entanglements.

The last thing he needed in his life was another complication.

3

MIKEL

M ikel turned the television up before taking a long sip of his cold beer. His pocket vibrated. He pulled his cell phone from his pants. The screen flashed an unknown number.

Unknown number: *Is it safe to text you? Or is this too dangerous for me as well?*

Mikel: *Depends. Who's this?*

Unknown number: *Remy.*

Surprise laced with concern spiraled in his belly. Vicious hope clawed at his insides as his chest tightened.

Mikel: *You should stay away from me.*

Remy: *I thought we were friends?*

He chuckled. Where had the shy little girl he used to know gone?

Mikel: *We are.*

Remy: *Friends have conversations, no?*

Mikel: *What could you possibly have to talk to me about?*

Remy: *I could think of a lot of things.*

She was persistent, he would give her that. Telling her

"no" was the right thing to do. But since when did he ever choose the right path in life? Those choices had been taken from him when he was born as an Evans. When he'd discovered his father's putrid secrets. When he'd taken a life.

What harm could friendly banter be?

Mikel: *Fine.*

Remy: *Is owning a business everything you hoped it would be? What else do you want for your life?*

Apparently, she was jumping right into the deep end. But what he wanted and what he was capable of were two very different things.

He'd go with a safe answer.

Mikel: *That's two questions.*

Remy: *Humor me.*

Mikel: *I love being a partner in our own business. It's more than I could have ever hoped for. In the future, I want to be successful with our contracting business, like your brother and I always talked about. You?*

Remy: *I love to bake and read. I'm working at a bakery for a year to see if that's what I want to go to school for. I like the idea of being my own boss. I'll take this gap year and then attend college for business.*

Of course she did. She wanted to bake treats—sweet things, like her.

Remy: *What is your best childhood memory?*

Pain clawed at his chest, eviscerating any lightness he'd had a moment before, shredding it into pieces. There were no happy memories from his childhood at home. Just abuse, loss, abandonment, and traumatic violence.

Fuck this. He threw the phone on the cushion as his rib cage tightened, making it harder to draw breath.

Mikel rose from the couch, switched the television off before walking up to his room. Lying on the bed, beer in hand, he dug under the mattress and swallowed the last two pills. He would need to go to Isaiah's later for a pickup. After draining the last of his beer, he set it on the ground before sinking into his sheets.

Sleep came, and for once he had a good dream—a memory. Darkness broken by the pinpricks of millions of stars. He was on the roof of his old house, peering at them with a telescope he had rigged by himself. It wasn't perfect, but it got him just a little closer to the light in the black void of his life. The book he had stolen from the library was open, guiding him as he searched for the Phoenix constellation. The story of the bird resonated with him, and provided him an escape for a little while. When he focused on the stars, he could leave his broken world. He pretended he was among the myths and legends painted in the sky in stardust, planets, and galaxies.

Mikel woke several hours later, rested. He couldn't remember the last time he hadn't had a nightmare in his sleep. It was flashbacks or nothing. He never dreamt.

He picked up his phone—seven in the evening. He needed to get some dinner and then head over to Isaiah's. He clicked Remy's message open, finally having something to answer her with.

Mikel: *Stargazing. I built a crappy telescope and tried to find the Phoenix.*

He set down his phone and jumped in the shower to get ready. He checked it one more time before he got in his car.

Remy: *Did you ever find it?*

When Bently hadn't been home, their father, Paul, would take his rage out on him. Mikel had been a willing sacrifice if it meant keeping that bastard away from Jasmine. He had closed his eyes and imagined he was looking up at a sky that mapped out the stories of Greek tragedies and made his family seem a little more normal. Some had given him hope that there were at least a few happy endings—like the

Phoenix. But even in that story, inspiration had been born from the ashes of pain and grief.

Mikel: *Nope.*

He didn't bother to knock at Isaiah's. He walked into the house, past the neatly organized recycling bin full of beer cans and glass bottles. The rooms were clean and modern. Several people were spread throughout the place, their stoned, glassy-eyed faces smiling as they rocked to the beat of the techno music. You would never expect the nice house in this suburban neighborhood to be a drug den. Moms, dads, husbands, wives, daughters, sons, people with different back-grounds all coming together for the same reason: to forget for a little while. To escape to a place where no one could hurt you and you were never powerless. A place of only euphoria.

Unfortunately, that high never lasted long enough. Each time, it seemed harder to get to. One pill turned into two, which turned into snorting white powder or shooting poison into your veins. Addiction was a ruthless oppressor—a dictator that ruled your thoughts and actions in selfish tyranny. It morphed you into the worst version of yourself while tricking you into believing you were at your best. Until nothing mattered anymore, except that high. Your next fix became your sole purpose of living, your constant focus.

Mikel didn't see himself as an addict. In fact, he felt sorry for all these people. He wasn't like them. He could stop if he really wanted to. He just didn't want to yet.

"Mikel! You finally made it, man," Isaiah said walking up to him, bottle of vodka in hand. No one bothered with pretense here.

"Yeah. You got something for me?" he asked.

"Joe sent a new shipment. He told me not to give you anything on credit though. He said you owe him." Isaiah shifted nervously on his feet and sniffed.

He would pay it back if only he could, but fifty thousand dollars didn't just grow on trees. And the money he'd borrowed from the loan shark wasn't the only thing Joe had on him. "Yeah. I'll catch up with him soon."

Isaiah tipped his head so that others couldn't hear when he spoke. "Don't know what business you got with him, man. None of my concern. But Joe ain't the kinda guy you want to owe anything to. Whatever you gotta do to pay him, you better do it."

Too late. Mikel nodded. "Sure thing." If his friend only knew what the man held over him, he'd understand there was no way he'd ever be free from Joe's clutches.

"Tell him I'll bring him some of the money next week," Mikel said.

"My sister's in the kitchen. She'll hook you up."

"Thanks." Mikel walked down the hall towards the lemon-yellow kitchen.

"Hey, sexy. Did you come all this way to see me?" June teased, her blond hair swinging from a high ponytail as she cocked her head to the side. Her smoky eyes raked over him like he was a prime cut of meat.

She ran her hand over his cheek and down his chest. Maybe this was what he needed. She could erase this sinking feeling if only for a fleeting moment, take his mind off what he couldn't have. He and June were both damaged goods, both from the wrong side of the tracks. He'd sampled what she offered several times over the past few years. She was always down for a quick and dirty fuck. Sex and drugs. Highs and lows. Love for the moment, hate for himself.

"You have something I need," he said, grabbing her hand before she slid it any farther into his pants.

She smirked. "How many?"

"The usual."

She backed away, and he let her hand drop. "It's upstairs in my room." She led him towards the dimly lit stairs, and he followed behind.

She pulled a bag from the large hidden safe she kept in a closet and tossed it to him.

He caught it and slipped it into his pocket. He paid her. "Thanks."

She turned and sauntered back to him before kissing him. Her lips were nothing like Remy's. June's mouth was pure empty lust. He grabbed her neck and pushed her away.

"Let me make you feel good." She licked her bright red lips.

Letting her touch him was simply a means to an end that promised release. A temporary vacation from reality. He was an expert in physical relief without the baggage of emotion.

She must have taken his hesitation for consent as she sunk to her knees, undoing his pants.

He was hard, aching for relief since last night with Remy. He wished to god those blue orbs looking up at him were brown. If he closed his eyes, he could imagine the creamy white hands pulling down his pants were dark as midnight.

Remy didn't belong with him. He'd taint her with his evil. He wouldn't do that to her. If he couldn't have Remy, he would have to settle and take what he could get. He just needed something to help him forget his past for a little while.

His phone buzzed as June kissed his stomach and hooked her fingers under the elastic of his underwear. Did it make him less of a man that he'd rather see what question Remy had come up with next than allow this chick to blow him?

This was wrong. She started to tug his boxers as the cell pinged again.

"Stop." He grabbed it off the floor.

Remy: *I need help.*

Remy: *Green Park. Baseball field.*

Panic seized his body as the jolt of adrenaline shot through him. He wrenched his pants on.

"Baby—"

"I gotta go," he said, on his way out the door as he buttoned the waist.

Remy was in trouble. What if he was too late? It was dark and she was in the park. Was she alone? Was she hurt? Fear and doubt swirled in his mind as he peeled onto the road, speeding towards the address. One thing was certain: if anyone touched her, he would kill them with his bare hands. He would murder again if it meant keeping her safe.

4

REMY

Remy hid in the bushes as the headlights swerved into the parking lot. The car screeched to a stop.

Mikel jumped out a moment later, slamming his door shut. "Remy!" he screamed, jolting her. "Remy!"

"O-over here." She walked towards him on trembling legs.

He pivoted to her, his shoulders raised and tense. After running to her, he grabbed her face in his hands. "What's wrong? Did someone hurt you?"

Confused, she said, "I'm fine. Nothing's wrong."

His shoulders seemed to relax a little before his voice grated angrily, "Why did you text me for help, then? I thought you were in trouble! What are you doing out here alone in the dark?"

She shrank back from his sudden outburst. "I-I'm sorry. I didn't realize it sounded that way. I just thought . . ."

He ran a hand through his hair, tugging on it. "What did you need my help for?"

"It's stupid. Never mind. I-I'm sorry I bothered you." She

turned to walk towards her car, feeling childish and defeated. *So much for a surprise.*

"Stop," he said.

She hesitated, slowly spinning around to find him illuminated in the moonlight. Dangerous and alluring. Even in the darkness he was beautiful.

She couldn't have walked away if she tried. It was like they were tethered, some invisible force winding them closer. Held hostage by a childhood crush, she just wished he would give them a chance.

"What did you need my help for?" he repeated, his tone even.

She nodded towards her trunk. "To find the Phoenix."

His brows furrowed as he studied her. She pressed the button on her key fob and popped the trunk. Her father had been able to borrow a telescope for her from the astronomy department in the college that he worked for on short notice. She lifted the bag out she'd packed with snacks and essentials for a stargazing picnic before she said, "It's really heavy."

Mikel shook his head as if in disbelief. He walked over and peered inside her trunk as she studied his reaction. Surprise. Astonishment. Awe. Each reaction fluttered across his shadowed face.

"You did this for me?" he asked, his voice sounding huskier.

"Yes."

Without another sound, he picked up the telescope like it weighed nothing. She shut the trunk and led him to a grassy spot on a hill overlooking the whole park. She laid out the blanket from the bag and picked out a beer and a soda.

"How'd you get that?" he asked, eyeing the alcohol.

She shrugged. "I stole it from the fridge."

"What happened to the shy little girl who used to tattle on

herself?" he asked, setting up the equipment like he had done it a million times before.

"She grew up."

He stared at her for a moment before peering through the scope. She moved closer, enjoying the moment. The warm June night had brought out a few fireflies blinking in the grasslands below them. Frogs peeped from the pond as crickets chirped—summer's background melody. Butterflies swirled inside her belly as she admired Mikel at work. His muscular arms flexed in his black short-sleeve shirt as he adjusted the dials. He kneeled on the ground next to her, peering into the heavens. She wished he would let her in, trust her with his heart, because she had given hers to him a long time ago.

"So, why the Phoenix?" she asked as he searched.

He smiled like a kid at Christmas and nodded towards the contraption.

She got closer. His scent was light and woodsy in the air between them. Her body heated as she leaned in and peered at the cluster of stars.

His hot breath tickled against her ear as he explained, "It was a sacred, mythical bird with the head of an eagle and red, purple, and gold feathers. When it was getting ready to die, it built a nest of incense and would light itself on fire. A new bird would be born from the ashes of its father."

She panted, more focused on the sound of his voice and his closeness rather than the stars. She turned towards him, her face only centimeters from his. "Like a second chance? Like, if the bird wanted to become someone different, someone better than its father, it could?" she asked.

Kiss me.

He swallowed. "Remy," he said, his voice husky. Maybe he was feeling the same need that coiled tightly inside her, winding her body, threatening to unravel life as she knew it. "We can't do this."

"We can't be friends?" she asked, hoping to lighten the intensity of her silent plea.

"You don't know what you're asking of me," he said, his eyes flicking to her mouth.

She licked her lips. Her body trembled as fear of missing her chance gripped her. Terrified of the consequences of not at least trying. He'd never make the first move.

Despite what he thought, he was a good man. He respected her brother's friendship and her, but he somehow had this twisted belief that he was never going to be worthy of her. It was the opposite. If anyone was the lucky one, it would be her.

"Please?" Begging wasn't beneath her, not for this man.

"I don't think I could ever just be your friend. I'm nothing but trouble. I'm darkness and you're pure light. We don't belong together."

His words reverberated through her, shaking her to her core. Compassion for his broken pieces and love for the strength of what it took to live through hell and come out the other side overwhelmed her. He wanted her. Mikel Evans wanted her. Her heart swelled and pounded in her chest as she inhaled a shaky breath. Mustering every ounce of courage she had, she said, "You can't have light without the darkness. The stars and the moon are only beautiful because of the night."

The mask fell, his expression once again vulnerable. A lifetime of untold pain flickered to the surface, visible in flashes. He bit his lip, looking towards the sky as if deep in thought.

Something inside her propelled her forward, tugging her in his direction. He needed to hear the words that tumbled into her mind, dancing and weaving into her spirit in whispers. His need to be loved overrode her hesitation and uncertainty. A primal force to care for the man and give him whatever he needed controlled her actions.

She climbed onto his lap, taking his face in her hands as she gazed into the windows of his soul. "I have cared for you all my life, Mikel Evans. I just never thought you would look my way. Everyone deserves to be loved, especially those who don't think they're worthy of it. They need it the most. Give me a chance. I'll be whatever you need me to be, as long as I get to be with you."

His body trembled, and his jaw clenched before his mouth crashed onto hers, hungry and seeking. Unhinged and uncontrolled. He drank from her as if she was his fountain of life. She gave everything to him, open and willing to let him take whatever he needed. His tongue invaded her mouth, meeting hers as his hands slid to her waist, pulling her tighter against him. He tasted like vanilla cupcakes. Sweet and mild. He trailed tender kisses along her neck, spinning her in a knot of passion and awareness.

He kissed her collarbone before saying, "You're so beautiful. If I was a better man, I would leave you alone."

She didn't know whether to laugh or cry at his statement. She'd had a lifetime of watching him from the sidelines as he cared for his sister, protecting and providing for her when he had only been a child. This was the man who had saved her from bullies. He was her fantasy come to life. "You are a better man. That's why I chose you."

He kissed her lips again, this time tender and reverent. As if he was cherishing every moment they were tangled together as much as she was. His hands kneaded into her hips possessively, sending a rush of desire through her. Fire bloomed in her center.

Mikel is kissing me.

He was touching her. After a lifetime of shooting stars and

birthday candles, her wishes were coming true. His palm skated over her thigh, blistering her bare skin with lust. Her body burned white-hot. Emotions and yearnings she had never felt before sent her tumbling and spinning into a boiling frenzy. She'd not felt as alive and empowered in all her life as she did kissing Mikel under the canopy of the stars.

5

———

MIKEL

ikel spent the week at the construction site. On his breaks, he slipped out his phone to see what new question Remy had come up with. She had far surpassed twenty by Friday.

Remy: *Wanna stargaze with me tonight?*

Excitement and nerves sparked in his belly. She'd felt like a dream—too good to be true. She was making him hope for things that he hadn't in a long time, like a future.

"What's got you all smiles this week?" Andre asked, setting his hard hat next to him on the bed of the truck before jumping to sit by him.

Mikel slipped his phone back into his pocket. "It's been a good week."

Andre took a bite out of his sandwich as he eyed him suspiciously. "I don't think I've ever seen this look on you."

"What do you mean?"

His friend drank from his bottle of water. "Happiness, bro. You look happy."

"I'm always happy." Mikel playfully smacked Andre's shoulder.

"This is a different kind of happy . . . You got a girl?"

Mikel bit into his own lunch, buying himself some time before answering. His mind was racing a million miles a minute. Could he do this? Could he date his best friend's sister? "I met someone, but we're taking it slow. Just talking right now." Vague honesty was the best approach.

"Mikel Evans is going slow?" Dre teased.

He shook his head. "She's really special and I don't wanna fuck it up with her." He hoped his friend would remember his words when the time came to tell him.

"Good for you," Andre said, crumpling the wrapper of his lunch.

Mikel sighed. He shouldn't have gone near Remy, but it was too late to turn back now. He liked talking to her, waking up to her texts. They were innocent, funny, and sometimes philosophical.

He had tried to stay away from her for her own good, but he was a selfish bastard. One taste of those sweet lips and he was done for. The way she looked at him, like she could see an ounce of good in him, gave him a high that he couldn't find anywhere else. She believed in him. That was what had made him give in. She was his vice now.

* * *

Mikel walked into Dolly's Bakery. The scent of baked goods and coffee hit him in full force as he got in line behind a woman blocking his view of the very gorgeous Remy. Even though he caught just a glimpse of her, she managed to steal his breath away.

"Look, I wanted this with three shots of sugar. This

doesn't taste like three, it tastes like two," the woman berated Remy.

"I-I'm sorry, ma'am. I did use three, but I would be happy to add another shot for you," Remy responded timidly.

"Throw in a free cookie too for my inconvenience." She slammed her cup on the counter and some of the contents splashed over the rim.

"I-I'm sorry. I'm not allowed to do that," Remy said, quickly adding another pump of sugar.

"I need to see your manager. This is ridiculous. Horrible service. I guess I should not have expected much from *someone like you*," the patron snapped.

Remy's eyes fell to the counter as her bottom lip trembled. Her shoulders drooped, hurt painting her features.

He balled his hands into fists and clenched his jaw tight. "Don't think you need those extra calories anyway. Seems to me you've had enough sugar to last you a lifetime," Mikel said gruffly.

The woman turned to look at him, horrified.

If she wanted to insult his Dove, he didn't mind delivering a low blow.

"Excuse me?"

"Don't like the service, then shut the fuck up and move on. We all have lives to live and you trying to take advantage of this smart woman because your cheap ass won't buy your own damn cookie is despicable."

She blinked several times with her mouth hanging open, her face turning bright red, before looking back to the counter where Remy had her drink waiting. The woman grabbed the coffee and stormed out of the café while screaming, "Well, I never!"

The few other patrons in the café had turned to watch the spectacle.

He chuckled and walked over to greet Remy, who was visibly shaking. "Hey, baby. You okay?" he asked. The endearment slipped from his mouth as if he had called her that all his life.

She looked up at him with wide doe eyes. "That was mean."

"Yeah, she was a bitch. I'm sorry she spoke to you like that."

"Yes, she was, but what you said was not very nice either."

"Excuse me?" he asked, surprised by the turn of conversation. He'd just stood up for her and she was calling *him* mean?

"She was obviously having a bad day. I think you really hurt her feelings. You should never talk about a woman's weight. We don't know her life. Maybe she'd just found out her husband was cheating on her. Maybe her dog died."

"Maybe she is just a racist piece of shit who gets off on putting other people down," he said defensively. He wasn't sure why *she* of all people would defend someone like that.

"Maybe. But you never know." After a moment of awkward silence, she said, "I'm not good with confrontation. I should have said thank you. I know you were trying to stand up for me, and I'm glad you feel that way. I just wish you didn't have to be so unkind about it."

"At least I didn't punch her," he joked, thinking of 'Handsy' at the bar. From her horrified expression, his little Dove didn't find an ounce of humor in his comment. "It was a joke. I would never lay a hand on a woman, no matter how much I may be tempted . . . Are you afraid of me, Remy?" he asked, searching her eyes for the answer. She should be, but if she was, he would be devastated. Because if this pure sweet woman didn't think there was hope for him, then there wasn't.

"I'm afraid *for* you."

Each word was an arrow shot through what was left of his

tattered heart. It was as though she had already found a way in, reclaiming parts of him that she had no business resurrecting.

* * *

Later that night, they set up the telescope under the canvas of stars splattered across the sky. The moon was waning, still bright enough for them to see without the use of a flashlight once their eyes adjusted.

He moved over so that she could have a turn with the equipment. It gave him time to admire the way her lips curved upwards when she spotted it. Even though she was the one looking into the sky, staring at her was pure heavenly beauty.

"What's this one?" she asked.

"Lyra. It represents the lyre instrument. It's comprised of nine stars and planets. The brightest star is Vega, Alpha Lyrae, which happens to be the fifth brightest star in the whole sky."

"What's the story?" she prompted, sitting back to look at him, her eyes sparkling with interest.

"Lyra is the lyre of Orpheus. He was a poet and musician in Greek mythology. When he was young, the god Apollo gave him the golden lyre and taught him to play it. He was known for his ability to charm anyone, or anything with his music. He saved sailors from sirens, and helped his buddy Jason and the Argonauts."

"Sounds like a great story." She smiled.

"Not really. He was married, and his wife tried to get away from a dude who attacked her. She fell into a pit of vipers and died."

Her hand flew to her mouth in shock, as if these were real people she was concerned for. Goodness and compassion oozed out of her every pore. "Was that the end of the story?" she asked. His Dove, always brimming with hope.

"No. He played such a moving song of grief after finding her body that even the gods took pity on him. He went to the underworld and made a deal. He was supposed to walk out of there, with her following behind, back to the land of the living without turning around until they both crossed over. Then, they could be together again," he explained.

"Oh, so they got their happy ending after all?" Her hand rested on his, sending blazing heat throughout his system. All it took from her was a spark and he burned hotter than the sun.

He struggled with whether to tell her the truth or not. Those brown eyes were full of possibilities, wishing for a happy ending. She was the embodiment of what fairy tales were made of while he was a Greek tragedy.

"Yeah, they made it," he lied, leaning back and admiring the black canopy above filled with countless other stories that all ended in heartbreak and death.

She laid her head on his chest, and he wrapped an arm around her. He had never done this with a woman before. Women provided him a physical release, nothing more. Everything with Remy was different. She fit against him like she was carved from his body. Yes, he craved her, but it was more than that. He didn't want to rush things and ruin it. He wanted to draw this out and enjoy every moment of it—while it lasted.

He never thought in a million years he would be here. What he did know was that right now, he wasn't worrying about his past, or stressing over what job Joe was going to have him do next. Remy gave him peace. He would cherish every moment with her, because nothing good in his life ever stayed that way.

"So, you want to own a bakery someday huh?" he asked, changing the subject.

"Mm-hmm."

"Got any names in mind?"

"How about Remy's Goodies?" She laughed.

Jealousy sparked. "I don't think you should be sharing your goodies with anyone else but me," he growled.

She looked up at him shyly.

"What?" he asked.

She bit her lip. "You want my . . . goodies?"

He smiled, trying to set her at ease. "I want every part of you, beautiful. That doesn't mean I can have it. I only want what you're willing to give, but we're a long way from that right now."

She nodded and relaxed against his chest once more.

"Are you a virgin, Remy?" he asked. He had his suspicions.

She hesitated a moment before answering, "Is that a problem?"

He squeezed her tighter against him, wondering what he'd done in a previous life to deserve her. "No, baby. It's the opposite. I just . . . don't want to destroy this. You deserve so much better than me."

"Then don't, Mikel. Don't screw it up. You can start by believing you deserve good things."

His eyes stung as the confession of his sins bubbled up in his throat, burning like the bile it was. He hammered it down as he had always done, swallowing hard.

"I'll ruin you before you can save me."

She remained silent, snuggling closer into him.

Time passed with a warm breeze blowing. Peeping frogs and all manner of insects joined together in nature's melody.

"How about we call it Stardust?" she asked, finally inter-rupting their silence, changing the topic back to the bakery.

"Why would you want the dust? It's just the leftover broken scraps of what used to be the beautiful whole star." He closed his eyes.

"Because stardust is what wishes are made of."

6

———

MIKEL

irds chirped loudly, waking Mikel from his peaceful slumber. A warm body pressed against his, smelling like heaven. He opened his eyes, blinking at the bright sunlight. Trees swayed in the wind overhead, framing the blue sky around him. He was outside. *Why am I outside?*

Realization hit.

Remy snuggled close, lying peacefully on his arm. They had fallen asleep like that under the stars, their conversation fading into the darkness as they'd drifted off into dreamland.

"Remy? Baby, it's morning," he said, gently waking her.

She stirred and blinked a few times before shooting upright in a panic. "Oh fudge!"

He couldn't help but chuckle at her inability to swear. She glanced at him before searching through the backpack she'd brought. "My parents are gonna kill me. I was supposed to be home by midnight."

"Shit, I'm sorry." He had been so tired from a long week in the hot sun on the jobsite, he hadn't even realized he was drifting off. He started gathering the equipment together.

"My phone is dead," she said, slipping it into her back pocket and hurriedly packing up the remaining items.

He glanced at his black screen. "Mine too. We can charge yours in the car. You gonna be grounded?" he asked, half-teasingly. He had no idea what it was like to have two caring parents who made rules other than to be completely invisible or you would pay dearly.

"They would have been okay if I had just told them I was gonna stay out at a friend's. Out of respect for them, while I'm still living at home, I just like to let them know where I am or when I'll be home."

"Let's get you home, then."

* * *

As soon as they pulled into her parents' driveway, Andre came down the steps, his eyes locked with Mikel's.

"Thank you, Mikel. I'm sorry I have to run off like this. I'll text you later, okay?" Remy said.

"Sure thing." He nodded, wanting more than anything to lean over and kiss her, but they had an audience who he assumed wouldn't be all that receptive.

"I had a lot of fun last night." She smiled, before hopping out of his truck. She said something to Andre in passing before rushing into the house.

Andre stared at Mikel with an unreadable expression. The cat was out of the bag.

He needed to man up and face the repercussions of his decision. Switching the engine off, he got out of the truck, preparing to get hit. Out of politeness, he would let Dre have the first swing. After that, it was game on. He was many things, but a coward wasn't one of them.

"How long has this been going on?" Andre asked, nodding

towards the door his sister had disappeared through only minutes before.

Straight to the point, as usual.

"Not long."

Andre crossed his arms, and asked, "Did you sleep with her?"

Mikel shook his head. "Not like you're thinking. We dozed off just talking and looking at the stars."

"How romantic," he said, sarcasm dripping from every syllable.

"I should have let you know sooner. I just wasn't sure what this was at first. I know she's too good for me," Mikel said, his body on high alert for retribution.

"Damn right she is." Andre crossed his arms across his chest. "But she's been crushing on you for as long as I can remember. You better not break her heart."

Shocked, Mikel took a step back as if his friend's words were a physical blow. "You trust me with her?"

"You want my blessing?" Dre asked.

"Yeah, I do."

"You better keep it PG with her. I'm serious, man. If I find out you . . . Just don't unless you're ready to offer her that white picket fence, a ring, and the family she wants someday." He sighed before he continued, "I know you got ghosts, bro. We all do. She's a good girl, but she's a little naive. She hasn't seen what this world is capable of just yet. She was sheltered, more so than me. Don't start something you don't intend to finish, because then we will have problems. But as far as guys dating my sister go, I don't think she could have picked a better one. You should give yourself a little more credit."

Mikel's chest tightened. He was speechless—honored that this man believed in him enough to give him his blessing. His warning was clear: *don't start something you don't plan on seeing through*. He had no plans of letting Remy go. The thought was physically painful. But could he really go through with this, take from her what could never be given back? He'd screw it up somehow, because he ruined everything.

But it was too late to turn back now. "Thanks, man."

He needed some air, and time to think. He nodded and got back in his car before starting the engine and driving off towards his house.

Mikel's head was a jumbled mess of voices screaming at him.

I believe in you, bro.

You'll never amount to anything.

You're just like me; you're nothing.

I see the good in you.

You don't do anything right.

You belong to me.

You are nothing but a failure.

You are ugly and weak.

Worthless piece of shit.

I hate you.

Guilt. Shame. A vortex of confusion and helplessness to the voices in his head suffocated him. He needed to drown them out—escape his past and the pain that came from a life-time of trauma.

His phone buzzed with a text message. Glancing at the screen, bile rose in his throat.

Joe: *Got a job for you. Same address as before. Give him the late payment special.*

Fuck! He had no choice.

He reached one of his shaky hands into his pocket, pulling out two pills, and swallowed them without any liquid. It wasn't working fast enough. He needed something stronger. He turned left and headed towards Isaiah and June's house.

7

REMY

Remy pulled out a fresh batch of chocolate muffins out of the oven before carefully placing them on a cooling rack. She loved the smell of the bakery after hours. The aromas of sugared frostings, pastries, and baked goods melded together with coffee. Coziness and comfort. It reminded her of so many afternoons spent baking with her father in her parents' kitchen.

Daddy was the baker and her momma was the decorator, showing Remy what it meant to work together as a team. Her parents were best friends. She wanted that for herself some-day. She had always fantasized that it would be Mikel, but never in a million years had she expected him to actually desire her.

She'd heard her brother talk. But as far as she knew, Mikel had never had a girlfriend before. Was she his first?

Emma sat across from her, piping white cream cheese frosting onto carrot cupcakes. "Why the long face?"

Remy sighed, slipping her phone out to check it one more time before returning it to her pocket.

"I texted Mikel after he dropped me off to make plans and he hasn't messaged me back all day."

"You think Andre scared him?" she asked, swiping a stray strand of blond hair behind her ear.

"I don't think so. I mean, they're best friends. He wouldn't do that. Would he?"

Emma gave her an incredulous expression. "He's your older brother, Rem. When have you not known him to be protective of you?"

Remy sighed. "Crap."

"You two make quite the couple," Emma said.

"How so?"

She set the piping bag down before reaching for the orange sprinkles. "He's the dark and mysterious type, a broody bad boy through and through, and you're . . . well, you're you."

"What's that supposed to mean?" Remy crossed her arms over her chest.

"You never lie. You've never cheated on a test. You don't even go above the speed limit. You're a rule follower. I'm just observing how opposite you guys are."

"He's more than just what you see on the outside. He has this whole other part to him that's sensitive and intelligent. We can talk for hours without running out of things to say." Remy came to his defense.

"Oh, shit, girl." Emma looked at her sympathetically.

"What?"

"You reeeeaaally like him. Do you, like, love—love him?" Emma asked.

Remy rolled her eyes, and let out a cleansing breath. "It started as a friendship and then a crush, or puppy love, as my momma calls it. I've always loved him in some capacity. He's been a part of my family since we were kids."

"Just be careful, Remy. I've heard the rumors. I know the Evans family have been through a lot. People don't just get over their mother killing herself in their basement and then their father overdosing. That shit stays with you for life," Emma warned.

"That's not fair. His past doesn't dictate his future."

Mikel had been changing his shirt at their house when Remy walked in on him. He was only fourteen, and she nine. He was staring into the mirror, a finger pressing into one of the large black bruises covering his ribs as he winced. He startled, noticing her, dropping his shirt to hide the evidence.

"What happened?" she asked, tears burning her eyes.

He stared at the floor. "I fell down the stairs."

The Evanses always had excuses of clumsiness, but she knew deep down what was going on. She shook her head. "You should tell someone. My dad could help protect you," she offered.

Mikel locked those dark brown eyes on her as his expression softened. "Remy, I just fell. That's it. I need you to make me a promise. Will you do that for me?"

She would have done anything to make him feel just a little better. She nodded, sniffling.

He walked over, reaching out his hand as if he wanted to wipe her tears away. He didn't though. "Promise me you won't tell anyone anything about this. I could get into a lot of trouble if someone knew. Telling would only make it worse."

Everything inside her screamed to do the opposite, but she agreed because she wanted to help him any way she could. "Okay."

"Earth to Remy?" Emma said, waving a cupcake in front of her face.

She snapped out of the memory, shaking her head. "Sorry. I was just thinking."

Her phone buzzed in her pocket. Remy jumped as her heart raced. Was it him? She read the message as her body rushed with excited tingles.

Mikel: *Come see me when you get off work. I'm home.*

"Judging by that look on your face, I'd say all your worries have been put to rest." Emma chuckled.

Remy's friend's smile was laced with a hint of concern. "He wants me to come over after my shift."

"I can finish up here and close. Why don't you clock out and go talk to him before you go crazy?" Emma offered.

* * *

Remy gripped the cupcake container tighter as she rang the doorbell to the Evans family house. She had been there countless times before, but something about this felt different. She was there to see Mikel. Unease and uncertainty wound around her, gripping tightly, making it hard to breathe.

Footsteps came closer, and the door opened to reveal Jasmine. "Hey, Remy. I didn't know you were coming over. I was just on my way out to meet a friend."

"I, uh, I'm actually here to see Mikel."

Jasmine crooked her eyebrow, studying her with an intense green-eyed glare. "You . . . and Mikel?"

Remy chewed on her bottom lip as she nodded. "Is that okay with you?"

"I just can't believe it. I mean, I know you've been ogling him for years, but I never thought he'd . . ." Jasmine waved her hands.

"Oh." Remy ran her shoe over the paint peeling on the porch.

"I didn't mean it like that, Remy. My brother is as closed off as they come. You're so open and trusting. I just never saw him settling down with anyone." She placed her hand on Remy's shoulder. "But I'm glad it's you. I wouldn't trust any other bitch with his heart."

Remy smiled as her heart filled with elation. Butterflies danced in her belly at Jasmine's acceptance. "So, does this friend you're meeting happen to be of the male kind?"

Jasmine's eyes fell to the ground and then returned to hers as she smirked. "Is there any other kind for me?"

"Be safe and have fun," Remy said.

"I always wrap it up." Jasmine winked.

"If you need anything, let me know."

"Will do." Jasmine nodded, looking past her to the driveway where a car had pulled up, driven by the captain of the football team.

"See ya later." Jasmine waved as she ran out to catch her ride.

They drove out of sight. She wasn't sure if she'd done the right thing for her friend, but the fact was that it was Jasmine's body and she could choose to do what she wanted. She just wished she would make some safer choices.

Remy walked into the house, closing the door behind her. She took the stairs towards Mikel's bedroom and knocked.

Mikel opened the door. He was shirtless—all his defined muscles were on full display, highlighted by the shadows of the dark hallway. She met his tired eyes. His hair was mussed, like he had just gotten out of bed.

"Remy?" he questioned as if he thought he was still dreaming. He rubbed his bloodshot eyes. He smelled like cigarettes and alcohol.

"I'm sorry. I didn't mean to wake you up. I brought you a carrot cupcake." She offered the container awkwardly.

He studied her for a moment before opening his door wider to let her in. "Let me shower really quick," he said, grabbing a towel that hung over the dresser in his room.

"Sure," she said, taking a seat on the bed and setting the treat on the nightstand amidst the empty bottles of Jack Daniel's.

He disappeared into the bathroom down the hall and she fiddled with her fingers, unsure what to do while she waited.

His walls were bare. Just plain light-grey paint. Clothes were scattered across the floor and his bed was unmade. A few empty beer bottles were placed throughout the musty room.

She stood and opened the window to let the fresh summer breeze filter in. Next, she stripped the bedding. Then went to the hall where Jasmine kept their sheets. Remy picked out a fresh set and began making the bed. Tucking the first sheet under the mattress, her hand grazed something. Remy pulled it out. It was a small plastic bag with several pills inside.

What the heck are these? And why are they hidden?

The shower knob squeaked, signaling the water being shut off. Remy shoved the bag back where she'd found it and grabbed the other sheet, hurriedly finishing the bed.

She had the pillowcases and comforter on by the time Mikel emerged from the bathroom wearing the same jeans he'd had on when he went in. He threw his towel on the floor, before opening the dresser. He pulled a grey T-shirt over his head and covered those muscles that made her mouth water.

He turned towards her, and then nodded towards the bed. "You didn't have to do that." His voice was gravelly.

Her heart raced. She was unsure and uncertain. The ground she stood on was trembling and shaky as his presence sent shockwaves through her. "I wanted to."

He glanced towards the side of the bed where she had

discovered the hidden pills. *What were they? Why was he hiding them?*

He cleared his throat and sat next to her.

"I'm sorry about this morning," she said, hoping to snap him out of whatever funk he was in and back to the Mikel whose arms she had fallen asleep in.

"It wasn't your fault."

"Are you mad at me?" she asked, afraid of his answer.

Confusion decorated his expression. "Why would you think that?"

"Well, you haven't texted me back since this morning. I wondered if Andre had said something to you and you were rethinking this . . . *friendship*." She would not be the first one to label this. He needed to do that. She didn't want to scare him away.

He blinked and shook his head, staring at the ground. "I just had a lot on my mind. I was tired and fell asleep."

He'd looked down when he lied all those years ago at fourteen, the same way he was doing now. He was lying. He needed space. She ran her hand over his scratchy stubble. "Do you want to try my cupcake?"

He smirked, those dark eyes locking on her. "Yes, I definitely want to eat your cupcake, Remy."

By the way he said it, he clearly didn't mean the carrot dessert she'd brought. The hunger in his eyes was for her alone. Her breath hitched as the anticipation in the room thickened. Nerves tied her insides into knots. He leaned and grabbed the box from the nightstand, his hot breath dancing along her neck with his closeness. She was nearly panting by the time he had it open in his lap. Discarding the paper container, he peeled the liner from the bottom. He dipped his finger in the frosting and offered it to her. She kept her gaze locked on his as she parted her lips. He slipped his finger inside and she sucked the frosting off.

He clenched his jaw as the brown in his eyes turned nearly black.

She had never intended for this little innocent cupcake to lead to such illicit territory. But something came over her. Her body rippled and throbbed with power knowing she made him desire her as much as she yearned for him. He swallowed, slowly pulling his finger from her mouth. He dipped it in the frosting again before painting her lips with the white sugary confection.

"My turn," he said before running his tongue delicately across her bottom lip, teasing and sucking on it, slanting his mouth against hers. She was consumed with lust and want. A wanton fire burned her from the inside out. He must have set the cupcake aside because both of his hands wrapped around her, kneading into her hips.

His kiss seared through her flesh, marking her heart. It had always belonged to him anyways.

8

REMY

Remy whimpered as Mikel pulled her close to him in a hug. She had somehow ended up on his lap again. His arousal underneath her made her yearn to have him buried deep inside where she throbbed and ached with hot emptiness for him.

"Why did you stop?" she asked, breathless. His own racing heartbeat matched hers beat for beat, pounding against her chest.

"If I don't stop now, you'll be spread out under me and I'll take the one thing you can never get back. I can't do that to you," he said, almost like it pained him to admit it.

"What if I want you to?"

His grip tightened around her. She'd asked the question aloud in her lust-induced haze.

"Let's go out to dinner."

She nodded. His arms loosened and she stood. She didn't have to miss his touch for long because he took her hand and led her down the stairs towards his truck.

"Where do you want to go?" he asked, opening her door.

She climbed in. "Pizza could be good. Pirate's Pizzeria does the best gluten-free crusts."

He shut the door and climbed in on his side. Starting the engine, he said, "How do you work in a place where you can't eat any of the baked goods?"

"I need the experience. It isn't so bad. I bake my own things at home for practice," she said, buckling her seat belt.

"Is your Stardust Bakery gonna have gluten-free stuff?" he asked, driving them towards their destination.

She smiled. "Yes. It will be a completely gluten-free and celiac-friendly establishment. I want to look into baking without any grains at all. After all my research, I've found new flours to experiment with so I can actually eat the food I cook. Something called cassava; have you ever heard of it?" she asked. Most people's eyes glazed over when she went into detail on the chemistry of baking.

Mikel just flashed her a smile and said, "Nope. I'm sure if you want to do something, you could pull it off, Remy."

Hope spiraled in her chest. He believed in her.

* * *

They slid into a booth at Pirate's, and she ordered an iced tea and the special on a gluten-free crust. Mikel ordered a beer. The server brought out their drinks as they settled into an easy conversation.

"Today, Dolly wanted us to make two hundred cupcakes for a wedding while she focused on the cake as I'm still learning how to work with fondant. It's kind of like clay. Anyways, it was fun," she said as he gave her his undivided attention.

"That's cool."

"How about yours?" she asked.

"Pretty good. We got the framing done for the garage of a client," he answered simply.

Mikel started tapping his foot on the ground.

"What is your favorite thing about your job?" she asked.

Mikel took a long sip of his beer. After setting it down, he began peeling the label off as he answered, "I like the numbers. The office end of things is probably my favorite, but I like being able to bring something to life with my hands too." He held up his palms. "Building requires a lot of math. I mean, I was never great in school because it just wasn't useful then. I think I learned better when the information was actually applicable. I had the basics, and then I figured out the rest through trial and error, or watching other people. It's also a nice way to tire myself out." He sipped his beer again.

Remy smiled as she listened intently, soaking up the pieces of himself he was willing to share with her. She was honored that he trusted her. "You're incredible."

He drained what was left of his beer before he shook his head. "Hardly."

Remy wanted to ask him why he didn't agree, but the server brought their hot pies. Mikel ordered another beer before she left.

"This smells so good." Remy inhaled the cheesy tomato pizza.

"Yes it does," he agreed.

While they waited for it to cool, Mikel adjusted in his seat, clenching and unclenching his fists. "Tell me more about what's going on with you," he said before plating himself a piece of the hot meal.

"Like what? I feel like you know almost everything about me."

"Tell me something I don't, then." He smirked before taking a bite.

She waited for hers to cool as she began talking about her plans for the next few years. Would he be willing to do a long-distance relationship when she went to culinary school in New York? Was it too early to ask? She ate her pizza.

"You'll be great at that, Remy. Your whole face lights up when you talk about your dreams. I know you'll get there someday." He sipped on his drink as she reached for her tea.

"Well, that's just phase one of my dream." She smiled.

He chuckled. "Don't leave me hangin'."

She pictured it in her mind as she told him. "I want to have the bakery all set, and eventually, I'll do catering for special events like tea parties and weddings. Then I want to have a couple kids. It would be so fun to grow up in a bakery. Don't you think?"

Mikel blinked a few times, eyes wide before his expression hardened, becoming unreadable once again. "Yeah."

Had something she said upset him? The tapping of his foot grew louder as the table began to tremble slightly.

Maybe it was best to change the topic. "Emma is going on her first tour with her band. I don't know what I'm gonna do without her. At least I'll still have Jasmine."

Mikel nodded. It was obvious something was bothering him, but if he needed her to fill the silence, she would.

"We had someone call in and ask for a . . . umm . . . special cake for a bachelorette party. I did the design and sent it off without Dolly checking the work. I had spent a lot of time on the details and it was so realistic, so I was surprised when the woman came back in to complain about it."

A triangle formed between Mikel's eyebrows. "What was the cake decorated with?"

"Several small roosters." Heat rose to her cheeks as he studied her for a moment before busting out in laughter.

"She asked for a cake covered in cocks, didn't she?"

"Apparently, she wasn't a bird-lover." Remy sighed.

"What did Dolly say?" he asked in between bouts of amusement.

Remy couldn't help but chuckle herself too. "She explained the euphemism and I was mortified that my seventy-year-old boss was talking to me about . . ." She leaned in and whispered, "Penises."

Mikel shook his head.

"Then she told me to check with her or Emma before I started designing anything in the future."

"I bet Emma lost it," he said, taking a sip of his drink.

Remy rolled her eyes. "You have no idea. She said she'd failed me as a best friend, and then continued naming other slang or sayings for every body part and term for sex."

"So, it's safe to say you won't be making any more roosters for cock parties in the future, huh?" he teased her with a smirk.

"My parents are professors. I was busy visiting natural history and science museums when other people were at the theater watching movies or playing in the park."

"How did Dre get out of all that?"

She crossed her arms and huffed. "Dre came sometimes, but he didn't have as much interest in it. He preferred to be more active. I actually liked going."

Mikel nodded as he ate another piece of pizza.

Towards the end of the night, he was fidgeting more and more. She hadn't ever seen him so antsy.

"Ready to get out of here?" he asked.

"Sure."

He pulled out his wallet before throwing cash on the table next to the bill and walked out, barely holding the door open for her as he rushed to the car. He was acting odd. She'd thought the rooster story would have reset his mood, but he'd been "off" all evening.

She opened her own door this time. He was too busy searching under his seat for something. Whatever it was, he was pissed he couldn't find it.

"Shit," he hissed.

"What's wrong?" she asked, buckling in.

He looked up at her, as if realizing she was still there. Shaking his head, he said, "Sorry. I just forgot something at a friend's house. I gotta stop by on the way home and pick it up." He climbed in and shut the door.

He drove faster than he had on the way to the restaurant. A nagging feeling had her stomach in knots. Was his behavior related to those pills she'd found? What were they? Should she ask him about them?

They pulled into the driveway of a house she didn't recognize. The neighborhood was quiet, except for the sounds of night drifting in through her open window. She reached to unbuckle herself, but his hand stopped her.

"I'll be right back." He left the car before she could protest.

As he walked into the porch light and knocked on the door, unease and curiosity rippled through her. He was acting weird. Mikel disappeared inside as she waited in silence.

She turned the radio on, flipping through the channels until she found one she liked. "Colors" by Halsey was playing. Remy sang along, the lyrics making her think more about his behavior.

Mikel was doing drugs. That was the only way to explain his erratic behavior, the pills she'd found, and where she was now. Maybe it was a one-time thing, or something he did on occasion. Mikel couldn't be an addict. He owned a business and his brother was the deputy, for crying out loud. If Mikel had a problem, surely Bently would know.

He walked powerful and commanding back onto the porch, heading towards the car. His shoulders seemed heavier. Her heart ached for him. Remy saw past the mask to the broken boy within. She wanted to hold him and assure him it was all going to be okay. Remy wished she could fix him, give him all her love, and solve his problems. She'd do anything to take his painful past away for a little while. He had secrets that he had never shared with anyone and Remy wanted to be the one to comfort him. To love him. To save him. Maybe if she gave him all the love in her heart, and if she was the perfect girlfriend, he would see how much he had to live for.

He opened the door and climbed in, seemingly calmer. A hint of some kind of smoke clung to him. She wasn't sure if she should speak first, or let him.

He started the car and pulled onto the road. "I'm pretty swamped this week with work, but do you wanna hang out next Saturday?"

She turned to face him, her worries fading as butterflies tumbled in her belly. He wanted to spend more time with her.

"Yes." She nodded in the dark cab as he reached over and brought her hand to his mouth. His warm kiss was so tender, it eased all her fears. Mikel was in this with her.

9
___

MIKEL

Remy bounded down the steps from her house towards his truck and he couldn't help the way his body reacted. She was like sunshine. Whenever he was around her, he felt lighter. That smile on those shiny lips made his knees weak and his cock hard.

He'd had every intention of knocking on her door, but she'd run out as he slipped into park. Seemed like she was just as happy to see him as he was to see her. How could that be possible?

He got out and jogged around the other side of the truck. He wrapped his arms around her tight little body, sexy as fuck in another one of those summer dresses she wore all the time. *Good god.* He needed to think of something else to get his arousal under control. Anything to stop fantasizing of how good those thighs would feel wrapped over his shoulders.

Slow down.

He inhaled and kissed her neck, her sweet scent intoxicating.

"I missed you," she said as he released her.

"We texted all week."

"Yeah, but I missed having you in person." She looked up at him expectantly.

"Me too." He leaned down and kissed her lips, tasting her cherry lip gloss.

"I might have missed that most of all," she said, her voice breathier as he released her and opened the passenger door.

"Same here, baby."

As they pulled onto his street, she asked, "Where are you taking me?"

"It's a surprise." Hopefully she would not be disappointed.

After parking in front of his house, he got out and helped her to the ground. Her confused expression made him smile. She didn't say another word—she just followed him inside.

"Close your eyes."

She studied him, seemingly unsure for a moment before she obliged. She trusted him. The thought brought him both relief and unease.

"No peeking," he said as he placed his hands over her closed eyes and led her safely through the living room to the kitchen.

This was the moment of truth. *Hopefully this isn't a stupid idea.*

"Okay, you can open them now."

He stepped in front of her, preparing himself for the disappointment on her face. Good thing he had a backup plan. He turned his head from her to the array of baking flours and supplies on the counter, then back again.

Remy's hands covered her mouth as she blinked away a tear.

Shit. He'd really messed up. "I have another option if this—"

"This is perfect!" Her hands fell, revealing the biggest

smile he'd ever seen on her face. Relief flooded through his system as she looked at him like he'd hung the moon.

"I figured, why wait trying out some of those recipes you wanted to experiment with? Took me four stores before I found that cassava flour you were talking about, and I got a list of other ingredients from Emma that you'd need. I can be your taste tester." He stuck his fingers in his pockets.

"No." She shook her head as she studied the items he'd set out all over the kitchen.

"You don't want to?"

Remy turned and wrapped her arms around him as she met his gaze. "Of course I want to. I just mean that you won't just be sitting there taste testing, silly. You're gonna be my assistant." She beamed.

He was out of his element for sure, but he'd do anything to keep that smile on her face directed at him. "Your wish is my command. Just tell me where you want me."

* * *

Three hours later, they had baked enough cupcakes and cookies to feed an army.

"Taste this one," Remy said, offering the chocolate chip to him as he sat on a stool.

He bit into the gooey warm deliciousness and groaned. "So good."

She smiled and he reached out his arm to swipe off some of the flour dusting her cheek.

Remy stepped closer into his space. "Thank you for doing this for me."

He shrugged. "It was no biggie."

"This was so special. You listened to me and then you spent your afternoon well outside your comfort zone for me.

This means a lot." She leaned in and kissed his cheek, before doing the same to the other side. Lastly, she landed on his lips, sucking the bottom one into her mouth.

If this was the reward I get for buying a few groceries, I'll do it more often.

Dipping his tongue into her mouth, he tasted her sweetness. His hands traveled to the backs of her knees and up to the soft flesh of her thighs.

The tiniest of moans escaped her as he pulled her closer. It was getting more difficult to keep his body in check. Desire blistered his skin. Every cell throbbed with raw sexual tension.

Slow down.

Mikel tore himself away as his body screamed to climb inside her. His heart raced at a punishing pace.

Remy's innocent eyes were glazed with her own need. If she only knew the things he could do to her body.

She reached behind him and smiled. "I have one more thing for you."

"I don't think I could eat another bi—"

Remy's finger slicked across his cheek leaving something sticky behind as she giggled. His arm wrapped around her, holding her in place as she tried to wriggle from his control.

He used his free hand to wipe his face, his fingers coming away with chocolate frosting. "You frosted me?"

She gasped for breath in between her playful laughter.

"You're gonna pay for that." He dipped his fingers in the frosting bowl and smeared it over her mouth before backing her up to the counter to tickle her with his other hand. She giggled and tried to defend herself from the onslaught of his attack. She laughed harder as she wiped his other cheek. His own laugh boomed through him as tension he hadn't known he'd been holding released. His palms settled on either side of her hips as they both panted, trying to catch their breaths. She was a mess, but she'd never looked more beautiful.

"You have a little frosting on your mouth," he teased.

Her eyes lit with fire. "Then maybe you should lick it off."

He leaned down, swiping his tongue across her parted lips. His kiss wasn't gentle, but possessive. He swept her into his arms and set her on the counter, swiping the bag of flour to the ground. The fresh cookies beside them tumbled to the ground and smashed on the tiles of the floor. Her nails dug into his shoulders as he ground between her thighs. His cock strained in his jeans against her hot core. Lust surged as she moaned into his mouth. She wanted this too.

All mine.

Flames licked his self-control as the need inside him coiled so tight, it was sure to snap any moment.

He slipped his hands up her bare thighs and over her soaked panties. Her body trembled as she kneaded her hands into his back.

"Do you want this?" he asked, breaking away from her mouth to kiss her neck.

"Yes." Her voice dripped with need.

He dipped his fingers underneath the flimsy fabric and she gasped, her eyes locking on to his. He started slow, exploring her sex like uncharted territory. He paid attention to the way her eyes dilated, her breaths increased, and the hundred other small ways her body reacted to his touch. He pressed one finger inside her, and she clenched around him.

"You're so tight." Adding another finger, he stretched her, moving in and out of her while his other hand found her clit.

"Mikel!" She gasped as her eyes rolled back.

"That's it, baby. Just relax and take what I have for you. I wanna see that sexy body come all over my hands."

She clenched her brown orbs shut as he increased the speed. She was so close.

"Open your eyes."

She obeyed.

"You want this?"

"Yes." She said it like a plea.

The moment it happened, pride tightened in his chest as the look of pained bliss painted her features. She cried out and he almost came in his pants. The expression of utter satisfaction on her face was the most stunning thing he'd ever seen. "That's it, baby. You're so beautiful. So goddamned sexy."

She slumped against him as he wrapped his arms around her.

"That was . . ."

"Perfect." He finished for her.

A door slammed and the sound of boots thudded in. Remy instantly tensed in his arms and pushed him away.

Mikel turned in time to find Bently studying the disarray of the kitchen. A fine snow painted the floor where the flour had spilled in their lust-fueled haze. Cookies crushed under their feet, leaving brown smears of chocolate against the white tile.

"Dre! Come here," Bently yelled towards the door as Remy took a timid step behind Mikel. Was it even conscious?

His brother burst into laughter a moment later. "You should have seen your faces!"

"You're a real comedian." Mikel shook his head.

"Remy looks pretty guilty. Do I even want to know?" Bently asked.

Remy wouldn't meet his gaze. There was no way of hiding the scent of her arousal mixed in with the baked goods.

Mikel shrugged. "We're just taste testing some of Remy's goodies." Remy's face snapped to look at his, her embarrassment clear. He licked his fingers that had been inside her only minutes ago and said, "Fucking delicious."

A smile cracked across her face as she burst out laughing.

Bently chuckled and grabbed a cupcake, his smirk evidence he knew exactly what Mikel was talking about. "You're just lucky it wasn't really Dre coming through that door or you'd be a dead man." Bently added a cookie to the other hand before leaving them alone in the kitchen.

"This has been the best day of my life," Remy said after Bently was out of earshot.

"Me too, babe. Me too."

His phone buzzed in his pocket. Pulling it out, Joe's name flashed across the screen.

All the lightness and mirth he'd felt only moments ago was ripped away and replaced with a sickening dread.

Joe: *Meet me at my office in an hour.*

"You okay?"

Mikel's head snapped to catch Remy's concerned expression. "Yeah. Why wouldn't I be?"

"Your whole body changed after reading that text."

He shrugged and tucked his phone back in his pocket before grabbing the broom and dustpan. "Just something I forgot to do. I need to head out soon and take care of it."

More like immediately, if I want to stay on Joe's good side and out of prison. The irony wasn't lost on him that whatever job Joe had for him could also end with him behind bars.

"Oh, okay. Do you want to hang out after?" Remy asked as she started putting the ingredients away.

"Not tonight." God only knew how messed up he'd be after he got back. The things he had to do sometimes made his own skin crawl.

"Okay, well, maybe tomorrow we can get together before the—"

"We'll see. I gotta go."

He didn't mean to snap at her, but pushing her away was the only way to keep her safe and slip into the other masks he had to wear to survive.

"Okay." Her voice sounded so small and he kicked himself for ruining their good time.

He pulled her into his arms and kissed her forehead. "I'm sorry, baby. I'm just stressed about stuff."

"It's okay. You can talk to me about anything, you know."

The thought of opening up and exposing all the putrid secrets that were hidden within him was almost as terrifying as the thought of her rejecting him after she learned what a monster he was. She'd never look at him the same. "I know. Now let's get this mess cleaned up and I'll drop you off at home before I go."

She gave him a peck on the cheek before they got to work. "Sounds like a plan."

10

REMY

The next month went by fast. Mikel would pop into the bakery for coffee, and once Remy had finished her shift on Saturdays, she'd swing by his house.

"Haven't you seen enough of each other?" Jasmine whined as she opened the door for Remy.

"No. You know we don't get any time for us during the week because of his work," Remy defended, stepping inside.

"Uck."

"Is it starting to really bother you, Jaz?"

Jasmine sighed and crossed her arms. "No. I mean, as long as you don't go into details about my brother's and your *activities*. It's just gross to know you think of him in that way."

Heat spread to Remy's cheeks. "Jaz, we aren't—I mean, we haven't . . ."

Jasmine put her hands up. "Nah, nah, nah! I don't want to hear *any* details of what you are or aren't doing."

"Okay, alright. Is he upstairs?"

"Yup," Jasmine said, leading the way. She turned into her

room. The music began blaring just seconds after the door closed behind her.

Remy knocked at Mikel's.

"Hold on a sec . . . alright, come in," Mikel's voice called.

She entered. He was lying on his bed, his laptop resting on his thighs.

"Hey, beautiful," he said.

Relief. *He's in a good mood today.* She exhaled. "Hey yourself." She walked over before sitting next to him, searching for any sign that he was off. His eyes seemed fine, his pupils a little small, but it was bright in the room.

She hadn't told anyone about finding the pills those five weeks ago, not even Mikel. She hoped the issue would resolve itself, and she would never have to broach the topic. Maybe he'd stopped and it was a one-time thing, like she'd thought. He hadn't been by that house again—at least not with her. It seemed whatever she was doing was working.

The screen was paused on a video of some sort of architect's plans.

"Working on your day off, huh?" She smiled and leaned her head against his shoulder.

"Ah, the life of the self-employed." He chuckled.

"What are your plans for this weekend?"

He set the laptop aside and wrapped his arm around her, kissing her forehead. "I'm pretty beat. I was gonna relax. Maybe have a few beers with Dre and Bent around the fire, maybe grill out for dinner."

"Oh, okay." *Was there an invite in there somewhere for me?* It sounded like a relaxing idea, but they'd done it every weekend this month. "I guess I'll get going, then, and leave you to it." She started to get up, hoping he wouldn't see the rejection on her face.

"What? Why are you going? You don't wanna hang out with us?" He seemed genuinely confused.

"I wasn't invited." She smiled, trying to lighten the mood and make herself sound more like she was teasing him.

"I didn't know I needed to. I just assumed you'd wanna spend the weekend with me again." His gaze flashed with his own rejection as he drew his hands away from her.

"I would love to. But . . ."

"But?" he asked, not looking at her.

"A girl likes to be taken out every now and then. You know, like on a date?" She was thankful for her midnight skin to hide the hot flush that burned her flesh.

She'd been careful to avoid topics that might send him into that place where he shut off. He never got angry with her, just distant. His body was present, but not his mind. Had she pushed him too much by asking for what she wanted? *Stupid! I should have kept my mouth shut and followed his lead.* Her own insecurities had led her speech, needing him to acknowledge they were dating and that she was his girlfriend, without having to come right out and ask.

Mikel finally turned back to her. "A date, huh?"

She nodded shyly and rambled. "If you don't want to, that's perfectly fine."

"Let's do it." He smiled.

Sweet relief. She was finally able to breathe normally again. "You sure?"

"Yeah. I got an idea."

"Care to share?" She grinned, butterflies returning to their happy dance in her belly.

"It's a surprise."

"The last one worked out so well. I can't wait to see what you have planned for us this time." She beamed.

"We have some time to kill. Why don't we go get some

lunch and then maybe ice cream? I'll drop you off at home to change and then I'll pick you up at seven." He stood.

"Sounds good to me."

He raked a hand through his dark hair and sighed. "Can I ask you a favor?"

Remy got to her feet and walked around to face him. "Anything." And she meant it. She'd give this man her own heart if his stopped beating.

"Jasmine's been acting off lately. I want to get her out of the house, spend some time with her. Do you mind if she comes with us?" he asked sheepishly.

This was the Mikel she'd fallen for. The one who cared for his family and who'd raised a child when he was one himself. The Mikel who protected fiercely.

"Of course not! I'll go get her." She reached on tippy-toes and kissed his cheek.

His arms looped around her as he pulled her against him. Heat spread across her body, tangling and weaving together with something deeper. A force rose between them, sparking the air with electricity. The way his strong hands held her, and his brown eyes devoured her, charged her body with sensations only he had ever elicited.

"We better go before I have you naked and screaming my name. And we both know you're not ready for that." His voice was like gravel, coated with desire.

Aren't I? What is my name again?

When he looked at her like that, everything left her mind except the intense need to connect with him in every way.

"Don't look at me like that," he said.

"L-like what?" She stared at his full lips as she licked her own.

"Like you'd let me do anything I wanted to you right now." His voice was part groan.

She met his gaze. Would her first time be in his bedroom with his sister in the house?

"No," he said, as if reading her thoughts. He took her hand and guided her briskly out the bedroom door. "Get Jaz and meet me at the truck in five."

She nodded as he shut the door. Staring into the bathroom, she hesitated. *Do I have time for a cold shower?* Wasn't that what people said worked to calm this . . . riot inside her? Maybe she didn't need to cool down. Maybe she was ready.

At some point, she'd fallen in love with Mikel. He held her heart captive and he didn't even know it. She was his, and the thought was euphoric. She trusted him with her most vulnerable parts. And she never wanted this feeling to end.

* * *

"Remy? Are you going to be gone tonight?" her mama, Tilda, asked, walking into her room.

"Yeah. I'll probably be out late, so don't wait up."

Her mother's kind face flashed with concern. "Are you hanging out with Emma?"

"No. I'm going to be with Mikel. He's taking me on a surprise date," she answered honestly.

Tilda hesitated, before she said, "Honey, you know we love you. We love the Evans kids too. I'm just worried about you. I want you to make sure you're being *safe*."

Embarrassment radiated through Remy. She slapped her hand across her eyes in mortification. "Mama."

"I'd rather you be safe than sorry. I know you've been on the pill, but I need to make sure you're using other types of protection too."

"Oh my God, Mom. We are not having sex."

"Okay." She sighed, relief painting her features. "But

when you decide to do that with someone, you'll use a prophylactic, right?"

"Yes, Mom. I'm not stupid."

"It's not about being stupid, Remy. Sometimes you can get caught up in the moment and you just . . . forget. Or sometimes the boy might pressure you to go without it."

Remy held out her hand, knowing the only way to stop the assault on her ears. "Yes. You've told me, Mom. I know. I'm taking my pill every day. When I decide to have sex, I will definitely use a condom. Now, can we be done talking about this?"

"Okay, fine. Just one more thing."

"Mooooom!" She groaned.

"There's a new box of condoms in the bathroom, just in case." She walked in and kissed Remy's forehead. "Have a fun time. Be safe. Please text me where you'll be just in case."

"I will."

"Love you, honey."

"Love you too, Mom."

Maybe she'd grab one to keep in her purse. *Just in case.*

11

MIKEL

Holding Remy's soft small hand in his as they walked into the carnival gave him a feeling of pride. This girl was all his for the night. After an afternoon of taking turns trying to make Jaz laugh and bring her out of whatever funk she was in, he'd thought he couldn't appreciate Remy more. The way Remy was quick to carry the conversation when he was lost for words was just one of the many reasons he was starting to care more deeply than he'd thought his dilapidated heart was capable of.

"I love carnivals." She smiled and it went straight through his chest like an arrow. Why did she affect him so much? Fear crept in, winding up his spine like a snake waiting to strike.

He looped his arm around her waist, pulling her small body against his large frame. Those tiny cutoff shorts she wore drew all his attention to her naked thighs. "Wanted to do something different. Show off my dart skills."

"As long as I get a candy apple, I don't care what we do." She laughed.

"It's a deal." He paid at the ticket counter before

guiding her around the grounds. Bright colors swirled beyond them as paper lanterns of all hues hung on lines above. Other couples and families milled about, playing games and eating the greasy fried food that the food trucks supplied.

A live band performed from the small stage, doing popular covers from an array of musicians as Remy and Mikel made their way from game to game. Mikel's skin tingled like someone was watching them. He surveyed the crowd. No familiar faces stuck out to him; only a few people's stares lingered longer than was polite.

"Let's do the Ferris wheel," Remy said, pulling him towards the line for the old metal contraption.

"You sure?" He eyed the rust. "Looks like it's older than your gramma."

"They wouldn't let people ride it if it wasn't safe," she teased.

So trusting. Didn't she know how dangerous blind faith was?

He gave the attendant the tickets and climbed on as the metal creaked. Nerves twisted his stomach with worry.

"Hey, at least if we die, we go together." Remy smiled.

"If you're trying to make me feel better, that sure as fuck didn't work."

Her grin faded a little.

Why did it feel like a sucker punch to the chest? He was screwing this up. He placed his arm around her and pulled her close. "I'm not scared of dying, honey. I'm worried about you. There's no way I'd ever let anything happen to you."

She leaned in and kissed him. Soft and sweet. Like she knew just what he needed to feel at peace. The tension in his shoulders eased as he relaxed onto the metal seat. His hand moved up and down her shoulder, her closeness grounding him.

The sun was setting, casting the sky in cotton candy colors as they rotated on the ride.

"The view is so beautiful up here," she said, snuggling into his chest.

He studied the curves of her face, her long dark eyelashes, and button nose. "Absolutely stunning," he agreed.

If he could freeze time and stay trapped in a moment forever, this would be that one. Up here, he could forget everything else and just be. Remy did that for him better than any drug he'd ever tried. He'd never be able to let her go now.

"Sometimes you gotta take risks to enjoy the beauty." Remy sighed.

"Since when did you become a risk-taker?" He chuckled.

"Hmm . . . since that first night at The Shipwreck. It paid off, so I've decided to take a gamble every now and then."

She meant *him*. He'd been her reward. Gratitude and pure adoration battered against his rib cage. She thought he was worth something. It didn't matter if she was wrong. He'd soak up the warm feeling that wrapped around him like a hug.

"Have you learned anything new lately?" she asked after a beat of silence.

He told her about the video he'd watched and how he'd been able to enhance the efficiency of his and Andre's building process.

"Working smarter, not harder, huh?"

"Something like that. We're hoping we can fit more contracts in and be able to hire a crew, eventually branch out into bigger projects like homes."

"With your business sense and Andre's skills you'll get there in no time."

"I got skills too," he teased.

She smirked, lust in her eyes. "You sure do."

Was she making a sexual reference? *Wow.* Remy sure was

coming out of her shell. He liked this newfound confidence in her.

They got off the ride and meandered around to a few games before stopping at one of the food trucks.

"One candy apple, please," Mikel ordered, fishing for cash in his wallet.

The bored teenager handed the candied fruit over and Remy greedily took it as he paid the lady. They walked around, hand in hand. It felt so good to be close to her, to be in Remy's space.

Her little pink tongue darted out, licking around the candy apple. He was hard as steel, as she enjoyed the sweet treat, taking little bites here and there.

"Want a taste?" she asked, offering the confection to him.

Unable to restrain himself any longer, he leaned in and swept his tongue across her mouth—a sugar rush of Remy and candied apple ensued. She parted her lips, allowing him access as he deepened the kiss. She let out the smallest of moans. He slid his hand to her neck and under her long braids. She was hot to the touch. He wasn't in this firestorm alone.

He pulled back before he took her right there. It was commanding every last shred of control to not move too quickly with Remy. She was different, and he didn't want to do anything she'd regret. This all had to be her choice. He'd follow her lead. "Let's go listen to the band."

She nodded before he led her around the grounds towards the stage. His phone buzzed in his pocket. He'd ignore it, just this once. Mikel didn't want his world to taint hers.

"What's wrong?" Remy asked as she stopped walking.

She must have sensed him grow tense. The phone vibrated again. Slipping it out of his pocket, he held his breath. Joe was calling.

"Can you give me a second? I gotta take this."

"Sure."

He turned and walked out of earshot. "Yeah," he answered.

"I got a delivery for you." Joe coughed.

"I'll do it first thing tomorrow."

"No. Tonight."

Mikel tugged on the ends of his hair and bit his lip. "I'm busy tonight." He'd never told Joe no before. There were consequences, but if anyone was worth it, it was Remy.

"Excuse me? Maybe your brother wants to hear about that little secret you've kept all these years. Think Mister Rent-A-Cop would be willing to look the other way for his little brother?"

Mikel swallowed the curses he wanted to yell at the man who held his life hostage. *No. Bently would kill me.* His brother's moral compass would tear them apart. "Text me the details and I'll be over soon."

"That's a good boy." Joe's words cut deeper than any two-edged sword ever could.

Mikel hung up and balled his fists. Anger radiated through him in rippling waves. He had no one to blame except himself. He'd done this. Spotting a portable bathroom, he ran in, barely locking it behind him. Reaching into his pocket, he pulled out the little bottle of white powder. He hesitated.

I shouldn't do this. Not now. Not with Remy just out there, waiting for him. *I am stronger than this, damn it!* But how the hell was he going to face her and see that pretty face fall with disappointment when he told her he'd have to cut their date short? *Again?* It would destroy him. The powder spilled onto his hand before he knew it. *Just one small hit. One little bump to get me through.* His eyes closed, as he welcomed the rush.

He took another minute to compose himself and then put it away before going on a search for Remy.

She wasn't by the booth where he'd left her. Scanning the crowd, he caught sight of her boxed in against the side of a tent by two guys. One of the motherfuckers draped his arm around her.

Pure blind rage seared his body, taking control as he stalked towards them.

"You should come with us. I promise to show you a good time."

"No, thanks." She tried to pull away from him, but the guy wouldn't let her go.

No fucking way.

"There you are, baby." Mikel grabbed her hand and pulled her into his chest. Relief coated her expression as her shoulders relaxed.

"Ahh, come on now. We were just about to get to know each other a little better." The cocky voice of the one who had touched her said.

His fists clenched. He'd really love to show this guy some manners, but Remy's safety was the most important thing. Mikel surveyed their surroundings; only a few other families milled about nearby.

"Let's go," Mikel said, guiding Remy in front of him.

"Don't leave yet. The night is just getting started," one of the other guys said, stepping in front of them. His frame was bulkier, but he still stood a few inches shorter than Mikel, his eyes bloodshot and twitching. He was obviously on something.

Remy's body trembled against his. She was scared, and rightfully so. Two against one while trying to keep her safe would prove to be a challenge. Good thing he knew a thing or two about fighting dirty.

"Hey, wait a minute. I know this guy," one of the men said.

Dread crawled up his skin. There was only one place a deadbeat like him would know Mikel from. His two lives were about to clash, and Remy would be the casualty. She couldn't find out.

Mikel leaned towards her ear and whispered, "Run to the car and lock it. I'll be there in a few minutes." He slipped the keys into her hand as she tensed and shook her head. "Do what I say, Remy. Now!"

She took off towards the parking lot as he whirled around. His fist met with the bigger guy's unsuspecting faces in a flash. Searing pain erupted from the split flesh of his knuckles, but the release of tension was like soaring. The second guy grabbed Mikel's waist as he drove his elbow back with a bone-crunching thud. Grunts and groans erupted from the two men. Blood trickled down one's face while the other's filled with rage. A heavy body brought him to the ground. A woman's scream distracted the man long enough for Mikel to get to his knees.

He was kicked by a hard boot and pain radiated from his ribs. Mikel grunted as he jumped to his feet, fists in the air, ready to teach the men a lesson about touching a woman without her consent. The two of them took off, running towards the crowd in the carnival.

The wail of police sirens split the night air.

He jogged towards the parking lot through the crowd of spectators more interested in capturing his fight on video than lending a hand. A mother pulled her son closer to her chest as he passed, like he was the monster. He just needed to make sure Remy was safe.

The sight of her stricken face in the shadows of his truck made his heart ache. She clutched her phone to her ear, her mouth forming words he couldn't hear as her tear-filled eyes met with his. She hung up. She'd been the one to call the cops.

He climbed in the cab, wincing from the pain in his side.

"Are you okay? Are you hurt?" Remy asked, her soft hands gently searching his bruised form.

"I'm fine."

"Why did you do that? Why did you send me away?" Remy turned, the anger and confusion in her stare burning a hole into his heart.

Because I was reminded that I'm powerless, a slave to a piece of scum. Because that guy had touched her. He'd had to protect her. How had another great day gone to shit? Because as hard as he fucking tried, his past always caught up to him.

"So you'd be safe." He draped an arm over her and pulled her close. She inspected his torn knuckles in her soft palms before she drew them to her mouth, planting delicate kisses on his flesh. The act was so tender it nearly broke him.

She looked up at him. "I was so scared for you. It felt wrong to leave."

Her emotions were so potent he felt them trembling deep in his bones, thundering through him like a storm. "All I need is for you to trust me. And you did that. You were perfect." He kissed her forehead. "Now let's get you home."

Where she would be safe. Where his shadows couldn't touch her.

Joe was expecting him tonight. It was time to say goodbye to the fantasy and get back to his dark reality.

"Tomorrow night, let's go to the beach. Just you and me," she said.

"Sounds perfect."

12

REMY

Waves crashed in the darkness on the deserted beach. They snuggled in the back of his truck as the half-moon reflected off the midnight water. She tucked the soft plaid throw he'd spread out over her legs. The salty July air wrapped around their skin like a warm blanket. It was perfect, lying in his arms, with the canopy of stars splattered across the heavens above them. Everything felt right when she was this close to Mikel.

She turned to study his chiseled profile in the glow of the moon. He was beautiful. Strong and broken. A fallen star. Her dark angel.

He'd protected her. He'd supported her dreams. Their time together hadn't been all smooth sailing. But it was during small moments like this one, when his mask fell, revealing his soul in shattered pieces, that everything was perfect. She would give anything to chase his demons away, to connect with him in a way she had never connected with a man before.

She lifted her face to his. He gazed back at her as if she

were the most beautiful thing on the planet. In his eyes, she recognized the man he could be, the happiness he could have if she could figure out how to help set him free. She saw forever.

Remy leaned closer, erasing the space between their mouths, kissing him soft and slow, and purposeful. She wanted to remove the pain and infuse her lips with every last bit of love and compassion she had inside her, using her movements to tell him everything she was too afraid to say aloud. She pulled the hem, taking her shirt off, exposing her white lace bra.

He blinked and swallowed. A flash of fear and uncertainty in his eyes was quickly masked with lust. She unsnapped the back of her bra, letting her breasts fall free. She shivered as a wave of goose bumps spread across her skin. His glassy eyes stared back at her, watching her with rapt attention. Rough calloused hands caressed her dark nipple, his arousal hard and demanding underneath the heat of her core.

His white flesh contrasted with hers. Bending to kiss him, she reached for his pants button, fumbling in her nervousness. She gasped as he flipped her on her back before climbing on top of her, taking control. A sensation she had never known eclipsed her body. Something about the raw power he exuded made her insides quiver. His head dipped to her chest as his tongue licked her erect nipple. It burned so hard it hurt. He moved, grinding his hardness against her center. Even through his pants she could tell he was large.

"Mikel?" She panted as he sucked and laved her breast, sending sparks and shimmers of heat to her womb.

"I want to taste you so bad, Remy. Can I do that?" he asked, his voice heady with want.

His question sent a shockwave of anticipation rippling through her. She nodded, the word stuck in her throat.

"I'm gonna take care of you, baby," he said, trailing kisses down her belly towards her shorts. She drew in a shaky breath as he unbuttoned her cutoffs and slid them along her legs.

"You say the word and we'll stop," he assured her, before kissing the inside of her thighs.

She trembled as suddenly every sensation was amplified. The only sound she could hear was her thunderous heartbeat. The only touch of rough hands gently, reverently, pulling her panties down to fully expose her to him. She had never felt so vulnerable in all her life. Nerves and curiosity were swallowed by lust as he slipped a finger inside her wetness. All self-consciousness left her mind as pleasure soaked through her.

She moaned at the pleasant intrusion.

"You're so tight, so wet for me, baby." His breath tickled the sensitive flesh of her lower lips. A fever spread throughout her. Nothing else mattered in that moment but Mikel and what he was doing to her body. His tongue, warm and wet, slid inside her folds. His head bobbed between her parted thighs. His hands and mouth swirled, laving, flicking, and sucking. She came alive. An impending pressure built. He slipped another finger inside her as she winced and moaned. It hurt so good.

"You taste so sweet. You're beautiful, baby. Every part of you. I'm gonna make you see stars, beautiful. Gonna make you come."

His gravelly voice sent a bolt of white-hot need burning in every cell of her body. Inhibitions stripped, she arched her back, pressing herself against him, shamelessly seeking the relief he promised.

One hand reached out and pinched her nipple as his other fingers dipped inside her well, finding a spot that she had only read about in romance novels. The touch to the extra-sensitive area sent glittering flashes into her vision as she cried out, the pressure threatening to break her.

"Yes! Mikel, please!" she begged.

He sucked the sensitive pearl gently, giving her the final push into her orgasm. Intoxicating pleasure spiraled through her as she jumped freely over the edge, soaring, floating.

He lay next to her, holding her against his chest as she came down. Sated, relaxed, and limbless.

This is what heaven must feel like. The stars aligned. Everything as it should be.

She turned to Mikel, and tasted herself in his illicit kiss. Had she really just let him do that to her? Her cheeks heated as she snuggled against him. Trailing her hand down his abs, she lifted his T-shirt. He helped her take it off and lay back down.

She kissed his peck before licking one of his nipples.

"Do you like that?" she asked.

"Yeah."

She did it again, sucking one of his pink buds into her mouth as her hand slid down the trail of dark hair towards that perfect *V*. She moved to place a kiss in the center of one of the dips of his hip as she unbuttoned his pants.

His hand halted her exploration. "Remy, stop."

She turned towards him, confused.

"You don't have to do that. Tonight was about making you feel good."

She took a deep breath. "But what if I want to?" she asked. "What if this will make me feel good too?"

He clenched his jaw. His abdominal muscles tensed as his breathing increased. "Are you sure?"

"Yes," she answered, her voice not giving away the nerves she felt inside. She wanted to bring him the kind of bliss he had just shown her.

She removed his pants until he was as bare as she. She took in the sight of this naked man before her. His thick erect cock bobbed in front of her face. Her hand trembled as she reached out and wrapped her fingers around his hardness.

He hissed, and she looked back to him. *Was she doing something wrong?* "Is this okay?"

"It's perfect." He placed his palm over hers, moving it up and down his length. He was rock-hard, his abs clenched and taut. His gaze locked on to her. She lowered her head and licked the tip of his cock. He groaned his appreciation. He seemed so big and intimidating. Thanks to Emma's oversharing, she at least had some idea of what she was supposed to do.

She opened her mouth, taking him in as far as she could, moving her hand to the base. She moved him in and out of her mouth, slowly exploring him with her tongue. He groaned.

"That feels so fucking good. You're so sexy. So perfect," he said.

She sucked as he fisted her hair, guiding her head into the perfect rhythm, his moans of approval putting her at ease.

"Fuck, Remy. I'm gonna come." He slipped out of her mouth, grabbing her hand around his cock to guide her. He grew harder than she'd thought possible in her palm. She straddled his hips as he dropped his palms to her thighs, fully relinquishing control of his pleasure to her hands—trusting her.

"You don't want to come in my mouth?" she asked, licking her lips as his hot member pulsed.

"Fuck, Remy!" He growled as hot spurts of his cum shot out onto her breasts, dripping to her belly, marking her.

His whole body tensed and pulsed as he emptied himself.

His face focused and intense in the darkness as he orgasmed. A savage conqueror at her mercy.

They were both panting. She was revved up and ready for more. This was absolutely her new favorite thing to do. She hoped it was as good for him as it was for her.

"Was that okay?" she asked, climbing off him to sit on the blanket.

"That was a whole lot better than okay. That was fucking magical," he said, settling her apprehension.

He spread his arm for her and she snuggled against his bare chest. They lay together for a few minutes. His breathing slowed and his eyes closed.

She sat up and climbed out of the truck bed. The more time she spent with him, the more confident in herself she seemed to be.

"Where are you goin'?" he asked.

She turned back and nodded towards the water. "I'm gonna go wash up. Wanna go for a swim?"

He smiled and followed her. They carried their clothes down to the beach.

Remy was thankful for the cover of darkness and a deserted sandy coast. She turned her head towards their only witness: a sky painted with millions of bright bursts. Stories recorded in the heavens.

Would theirs ever be immortalized like the myths and legends?

13

REMY

Summer was passing in a blur. Days were spent at the bakery, and weekends with Mikel.

Remy: *Hey, baby. Want me to come over tonight?*

She sighed as she prepared herself to be turned down again. She never knew with him. He could be the kindest, most amazing boyfriend one minute and then distant the next.

Mikel: *Busy. Tomorrow?*

It was Saturday, and Andre wasn't working. What else could it be? His job took a lot out of him. Maybe he was just tired.

But he didn't say that. He said he was busy.

"Ugh!" She was obsessing. She just needed to keep herself occupied today.

Remy: *Up for a girls' day?*

Emma: *Yes, ma'am!*

Sunday morning, Remy grabbed her phone. Mikel hadn't responded to her goodnight text. Was something wrong?

Remy: *Good morning. Should I come over, or are you going to pick me up?*

Several minutes passed before her phone rang.

"Hey."

"Hey, baby. Listen, I got a few things I need to take care of this morning. Maybe we can hang out later this afternoon?" Mikel said.

"I could tag along with you and keep you company—"

"No." His voice was adamant.

"Oh, okay." She hoped she was disguising the hurt in her voice.

"I'd just rather get this done and over with and get to you. I'll text you when I'm on the way."

"Alright. I miss you." It had been eight days since they'd seen each other.

He sighed. "Miss you too, baby. I'll make up for it tonight. Promise." His smooth voice made her clench her thighs together in anticipation.

"Can't wait."

It was more evening than afternoon when Mikel finally messaged that he was on his way over to pick her up.

Remy's body wound tight with anticipation. It was getting harder and harder to stop herself from going all the way. The times they spent naked and tangled together brought them closer. She wanted Mikel to be her first. That condom was burning a hole in her bag. Was there something wrong with her? Was that why Mikel hadn't tried to take it further? For once in her life she wished she wasn't as inexperienced.

The smile that spread across his lips erased all her fears as she walked towards him. The way his gaze raked across every inch of her never got old. The jeans he wore fit snugly around his thighs, and she'd bet her life that his behind looked as good as his front. Her gaze lingered on his torso, admiring how his faded tee clung to his muscular tan arms. The arms that held her when she fell apart with orgasms, and those rough calloused hands that took her there.

"You look good enough to eat." His heated stare burned her skin.

"Well, I wouldn't want you to go hungry now, would I?" She winked.

The bags under his eyes were only getting worse. Worry was woven behind the mask he usually wore. His shoulders seemed to be weighed down with some unknown burden.

"I gotta make a quick stop and then we can have some fun."

She nodded. What she wouldn't give to make him feel lighter for one night. She'd do whatever she could to support him like he'd done for her. If only he'd open up more about what was troubling him.

He drove them to the edge of town. She'd only been here one other time, with him. Mikel pulled up to the house she'd suspected he got his drugs from, and it was the final straw. Several cars were spread out on the lawn as music bled into the warm night.

"I'll be right back," he said, grabbing the door handle.

Remy's arm shot out to stop him.

He turned to her, confusion written across his features.

"I know what we're doing here."

He looked down momentarily. "What do you mean? Of course you do. I told you, I just need to make a quick stop. My friend Isaiah is holding something for me."

"And you'll come back out with nothing in your hands, and pills in your pocket," she said, with sudden determination. *Where did that come from?*

Avoiding the topic hadn't worked. Maybe she just needed to let him know that he didn't have to hide it from her. That he could trust her.

"What are you talking about?" he asked, getting defensive. His voice was stone cold.

"You don't have to do this."

"Do what?" He steeled his expression.

"I-I found them," she said, suddenly less sure. *Maybe they weren't his?* Her belly twisted into thousands of intricate knots. Her world tilted on its axis. She wasn't sure what was right or wrong, what she should do.

"You found what?"

"The pills," she answered, her voice quieter than she intended.

He was silent for a moment, looking towards the house as if deep in thought.

Distant again.

She unbuckled and moved closer to him, laying her hand on his chest as she spoke. "Mikel, I don't know what you're going through, but I want you to know that I'm here for you. Whatever you need."

He flinched as if her words had somehow hurt him. "Were you snooping around in my shit?" he asked in a low growl.

Anxious worry curled in a ball, skittering around in her stomach. His anger had never been directed at her before. "No!" She defended herself. "A few months ago, when I made your bed, I found the bag by accident. But I've put two and two together."

He swallowed hard, still not looking at her. His heart was

pounding below her palm. "Have you told anyone else?" he asked, his voice a little kinder this time.

"No, Mikel. I haven't said a word to anyone."

He turned towards her, his eyes pleading. "Please don't. Keep this between us. I don't use that much. I'm not an addict or anything. I just need some help sometimes to get through the day. I take it to keep the memories away, to help me sleep."

A tiny voice inside her protested at his request, this was a bigger deal than he was making it out to be. Another part of her wanted to believe the man she loved wasn't an addict. Addicts were supposed to be horrible, selfish people. Mikel cared for her, Bently, and Andre, and helped provide for Jasmine. She wanted to believe him.

She couldn't turn him down when he was being so open and honest with her. This was what she'd wanted—his trust. "I won't. I promise. But will you try to cut back?"

"Yeah. I can do that. No problem." He nodded vigorously, wrapping her in a hug tightly to his chest.

She breathed out a sigh of relief. He would make an effort.

"Well, now that you know. Wanna come in and meet my friends? They're having a little party. We don't have to stay long," he assured her.

She smiled. He was letting her into his world, granting her access to a hidden part of him. There was no way she could turn him down. "Sure."

They entered the house. Remy was surprised at the small crowd of people all seemingly relaxed and happy. *Normal.* A few lines of white powder were being cut on a glass table by the couch. Several others were dancing to the music that thumped from the sound system. She recognized one of the faces from her high school, and a few others she'd seen around town. Nothing could have prepared her for this. But her parents had always taught her to try and see the good in people, to give them the benefit of the doubt. She didn't know their stories, or what led them here.

"You okay?" Mikel asked, squeezing his arm tighter around her waist.

She nodded, at a loss for words.

A man with red hair approached them. He had black circles under his glassy eyes and a bong in one of his hands. "My man." He reached out to greet Mikel.

"Isaiah, this is my girlfriend, Remy." Mikel introduced them.

Girlfriend. Hearing him say it never got old. She did a happy dance internally. A new sense of belonging washed over her, and she smiled and waved. "Hi."

Isaiah looked her up and down, making her a bit uncomfortable.

"You want a hit? First one's on the house," Isaiah said, offering her the glass instrument.

Mikel answered for her, "Nah, man. She's a good girl."

Isaiah's gaze turned to scrutiny before he spoke to Mikel. "I'd offer you one, but I know what you like. Joe's coming by soon."

Anxiety twisted around her, fear slithering up her spine.

Mikel tensed for a moment before he said, "Saves me a trip to go find him."

"Well, well. Look what the cat dragged in," a female voice purred.

Remy turned as the blond woman approached. *The same woman from the bar that first night we kissed.*

She raked her eyes over Mikel as jealousy flared within Remy, hot green flames searing her insides. Remy waited to see how Mikel would react.

"June. Been a while. I don't think you've met my girlfriend, Remy," he said.

June turned her attention back to her, scowling. She looked Remy up and down, as if measuring her on a scale and finding her wanting. "I was wondering what kept you away. I have to say, I'm surprised she's held your attention that long," June said, looking back to Mikel.

Remy's stomach churned. Vomit rose in her throat as acid burned her stomach. *Mikel has been with her?*

"Stop being a bitch, June," Isaiah said, still not taking his hungry gaze off Remy.

Mikel pulled out his wallet and removed some cash. He handed it to June. "Here. Why don't you go get me the only thing I need from you and don't say another word here about my girl, or we're gonna have some problems."

June snatched the cash, acting as if she was hurt by his words. She pouted. "You sure you don't wanna come with me for old time's sake?"

"Just go get what the man asked for," Isaiah said.

June cut him a look and then disappeared up the stairs.

"Sorry about that, man. A woman scorned, you know how it goes," Isaiah said.

"Don't worry about it," Mikel said, tightening his grip on Remy.

Suddenly his arm felt heavier around her. It was getting harder to breathe. She needed a moment to herself, and some air. "Do you have a bathroom I could use?" she asked.

Isaiah pointed towards a door. She walked out from Mikel's grasp towards the restroom before shutting herself inside.

She glanced at herself in the mirror. Her dry eyes quickly turned glassy as tears burned, threatening to slip out. Remy took some deep cleansing inhales.

It was no secret Mikel had been around the block. She just hadn't expected to meet any of his earlier conquests, or have their relations thrown in her face. Reality hit, spinning her in a web of uncertainty and worry. She had never dealt with something of this magnitude. It was like Mikel was living two different lives.

She had a feeling, a knowing deep within her soul, that Mikel's problem was much bigger than he was letting on, and a whole lot more than she wanted to admit. But what could she do? He was finally letting her see this other side to him she hadn't known existed. She couldn't base her decisions off of fear. Telling someone else would break his trust.

Remy let out a deep breath. She needed to stand by his side and give him the love and support that no one else could. The same as he'd done for her. They'd figure this out together.

With a new plan, and a clearer mind, she washed her hands and stepped out of the bathroom. Mikel stood by the door, arguing with an older man with black-and-white-peppered hair. His only menacing feature was the scar that ran down the side of his face. Goose bumps prickled across her skin as a warning resounded within, embedding itself into her every fiber. The hair on the back of her neck stood on end.

Mikel handed the old man a wad of cash he'd pulled from his wallet. She couldn't see how much, but the bills were hundreds. The man tucked the cash into his own pocket before he grabbed Mikel roughly by the shoulder, speaking into his ear.

Remy pulled her cell phone out of her back pocket. She clutched it, ready to call someone for help if this got ugly. Her body tensed, adrenaline pulsing in her veins, ready and alert. She was confused and unsure, wishing she and Mikel could just run out those doors and never return.

She walked up to them on shaky legs, hoping her presence would halt the threat. If he asked her to run again, she didn't think she could do it.

Mikel spoke as she approached. "I will. Next week."

The man backed up, turning to her. His cold, dead eyes locked on hers as a sinister smile spread across his face. "I'll hold you to it. And who do we have here?" the man asked.

Mikel grabbed her hand, his jaw clenching before he spoke. "We're just on our way out."

"It's like that, is it? You know I like to get to know the people who work for me, and the special people in their lives. I'm Joe Canoby."

Remy held her breath. Mikel squeezed her trembling hand, offering her some comfort. Confusion swirled. Mikel didn't work for anyone. He was a business partner to her brother with their own company, Seaview Construction. "You're a client of Mikel's?" she asked.

Joe laughed again, slapping his leg. This time he ended in a fit of coughs. He pulled out a pack of cigarettes from his pocket, lighting one up and taking a few drags before blowing smoke in their faces.

"No, doll. Is that what he told you?"

"Come on, Remy. Let's go." Mikel pulled her arm towards the door.

She didn't resist. She followed him outside. When they had entered Isaiah's, she'd been feeling like she was finally getting through to Mikel, making progress, breaking down the walls that surrounded his wounded, fragile heart and knowing him more deeply. Yet somehow as they left, it was like she didn't know the man next to her at all. This Mikel was a stranger.

She put one shaky leg in front of the other as she climbed into the truck. He shut the door behind her and went over to his side before starting the engine.

"Remy, look—"

"Stop," she said, shaking her head. "I just want to go home." *Back where I know I'm safe.* Where she knew a truth from a lie, up from down, and everything could be neatly organized into categories.

He slammed the steering wheel with his hand, making her jump as he yelled, "Fuck!" He whipped the car into reverse and sped down the road. She focused on the passing trees out her window. They were blurring fast.

It wasn't until hot tears streamed down her face that she realized she was crying.

14

MIKEL

Mikel had let her walk out of his truck without a word. He'd had a piece-of-shit day, and he needed to make a run. It was his own weakness and negligence that had made his two worlds collide, leaving Remy to witness it. Why hadn't he known better?

Because I needed a fix.

Whether she knew it or not, she deserved the space to really think things through, and he'd give it to her.

The week came and went. He didn't stop into the bakery in the mornings like usual.

Friday night, he sighed and rubbed the back of his neck, his muscles sore from a long day at work.

"You wanna meet up at The Shipwreck?" Andre asked, putting his toolbox in the back of his truck.

"Sure. I got some shit to do and then I'll stop by."

"You okay?" Andre asked.

"Yeah. Why wouldn't I be?" he lied. If Remy told Dre what she'd seen, her brother would probably kill him.

"You've been quiet all week. Everything okay with you and my sister?"

His chest squeezed. His traitorous body just wanted to be near her again, but it was better for her if he stayed away.

"Why wouldn't it be?"

Andre shrugged. "You both look like your dog died."

Anguish sluiced through his rib cage. Remy was in pain and he'd caused it. "Just got a lot on my mind."

"Well, come have a few beers with me and forget it for a little while," Andre said, getting into his truck.

"Will do."

His friend drove off as Mikel climbed into his vehicle. All he wanted was a hot shower and to go to bed, wrapped around Remy's soft curves. But that was why they called it a fantasy—because it wasn't really going to happen.

Mikel shifted into gear and drove towards the address he'd come to know all too well.

* * *

Mikel hated himself for what he had to do to survive and keep his family safe. But this was his life.

"I'll have it next week. Tell Joe I promise. I swear I'm getting some money in from my aunt, but she doesn't get paid until Friday. I'll have the cash then."

Mikel pulled back his fist as the balding man winced. The stink of fear on this man was almost as rancid as the self-disgust on Mikel's tongue.

If Remy ever saw me like this . . .

"You better have every fucking penny or I'll be back to finish the job," Mikel threatened.

He hadn't had to do it yet, but Lou Barrenger was the

closest he'd come. A compulsive gambler who'd borrowed money from the wrong loan shark. Usually, if Mikel beat them hard enough, they'd do anything short of robbing a bank to get the funds. Lou must have had a death wish, because Mikel'd had to visit him more often than all the others.

There is a special place in hell for people like me. As long as he did Joe's bidding, heroin deliveries and debt collecting, his family was safe, and he wouldn't land in prison for the life he had taken.

"I will," Lou promised for the umpteenth time. As if his word was any good.

Mikel unclenched his fist and dropped his hand to his side as the man cowered below him. "For both our sakes, I hope you do." He crouched low, looking the terrified man in the eyes. "Whether you do or don't get the cash, you better leave the state and never come back." *I don't want to kill you.* He hoped the man would value his life enough to listen.

Lou looked up at him, understanding flashing in his eyes. He nodded vigorously. "I will."

Mikel stood and wiped his fist on his shirt, leaving a smear of red behind. He tore off the bloodstained tee before throwing it in his truck.

He drove home with the windows down, letting the crisp fall air numb his skin, much like his insides. When he made it home, he threw his shirt in the trash and headed for his bedroom.

Lifting up the lamp on his bedside table, he pulled the bag of pills out before swallowing three and heading for the shower.

The hot spray of water was damn near scalding on his cold flesh. He grit his teeth and sunk to his knees. Everything felt so heavy. Everything hurt. Remy's beautiful face popped into his mind, radiating sunlight and warmth until it spread over every dark and empty area within him. She enabled him to feel something besides pain. Remy was a gift as potent as his first high, only it lasted longer with her. He needed her. Too bad a man like him was only good at one thing—causing people pain.

15

REMY

After clicking open the web browser, Remy surveyed the information on one of the countless sites she'd found about addiction. The past week without contact from Mikel had torn her into pieces. She'd been getting through to him until she had messed it all up by shutting him out. But she'd been so scared and unsure of what to do. Remy loved Mikel, and she wanted to help. She just wasn't sure what that meant.

She'd pored over research online and found an interesting piece in her quest for information stating that the opposite of addiction was not sobriety, but connection. How could she provide that for Mikel beyond what she was doing? She'd done everything she could to let him know she was there for him. Had she done something wrong? One thing was clear: enabling the behavior was the absolute worst thing a person could do for an addict. But what was the difference between enabling and compassion? Could she draw a line like that with him? Creating a boundary between them was the antithesis of showing him love, wasn't it?

The screen door creaked, bringing her back from her thoughts. Crisp September air blew through the back of the bakery, melding perfectly with the apple, pumpkin, and cinnamon swirling into a delicious aroma in the small space. It was Remy's favorite time of the year—warm days and cool nights.

"Are you going to invite me to this bonfire at the beach that Andre is putting together this weekend?" Emma asked.

Remy weaved the pie crust together over the warm apples. "You're always welcome. But I'm not sure if I'll be there."

"Why? You and that man of yours have other plans?" Emma smiled as she teased.

Guilt and pain squeezed her chest. She hadn't told anyone that she and Mikel had had an argument. It was like he'd dropped off the face of the earth. He hadn't tried to reach out to her, but neither had she tried to reach out to him. Loving an addict was isolating.

"Remy? Did something happen?" Emma asked, sounding concerned.

"We kinda had a fight. He hasn't tried to talk to me since."

"I'm sure he'll come around. What was the argument about?" Emma asked, wrapping her in a hug.

Remy relaxed into her friend's arms. She couldn't give her all the details and betray Mikel's confidence. He'd asked her to promise to keep his secret. One of many she held inside for him. "It was a week and a half ago."

"Ahh, Rem. I'm so sorry. What can I do?" Emma asked, backing away to look her in the eyes.

"Just being able to tell you has helped."

"How about you walk me through what happened? Maybe I can shed some light with my years of dating wisdom." She laughed, lightening the mood.

Remy searched for the words to cultivate an example

without spilling his secrets. "He kinda lied by omission about something. Questions came up and I was afraid of the answers. Someone told me something about him that didn't make sense."

"Ummm . . . okay . . . Not giving me a whole lot to go on here, are you? Did you try to talk to him about it and see what his explanation was?" Emma asked.

"No. I shut down. I just needed some space to get my head clear. When I'm with him, I'm sucked into all things Mikel. He clouds my mind like a fog."

Emma smirked. "He puts you in a haze of lust-induced fantasies, I'm sure."

Remy smacked her friend's arm playfully, her cheeks growing hot.

"Ouch! Okay, so it sounds like you're saying you didn't give him the opportunity to explain. Maybe reach out to him and try to talk it through."

"I was hoping he would make the first move."

"Sometimes boys are dumb. They need direction. They do the opposite of what we need and want. Trust me. I have lots of experience in that department."

Remy smiled, hope bubbling in her belly. Maybe she needed to bite the bullet and be the one to make the first move. Mikel needed her to be strong for him.

* * *

She pulled her car into her driveway, nerves tangling with drunk moths in her stomach suddenly. Mikel's truck was parked in front.

She walked into the house tentatively as deep, rumbling laughter came from the living room. Mikel sat with her father, having a beer. She nearly stumbled when he turned to face her. The man's presence was as potent as always, stealing the breath from her lungs. It stirred and blurred the lines around her carefully crafted world into a vortex of raw need.

"You're home, sweetie. I was just telling Mikel here about the time I found out you were being bullied at school. You told me to not worry about it because your angel had handled it. For so long we thought she'd gone religious." Her father grinned, turning back to Mikel. "Then Andre said that you'd gotten suspended for getting into a fight with the same boy who had been teasing my little girl. I don't think I ever got to thank you for that. I never condone violence, but the fact that you stepped in for Remy when I couldn't be there meant a lot."

Mikel's jaw clenched as he smiled. "I'd do anything for her," he said, stealing the only piece of her heart remaining.

She swallowed in the silence that descended upon the room. Her father stood, still wearing his sweater-vest and bow tie from work. "I'll leave you both to your evening. Have fun. But not too much fun, you hear?" he joked.

"Yes, sir." Mikel got to his feet and nodded.

Her father kissed her forehead and patted her shoulder. "I'm gonna head out. Promised I would meet your mom for dinner. You'll have to fend for yourselves." He grabbed his keys and left them alone. The sound of the door closing quickly was swallowed up by the stillness in the room.

She turned to Mikel as he stepped towards her. Tentatively, she met his gaze, afraid of what she would see there—pain, sorrow . . . regret?

"Can we talk?" he asked, clenching his fists at his sides.

She nodded, her voice held captive by the war that waged inside her—confusion, hope, and disappointment roiled and tangled, taking up space in her chest.

"I wanted to apologize. I need to explain," he started.

"What work do you do for Joe?" she asked.

He winced and looked at the ground before meeting her gaze. "I moved some product for him. Collected some debts." The words scraped from his voice like he had swallowed shards of glass.

Afraid to ask for further details, or of what she might uncover, she asked, "Why did you pay him that money?"

"I owe him a debt."

She nodded. "You used to be . . . intimate with that woman?" she asked. White-hot jealousy curled, licking flames of unease in her belly. *Please tell me that was a lifetime ago.*

He bit his lip and nodded. "I haven't been with anyone since you."

His answers seemed earnest. She sighed with some relief. "What did your friend mean? Which drugs are you doing?" If he was going to be open and honest with her, she'd better take advantage of it.

He hesitated before answering, "The pills were oxys. Sometimes I use H, or a little coke here and there if I'm going through a rough patch. The pills help me sleep. Keeps the . . . flashbacks away. Makes me . . . feel something besides . . ." He pounded his fist against his heart. Her eyes narrowed on the fresh cuts and bruising around his knuckles.

"Besides what?" she asked, her hand covering his.

"Empty. Pain. Rage. Hollow. Most of the time I feel like I'm the walking dead. This is why I never wanted to start something with you. Because I'm no good for you. I didn't want to get you wrapped up in all of this," he said, his voice breaking, shoulders slumped.

The once-strong warrior before her now seemed defeated. She wrapped her arms around him, holding him tightly in her embrace, trying with all her might to infuse him with every-thing bright and good.

"The thing is, Remy, I'm too selfish to leave you alone. I tried. For ten days, I've tried. But you made me feel happy for the first time in my miserable existence." The guarded, broken man was letting his walls fall, showing his most vulnerable and aching parts to her. This was what she had wanted. *I am getting through to him.*

"I love you, Mikel. I love every part of you. Thank you for telling me this, for trusting me. I promise that I'll always be here for you. You make me feel that way too. I just . . . want to know that you are going to be safe and try to stop all of this. It's too dangerous."

He nodded, his chin rocking against her head. "I will. I'm done. I promise. I want to be the man I see when you look at me. To be able to love you the way you need me to. I promise I'll do whatever it takes to be better."

Tears of joy spilled from her eyes. He kissed her forehead.

That weekend, she snuggled up close to him as the waves roared and crashed in the background. Their siblings and friends all laughed and joked together around the fire pit at the beach. The salty breeze carried the crispness that the changing leaves alluded to. The red glow of the fire cast a comforting warmth around the circle.

Mikel leaned and whispered into her ear, "Remember that night I showed you the stars at this beach?"

A blush crept across her cheeks as she bit her lip and giggled. She whispered back to him, "Shhh, my brother is sitting right next to me. He'll hear you."

Seemingly not caring, he kissed a trail from her jaw to her ear, continuing, "I can't stop thinking about the first time those sweet lips were wrapped around me, the way I came all over you. You're all mine."

Good god. The man knew exactly what to say to make her panties wet and have her body burning with a fever only he could cure. She swallowed as the crowd around them blurred into the background noise. Turning to him, she kissed him, soft and slow.

"Hey now! Dude, that's my little sister," Andre interrupted.

Mikel backed away from her, laughing. "You know we've been dating for months. What are you yapping about?"

"Doesn't mean I need to see it. Come on, man, have some respect." Dre shook his head.

"Like I haven't had to watch you suck face with your dates before?" Remy teased sarcastically.

"That's different."

"Why?" she demanded.

"It just is."

She rolled her eyes. "Wow, that's quite the winning argument. Congratulations. You should join the debate team."

"Smart-ass. Don't think because you're grown I can't take you over my knee."

"Come on, if anyone is going to be spanking Remy, it's gonna be me," Mikel teased interrupting the fighting siblings.

Andre snapped to standing. "The fuck did you just say? I know you didn't just make that comment about my little sister."

Bently's eyes followed the scene. "Come on, guys, cool down."

Remy wasn't sure if her brother and Mikel were still just poking fun at each other, or if Mikel had gone too far this time.

"Nah, man. I definitely wasn't joking," Mikel said.

Remy held her breath, waiting to see how her brother would react.

Silence stretched across the beach, no one in the small gathering making a noise, as if one wrong sound could cause everything to come crashing down.

Andre suddenly burst into deep laughter with Mikel following.

"You're lucky I love you, bro," Andre said, slapping his hand harshly to Mikel's shoulder.

"You are such cavemen," Jasmine said, rolling her eyes.

"Yeah, well, it's in the blood." Mikel's gaze grew dark, narrowing towards the fire as he sat back next to her.

"It's a choice," Bently said aloud, seemingly to himself.

The rest of the night passed without incident. Emma showed up late with a date, and they sang a few songs. Stories were told, drinks were shared—a perfect ending to summer in Shattered Cove.

Over the next few weeks, Mikel was extra attentive. He showed up at work surprising her with small gifts and planned dates. She didn't see any sign that he was doing drugs. Just like he'd promised. Everything was better than it had ever been. She could tell he was working hard towards bettering their relationship. He was more open about things, and not as distant.

It was time. She wanted to take the next step and help them connect in a way she had never done with anyone before. Mikel would be her first.

16

REMY

Remy climbed out of the tent. Mikel had the telescope all set up, pointing towards the meteor shower. Butterflies tumbled drunkenly in her belly as she inhaled the brisk night air until her lungs were full. She relished the solitude. Her heart was racing; tonight would be different.

Her legs wobbled as she walked over to the fire to warm herself. The cool September air rustled through the trees, causing some of the leaves to fall. The fire pit was surrounded by a few overturned logs turned into makeshift seats. They had pitched a small tent, complete with two sleeping bags and pillows. Their camp was perched on top of the Black Cliffs. Far below them, the ocean quaked and crashed against the rocks.

The campfire smoke rose with sparks of embers towards the midnight sky. The new moon was hidden. The black sky was splattered with millions of stars and planets out in the cosmos.

"Wanna see?" Mikel asked, beckoning her closer.

She walked to sit by him on the blanket he'd laid on the ground. As she exhaled, her hot breath came out like a puff of smoke in the cold air. She shivered as she drew closer.

He wrapped his arm around her as she peered into the telescope. Shooting bursts of light darted across the dark sky.

"It's pretty cool," she said, turning to face him. "What got you so interested in all of this when you were younger?"

He squeezed her closer and kissed the top of her head. "You really wanna know?"

She turned to look up at him. "I want to know everything about you, Mikel. I want you to feel like you can trust me with your secrets. I meant it when I said I loved you."

He cleared his throat and nodded. "You know my childhood was different than yours. My dad was a drunk, and he used to smack us around and stuff." He turned to face the fire, seeming to become distant in a moment of silence. His breathing increased in pace.

She laid her head on his chest against his pounding heart. "I'm listening."

He blinked rapidly a few times as he adjusted in his seat, appearing jarred. The rumble of his voice continued. "He was a monster. He did horrible things. I tried to protect Jasmine as much as I could from him. Bently took the worst of it. If I was about to get into trouble, he did something to turn the man's rage on him. When he wasn't there, I did the same for Jasmine."

Mikel took a deep breath, frowning at his hands in his lap before he explained, "When Mom killed herself, it only got worse. I did things to survive. Things I'm not proud of. I'm not a good person." His body shook, quaking as long-held secrets erupted from the depths of his soul.

"Why did you ask me to keep the bruises I saw a secret?"

she asked, wrapping her arms around him and climbing into his lap to face him.

He sighed. "Because if CPS did manage to come, we might have ended up worse off. We'd been taken before, and they separated us. Sometimes the foster families liked to smack us around, so it didn't make a difference where we were. But it was hell not knowing if Jasmine was okay and not being there to watch over her. We were eventually returned, and we made sure not to tell anyone. It was easier knowing the devil you lived with; we could avoid him most of the time. We thought we could protect Jasmine from him." His eyes grew darker. "But we were wrong."

She wanted to ask, but it seemed he was nearly at his limit—teetering on the edge of the precarious cliff that could send him crashing in the wrong direction. He had poured his heart out to her, painting her a picture of a horrific childhood existence. It was no wonder he wanted the drugs to dull the memories.

"Thank you," she said.

He looked at her in confusion. "For what?"

"For trusting me enough to show me that piece of you."

He looked at her in awe. "What did I do to deserve you?"

She searched his eyes before she leaned in and spoke against his lips. "You deserve so much more than you think." Maybe if she said it enough times, he would believe it someday.

His mouth slanted against hers, hot and demanding. Strong hands dug into her hips, forcing her tighter against his growing hardness. His tongue darted and danced with her own. Heat blossomed and filled every cell of her body with lust and longing. She was aching to become one with him, to show him just how much she cared for him, how amazing he was. Fear wound around her with questions of uncertainty.

What will this feel like?

Will it hurt or will I bleed?

What if I do something wrong or I'm terrible at this?

A hot blush crept up her cheeks.

"Are you okay?" he asked, pulling away.

She nodded, her voice locked in her throat, too shy to ask for what she wanted.

He kissed her softer this time, taking his time to caress every inch of her mouth with his tongue. He gently squeezed her closer, tighter against him as he hardened beneath her. She rocked against his pelvis with her own need, moving to a rhythm that felt right. She studied him as he reacted by strengthening the kiss. Pride glowed in her belly, what she was doing was pleasing him. A sense of power enveloped her with the revelation that she had the ability to capture this god-like man's attention and make him desire her.

"I want you," she gasped, a crashing avalanche of emotions surging through her. Her embarrassment of her forwardness was drowned by a renewed sense of confidence infused with lust and curiosity.

Mikel froze. He backed away to look at her, searching for an answer she hoped was painted on her expression. "Are you sure you want your first time to be with me?" he asked.

"I've never been surer of anything in my life." She panted, her body vibrating with need.

He cleared his throat before he spoke. "I would wait, you know. I don't need this to be with you. I want you more than I want my next breath. But, baby, I need you to be absolutely sure because this is something I can't give back. Are you certain you want me to make love to you?"

"Yes. Please?" Her voice came out breathy and needy. His care for her only solidified her answer, erasing any lingering uncertainty from the shadows of her mind.

His gaze never left her as he laid her on the blanket, the flames casting him in an orange glow. Shadows played with the chiseled edges of his face. Power, control, and reverence oozed from his every pore. Her body trembled from the magnitude of energy he exuded—it swirled between them.

The air was dense, so thick she could taste it. Dark and heavy, it crackled with sparks of anticipation like the moment before a lightning storm. This man was beautiful, hovering over her as he slowly undressed her layer by layer until she was naked: bared before him as an offering, a pure sacrifice in exchange for his redemption through love.

She shivered. A cool breeze of warning spread goose bumps over her exposed flesh. He stripped, eliminating the last of the boundaries between them. They were exposed to each other. Trust glowed from her heart, connecting, tangling, and weaving her together with him.

She gazed at every hard inch of his toned body. Mikel was all man. A sensitive and attentive heart encased in muscular perfection. He lowered himself onto her, resting his weight on his arms as he kissed her, igniting her body with the blaze of one thousand suns. Skin against skin. Heart against heart. Two souls connecting, woven together by the threads of fate.

He found her wetness, dipping inside her before swirling around her sensitive nub. She hissed, gripping his back, hanging on as he expertly built the pleasure that compounded and was magnified with each stroke. She was safe with him. He had always been her protector. Now, he would be her lover.

His hot mouth pressed kisses on the sensitive flesh of her neck. His other hand caressed her breast. Static shivers of building desire sparked through her, cascading like a waterfall as the pressure against the dam increased. His touch, his taste, the sounds of his heavy breathing all adding to the stream of her wanton lust.

She whimpered as he drove her closer to the edge.

"You're so beautiful, so goddamned sexy."

He sucked her nipple into his mouth. She let out a moan. Both his fingers worked in tandem, one sliding deep inside her finding the inner spot that made her squirm as wetness seeped from her. His other swirled and rubbed her tender, throbbing pearl. Pressure swelled into a boiling frenzy, an avalanche of sensations blossoming in every atom. She came apart, breaking and shattering in the best of ways. Ecstasy laced with euphoria crashed over her in waves as she cried out and the dam burst.

He held her as she came down, panting and breathless. She'd never been surer of any decision she'd made in her life.

"I want you inside me," she said, stripped of all inhibitions. She reached into the pocket of her discarded pants and pulled out the foil packet she'd been carrying around for months and handed it to him.

He nodded, his eyes half lidded in his own lust.

Something about the act of watching him prepare himself to enter her, and go where no man had gone before, was erotic.

"Are you sure about this?" he asked for a third time.

"Yes." She nodded, eagerly.

"I'll go slow," he said, assuring her. Spreading her thighs apart, he aligned himself with her entrance. Rubbing the tip of his hardness against her clit, he growled, "Are you ready?"

"Yes. Please. I need to feel you."

"It might hurt, but only for a second. I promise I'll make you feel good."

"I trust you. Do it." There was a hollow ache inside her. She was greedy for more and urged him on.

He nudged in, inch by inch, slowly stretching her. Her inner walls burned as he entered her. A sensation she hadn't known radiated through her—a different kind of flame. Primal need. Carnal lust. Bliss sparked and shimmered as her hunger grew.

A bolt of pain shot through her core as he thrust the rest of the way inside her. Sweet agony. She dug her nails into his back and held on as he rocked her, quickly masking any discomfort by the erotic rhythm. That same pressure returned as he intimately connected with her, moving in and out. She winced at the pleasured mix of sensations. He was big, filling her up in ways she didn't know were possible, fueling the delirium-inducing euphoria gathering in her womb.

"You're so tight. You feel so fucking good. Heaven," he growled.

Pressing the heel of her feet into his ass, she pulled him closer, needing more. Her skin burned. Fire and ice. Dark and light. "Faster," she commanded.

He increased his thrusts, sending her spinning and tumbling into her second orgasm. Bursts of light shot through her vision as she soared with the stars. Every muscle clenched around him—her only tether to this world.

"Yes! Mikel. I love you."

Focused on her, his expression grew more serious. The fire illuminated his eyes, flames burning in their dark depths promising ecstasy and rebirth. "I love you too, little Dove."

Pure joy filled her chest as she melted from the inside out. *He loves me.* Mikel, the man whom she had wanted for as long as she could remember, loved her.

"I'm gonna come," he grated.

"Yes," she said, wanting nothing more in the world than to feel him pulse within her walls, capturing just a little more of him.

His mouth parted just a little. His eyes widened, his pupils dilating, as he emptied inside her. He tensed around her, each muscle growing taut and rigid as a flash of pleasure rolled through her unlike any she had known before. He growled, possessing her as he invaded her heart.

Mikel kissed her slowly and intimately before he slid out of her. She still burned inside, just the slightest bit. He stood, disappearing into the tent as she caught her breath. He returned with a water bottle and a cloth.

"What's that for?" she asked.

"For you," he said, soaking the material with the cool water. Kneeling between her legs, he used the cloth to clean her up. Embarrassment heated her body. She had bled after all, but he didn't react disgusted like she'd assumed he would. He was gentle—his movements reverent. Somehow this felt even more intimate than having him inside her.

He pulled the material away when he was finished, the crimson streaks on the cloth evident in the firelight—a symbol of everything she had given him and that she was no longer a virgin.

He put his clothes back on and pulled out the double sleeping bag from the tent before laying it on the blanket while she got dressed. She climbed in next to him and cuddled into his side like he had been made for her. He wrapped his arm around her, holding her close.

They were silent for a long time, the crackle of the fire the only sound melding with the faraway crash of waves. The smoke rose towards the dark sky.

"I love you, Remy." Mikel's deep voice reverberated through her. He'd said the three little words she'd wanted to hear more than anything.

Her chest was so full, it might burst. Everything she had ever wished for was coming true. "I love you too, Mikel."

17

MIKEL

Mikel woke to the sounds of birds and the smell of campfire. He pulled Remy closer to him, breathing in her scent. She had given him complete trust. He would do whatever it took to deserve her love.

When he'd told her he was done weeks ago, he had meant it. He was done working with Joe, was cutting back on his pills, and had stopped using the heavier stuff. He only took the oxys when he really needed them. As he studied her sleeping profile, a wave of determination came over him. He was gonna get clean for *her*.

The following weekend, Mikel drank the last of his beer, signaling to Charli, the bartender, that he was ready for another. She set an ice-cold bottle in front of him while collecting his empty before helping another patron.

"So, how is everything going with you?" Bently asked, his

voice raised to be heard over the reggae band playing on stage.

"Fine."

"Haven't seen much of you lately." Bently searched the crowded room, no doubt for his conquest of the night.

"I've been busy." His sex drive had been in overdrive since cutting back on the pills. He wanted Remy constantly, and when they were together, she was more than happy to oblige. Sometimes she even initiated it. It was like he couldn't get enough of her. Remy was his new high. Sinking inside her every day was the highlight of his existence, each time seeming better than the last.

Bently turned to study him. As if reading his thoughts, he smirked. "I bet you have. I've never seen you so wrapped up in a girl. Who would have thought my little brother would fall for Remy Stone?"

Mikel took a long drink from his beer before he responded, "I love her."

"You think that's some big revelation?" Bently laughed, his eyes darting back to the growing crowd at The Shipwreck.

"What the fuck is that supposed to mean?"

Bently stood and patted him on the shoulder roughly. "It means, baby brother, that sometimes you're a little slow on the uptake."

Mikel swung his arm, hitting Bently in the chest.

"Hey, now. That's assault on a police officer." His brother laughed.

"You still using that same old line?" Andre said, walking up to the empty stool beside them. "Dude, it got old the first time you used it fresh out of the academy. It was funny once. It won't be again."

"Well, if you'll excuse me, ladies. I have another engagement to occupy my time with rather than your sorry excuses."

Bently laughed as he walked towards a group of women. He had them giggling at something he said within thirty seconds.

"Is he ever gonna learn?" Andre asked, waving Charli over.

"What can I get you, honey?" She wiped the counter with a white cloth.

"Rum and Coke, beautiful," he flirted.

"Coming right up." Her long dark hair flicked behind her as she left to prepare his drink.

Andre turned his focus back to Mikel. "How ya doing? Been a while since we hung out without my little sister hanging off you."

"Hey, I can't help that she's cooler than you," Mikel teased.

Andre laughed, before his expression grew serious. "I'm happy for you two, man. I gotta say, I was worried in the beginning. I can tell you really are treating her right."

"I love her," he said, hoping to put his friend's mind at ease. Saying it out loud brought a comforting warmth to his chest. The more he said it, the easier it got. He'd never thought he was capable of letting someone in, but Remy had somehow slipped past his barriers, going where none had gone before.

"Really? Have you told her that yet?"

Mikel nodded.

Andre smiled and looked towards the entrance. "He's not as dumb as he looks, folks." Dre winked at Charli who left his drink before smiling and returning to wait on another customer. "I'm happy for you, man. But now, I have to go greet my date for the night. This chick might just be *the one*."

"You're leaving me all alone? I thought this was a guys' night?"

"Don't worry. Your date's here too. You can thank me later." Andre smirked and nodded towards the door.

Remy had slipped in with another woman he didn't recognize. Andre walked towards the women and introduced them. "Tiffany, this is my brother from another mother, Mikel."

"Nice to meet you," she said, her eyes raking over him.

"You too," he said, shifting uncomfortably before turning his attention to Remy. His eyes skated over the short light-pink dress she wore that hugged all her curves in the right places. She'd changed her hair. Long braids fell around her shoulders with gold embellishments strewn throughout. His very own Cleopatra.

"Let's leave these two kids to their own fun." Dre winked and led Tiffany off to the bar.

Remy smiled, shyly. "Are you surprised?"

"Yeah. I was counting down the minutes until I could leave these two assholes and come find you."

Her eyes lit up.

"You look gorgeous."

"Thank you."

"That dress should be illegal. Don't know how I'm gonna be able to keep my hands off you."

She walked up and kissed him. "Dance with me?"

"I'd do anything for you." He smiled, taking her hand and leading her towards the crowd.

He pulled her against him in the center of the masses, surrounded by walls of people. His hands weaved around her hips as his leg nudged between her thighs. The smell of sweat and mixed perfumes enveloped them. She gripped the fabric of his shirt, leaning up to kiss him as they moved to the beat of the music. The song was slow, perfect for grinding her hot little body against his.

They swayed, caught up in every sensation. Compounded

and magnified. He ached for her with every cell in his body. Her scent coated him in a haze of lust. When she was with him, something inside him snapped every time, causing him to become uncontrolled and unhinged. Emotions he'd long ago buried, some he had only dreamt about, came rushing to the surface, threatening to drown him. Love possessed him, warring with the alarm pulsing in the back of his mind, cautioning him. Being this vulnerable would eventually break the parts of him that remained into jagged pieces.

"Let's get out of here," Mikel suggested.

Remy nodded, arousal evident in her eyes.

He led her to his truck before opening the door for her. She climbed in and he walked over to his side of the car. A scrap of paper on his windshield caught his attention. He picked it up, unfolding it carefully.

You owe me. I'm gonna collect. One way or another.

Chills skated down his spine as he crumpled the paper, searching the parking lot. A dark and ominous warning threaded through every nerve ending.

He needed to find a way to pay Joe back without working off his debt, in order to keep his promise to Remy. Fifty grand was a lot of money to come up with out of thin air. Not to mention that Joe knew his secret.

If the truth came out, it might be too late to send him to prison, but it would destroy his relationship with his family. Legal options were out of the question. He couldn't ask Bently for help and risk the inquiry and the disappointment. His brother's moral compass would only cause a gap between them.

But that left one burning question. *What am I gonna do?*

18

MIKEL

Later that night, Mikel tossed and turned in a fitful sleep. Vicious flashbacks assaulted him: his father's accusatory eyes as he convulsed on the ground at his feet, foam dripping from his mouth. His mother's lifeless hanging body, her face tinged with blue from the lack of oxygen. The sounds of grunts coming from the closed door, laced with cries and whimpers. The paralyzing fear that turned the blood in his veins to ice. A gut-twisting knowing that if he found the strength to open the door, his life would be forever changed. The look on *her* face as her innocence was stolen.

"Mikel, baby, wake up. It's just a dream." Remy's angelic voice broke through the nightmare, bringing him back to life.

He blinked open his eyes, the room still dark. His mind was spinning as he turned to focus on her soft arms wrapping tightly around him. *Where am I?*

Right. Dancing at The Shipwreck, and then they'd come back here to his room and fucked his worries away. He'd lost himself, driven his demons back to the shadows of his mind while inside his Dove.

"Shhhh. You're safe. I'm here," she soothed.

He relaxed into her arms, resting his head against her damp T-shirt-clad chest. Reaching out, he found the source of the wetness was coming from his own eyes. He was crying. He never cried.

Boys don't cry, only sissies do.

Are you a sissy?

You like dick?

His father's words rang in his mind.

An all-encompassing need to prove he was a man, that he was strong, possessed him. Grasping at anything to shake this feeling from him, he kissed Remy, lifting the shirt to expose her bare stomach.

"I need you." The words grated from his throat, raw and revealing far too much.

She kissed him back, her hands pulling him closer in her sweet silent consent. Climbing on top of her, he spread her thighs apart. His chest ached. Shame and guilt crawled up his spine, slithering around his rib cage, and squeezed. "I need you. Make me feel better, Remy." *Take the pain away.*

She kissed him harder, infusing her brightness into him. He drank in her goodness, seeking the relief she always brought. The urges inside him raged. Everything was splintering and cracking, brutally shredding him to pieces.

You're nothing.

You're a failure.

You should kill yourself and put us all out of our misery.

You weren't good enough.

You failed her.

You're weak.

Selfish.

Fuckup.

Pussy.

Obliterating pain coursed through him until he buried himself deep inside her. Instant bliss. He thrust, chasing the ecstasy, the high, like a violent sickness holding him captive.

His ears rang as the pressure built with his impending orgasm. He gripped her thigh with one hand and fisted her hair with another as he slammed into her. He came with an unstoppable force, his vision shattering. White-hot light pierced the darkness. But it was only temporary.

"Wait."

His heart raced in his chest, his euphoria cut short. Remy was looking up at him with wide eyes. *What have I done?* He pulled out of her, his semen dripping down her thigh. *Fuck!* In his emotional state, he hadn't thought to use a condom.

"Remy, I'm so sorry. I wasn't thinking straight." Worry tightened his chest. He'd been so selfish, seeking pleasure to pull him out of the dark pit his memories always thrust him into.

She wrapped her arms around him comfortingly. "It's okay. I'm on the pill. I trust you."

Her words took his breath away. He buried his head in the nape of her neck and squeezed her tightly against his chest.

He couldn't be a dad. He was a killer, and he carried a monster's DNA inside him. He couldn't pollute this pure creature with his darkness. Why hadn't he used his head? *God, I need an oxy.* Just to help him clear his mind and think straight.

Don't do it. Remy's voice reverberated in his mind. Everything was a jumbled mess again, twisting and tangling into a storm of chaos in his body. Remy probably wanted a family one day. Why hadn't he thought about that before he'd started this with her?

Because you're selfish. That's why. What had he done? How was he going to fix this?

You'll never amount to anything.

Murderer.

You deserve this pain.

You are nothing but a failure.

You are ugly and weak.

Worthless piece of shit.

I hate you.

I hate me.

He just needed it to all stop. The pain, the confusion, the hollow emptiness, and the shadow of the future looming overhead that threatened his destruction. He had to escape it, just for a little while.

"I need some air." Mikel stood, pulling a pair of sweatpants on and grabbing a tee in the dark from his drawer.

Remy slid those perfect brown legs out of bed as she reached for her clothes that had been strewn about the room in a lust-induced haze hours ago.

"I'll come with you," she said, her tone worried.

She had every right to be. He had just taken advantage of her, used her in the worst way. He was just like his father. The thought made his stomach twist, bile rising in his throat.

"No, baby. You stay here and get some rest. I'll be fine. I'm just gonna go for a drive and clear my head."

"Are you sure?" she asked, confusion written across her beautiful features.

He walked over and kissed her forehead, trying to set her at ease. Pulling the facade from one of the many personas living inside the circus that was Mikel Evans. "Yeah, baby. I promise I'll be okay," he lied.

"I love you," she said. The girl was so good and pure. He just tainted her. Taking, always stealing, from her.

"I love you too." He kissed her on the lips, thieving a little more like the selfish bastard he was before he turned his back and walked away. Before she could see the cracks in his mask. Before she asked him if he intended to use.

He'd already told enough lies for the night.

19

REMY

Remy stared at the ceiling for hours, waiting for Mikel to come back to his bed. She must have drifted off at some point, waking to an empty spot beside her. She searched around the room for any sign that he'd returned. She sat, rubbing the sleep from her eyes before grabbing her phone.

No texts. No missed calls. *Nothing.*

Worry tightened her chest.

Remy tapped the screen to call him just as the sound of deep voices rumbled from outside the door. She jumped out of bed and hurriedly pulled her clothes on from the night before. She had never done the walk of shame, but right now that was the least of her concerns.

She made her way down the stairs to the kitchen where Mikel sat drinking a cup of coffee, talking with Bently.

"I still can't believe you two are together. It's weird seeing Dre's little sister coming down the stairs, knowing she's been in your bed all night," Bently teased his younger brother. Mikel's smile faltered as he turned to face her.

Her legs wobbled with uncertainty and she held her breath. How was he going to react? How should she respond?

Mikel walked over before putting his arm around her shoulders and kissing her cheek. He smelled like coffee with a hint of cigarette smoke. She winced.

"Well, get used to it, brother, 'cause she's definitely stayin'." Mikel smirked.

His eyes were glassy and bloodshot. But that was probably from the lack of sleep . . . or had he used? He seemed okay. Was it best to pretend like nothing had happened? She'd follow his lead. "If I am going to stick around, I better get a change of clothes. I don't think this dress is gonna work for my shift at the bakery." She forced a smile, hoping it masked her worry.

"You looked pretty great in my shirt last night," he teased.

"Okay, that's enough. I've had my fill of young love to last me a lifetime," Bently interjected holding out his hand in protest.

"He's just jealous," Mikel said as two women she didn't recognize came down the stairs.

"Good morning." The redhead smiled, eying the door.

Bently walked over, stopping to smirk at Mikel and whisper, "I'm not sure I have anything to be jealous about."

Remy was awestruck as Bently wrapped his arms around both women and led them out.

"Did they . . .?" she whispered as they exited the house.

"I didn't think he had it in him." Mikel laughed.

A pang of jealous curiosity prickled in her chest. "Would you ever want to do that?"

He turned back to her, his gaze heated. "You're the only woman I want in my bed."

She let out a breath she hadn't realized she'd been holding

in relief. "I was worried when you didn't come back last night."

He drew in a deep breath. "I'm sorry. I just needed to clear my head. I'm feeling a lot better now. I apologize again about last night. It was reckless."

"Well, teen pregnancy isn't high on my to-do list, but it wouldn't be the end of the world." She laughed, hoping to set him at ease and let him know she was in this for the long haul.

Panic flashed in his eyes, his body tense and rigid. "But you're on the pill, right?"

She nodded, obviously the humor had been ill-chosen. "I've been on the pill since I was sixteen. In fact, I just got a new prescription—switched over to a different kind that's supposed to be a smidge more effective."

He nodded vigorously as he exhaled and wrapped his arm around her. "That's good because I can't . . . we can't have any more accidents like that. It's too much of a risk."

Unease slithered over her, coating her in caution. He had a lot going on in his life, dealing with his issues. She was too young, about to go to college and start a business in the next couple years. A baby would not be ideal, but it would be something they'd created together—a part of him growing inside her. Couldn't he see that it might not be all bad?

"Let's get you home to change before your shift at the bakery," he said.

His kiss put all her concerns out of her mind. She grabbed his shirt and pulled him into her. "Maybe we have time for a quickie before we go?" she asked, needing to feel connected with him and erase the upset of the last several hours.

He smirked. "You want me again?"

"I want you all the time." She kissed his neck, her cheeks heating with her confession.

He chuckled, low and deep, sending shivers tingling through her. "You can have anything your little heart desires," he said, as the smooth Mikel took her hand and led her back up the stairs to his room.

* * *

The feel of his strong grip wrapped around her hand as they pounded the hammer against the nail jolted her body. The hard hat he'd insisted she wear barely fit over her goddess braids. It was cute how much he worried about her.

It had been almost a week since he'd left in the middle of the night. Since then, he'd withdrawn from her. Remy was hoping that today would change all that.

The room smelled like fresh-cut wood. Sawdust floated through the air as Andre trimmed a few pieces down to size. The whine of the blade shut off, so they could hear each other once again.

"Now we have to make sure these pieces are flush before we connect them," Mikel said, motioning to the corner where the two lengths of wood joined. The flannel shirt he wore was folded to his elbows, showing off his sinewy forearms.

His stare bore into her, her eyes meeting his amused expression. *What was he saying again?*

"Don't keep looking at me like that. I won't get any work done." His voice was all gravelly.

She smiled. She loved that she had this effect on him. "Sorry, boss. Show me how you like to nail again." It was bold of her to be openly flirting like this, especially with Andre nearby. But she couldn't resist. She'd have to remember to thank Emma for all those euphemisms someday.

Mikel shook his head and leaned to growl in her ear,

sending shivers down her spine. "You're gonna pay for that later."

"Come on! At this pace, we won't finish before Christmas," Andre whined.

"It's all Remy's fault. She's distracting me," Mikel teased and gave her a wink.

"Hey. I'm here to help." She held up her hands and hoped she was giving her big brother her most innocent expression.

"Then get to it," Andre said.

"Yes, sir." Remy mock-saluted.

"Hold this piece here," Mikel directed. She wrapped her fingers around the soft pale wood. He lined up the nail and drove it all the way in with just a few powerful strokes. Watching him in the zone was fascinating—the way his body moved confidently, never second-guessing as he connected the pieces, checking his carefully crafted blueprint from time to time. She admired the way he fit in the tan Carhartt pants and scuffed work boots. Something about the sight of a hard-working man—*her* man—had her insides tied up in knots with need. How did she get so lucky that this *man* wanted her? That he loved her?

She followed directions, holding pieces, hammering, and using the screw gun. As much as her brother loved construction, she hadn't known the first thing about it—until today.

"Here, drive this in," Mikel said, holding what she now knew was a sixteen-penny nail. She lifted the hammer, much more confident after they'd been at it for hours, and swung. The tool hit its mark with a clang.

"Oww!" Mikel screamed, pulling his hand away to his chest quickly. Fear and shock held her like a vise as her hands slapped across her face to cover the panicked *O* of her mouth. The hammer clattered to the floor.

"I'm so sorry! Let me see," she said, gingerly reaching

towards his shoulder. He flinched away, his shoulders slumped over and shaking.

"Is it broken?" Andre asked.

Oh crap! Had she broken his finger? Horror at what she'd done brought fresh tears to her eyes. "I'm so sorry, baby."

Mikel's shoulders were heaving up and down now as he made a rumbling noise. *Is he . . . laughing?*

Mikel sat up, holding his stomach as he doubled over in hilarity. "I got you! Ohhh, you should have seen your face."

Relief flooded over her. "You are terrible." She wiped tears from her eyes. "I thought I really hurt you. I'm never hammering anything ever again. You . . . big . . . meanie!"

Mikel's arms wrapped around her as he held her in a bear hug. She feigned trying to get away before she relaxed back into the warmth of his embrace. *There is nowhere else I'd rather be.*

"I'm sorry, honey. You gotta admit it was funny. Just wanted to keep you on your toes."

Remy shook her head and glanced over to Andre who was grinning. "Were you in on this?"

"Ahhh, Rem, it's all part of being a rookie on the jobsite. Now you've officially been welcomed onto our crew," her brother said, pulling a measuring tape from his tool belt.

"Part of your crew, huh? So, I get wages as your first employee?"

Andre scoffed, taking a pencil from behind his ear. "I wouldn't go that far."

Mikel kissed her cheek.

"No more teasing me. You scared me to death." She searched his face for confirmation.

"Alright, no more scaring you; you have my word," he agreed. "Just one more thing, Remy?"

"Yeah?"

"Can you get the board stretcher from my truck?" Mikel asked, deviousness flashing in his eyes.

Andre burst out laughing.

What is so funny? She placed a quick peck on his lips before she stood. "Of course I can. What's it look like?"

20
<hr>

REMY

Two weeks later, Remy walked into a clean industrial building with Mikel by her side. He'd been quiet for most of the ride to the city. Her brow creased as she studied him. Anxiety swirled in her belly as a weight settled on her shoulders.

They took their time perusing the shelves filled with more baking and cooking equipment than Remy would know what to do with. Running her finger around the bumps of a porcelain mixing bowl, she checked him out again over her shoulder. Under his eyes were dark rings of exhaustion. He was pushing himself too hard. Was it part of the withdrawals? Would he still be affected weeks after stopping?

He scowled at his phone.

"You okay?"

Mikel snapped his head up, as if he'd forgotten she was with him. "Yeah." He pushed the phone into his pocket. Looping his arms around her waist, he breathed in the crook of her neck. His grown-out scruff tickled her sensitive skin and somehow turned her on at the same time. She giggled. "If you could pick out anything for that bakery of yours, what would you need?"

She surveyed the line of KitchenAids and other mixers. "Probably a few of these. Maybe an industrial-sized one."

"That's a lot of cookies," he joked.

"Mm-hmm."

"What about pans?" he asked, stepping away from her to pick up a few metal ones.

"Yes, I'll probably need, like, fifty sheet pans. Oh, and cooling racks."

He led her through the store, holding her hand as she looked around. As time wore on, his phone became glued to his palm and the frown on his face deepened. She could spend all day in a store like this, feeding her dreams of *what if* and *someday*. Mikel had been sweet to offer to come with her. But now he wasn't fully present. *He sure is distracted and on his phone a lot.*

"Are you sure nothing is the matter?" She turned towards him. Mikel didn't respond, so she reached out and touched his face. "Babe, what's wrong?"

Mikel's jaw clenched under her fingertips. "Nothing. Can you stop asking me that?" He was short with her—a side of him she'd been seeing more of—but it was unpredictable when this version of Mikel would come out.

"I'm just worried about you." She had a right to be, after all that had happened.

He sighed and wrapped his arms around her. "Well, don't be. I'm fine. But if I say I'm in need of some of your goodies for stress relief, would that convince you to get out of here with me faster?" He wiggled his eyebrows up and down, making her laugh.

"Oh, I see. You're bored. Well then, I suppose I could be persuaded."

He leaned in for a kiss, but she halted him with a finger to his lips.

"But first, I need lunch."

He enveloped her hand in his and kissed her palm. "There's a café down the block."

* * *

As she set her fork on her empty plate and leaned back, Mikel's thumb swept across the glass screen of his phone for what seemed the millionth time today. Was it another woman? Pain squeezed her chest like a vise as her stomach rolled over in protest. Mikel wouldn't do that. Would he? "Is there a reason you've had that thing glued to your hand all day?" she asked, the bite of jealousy lacing her words.

Mikel glanced at her. Seconds ticked by as a myriad of emotions played over his features.

"Is it . . . a woman?" she asked, so quiet she wasn't sure if he'd heard her.

Mikel's expression turned angry as he leaned in and captured her hand in his. "You think I'd step out on you?"

The look in his eyes told her no, but her insecurities were eating her alive. Sometimes being around him was like walking on eggshells; she was afraid to say or do the wrong thing to set him off.

A server came over and collected their plates before asking, "Is there anything else I can get you? Perhaps a dessert menu—"

"No," Mikel snapped, his eyes never leaving Remy. "Just the check."

The stunned waitress nodded as she hurriedly left the table.

"Answer me," he said, his grip on her hand tightening just a little.

"I don't think you would. But you've been distracted a lot these past few weeks. You've been paying extra attention to your phone." She nodded as the very device vibrated on the table.

Mikel stood abruptly, dropping her hand before pulling out his wallet. He threw some bills on the table and motioned to the door. "Let's go. I'm not having this conversation here."

She grabbed her sweater and slid out of the chair, quick to follow on his heels as she fought back tears. He opened the door of his truck for her and she climbed in, swallowing the ball of hurt bubbling in her throat before he joined her.

With a sigh, he slammed his fist into the steering wheel, making the horn honk. She jumped.

Mikel shook his head and turned to her, his eyes glassy and red with tears. Her heart broke for him, terrified that she'd been immature and acted on impulsive insecurities rather than confronting him a better way.

"I would *never* cheat on you, Remy. It's physically impossible. You're . . ." He took a moment as if another word would break the dam of tears. He blinked a few times. "I love you, Remy. I'd never want to screw that up. You're the best thing in my life. I've just been under a lot of pressure. I'm not sleeping that well."

Remy scooted closer and pulled him into her chest as she cried the tears he was too stubborn to. "I'm so sorry. I'm here for you. You can come to me and talk to me about anything. I'll always listen."

He nodded. "I know. I just need you to trust in my love, baby." Mikel pulled away, wrapping firm hands on either side of her face. "I'm sorry I'm such a downer today. Let me make it up to you."

She shook her head. "No, I shouldn't have jumped to conclusions. I've wanted you to look at me like you do now for so long. Sometimes it's still hard to believe this is real. What I feel for you—sometimes it's overwhelming. I'm just terrified to lose you."

"Never." His promise was spoken across her lips as he nuzzled her nose with his own. "I'm gonna take you home and remind every part of you how much I love you." He slanted his mouth against hers.

She leaned into the kiss, happy to give whatever he wanted to take. Mikel was everything—the very next breath her lungs craved. She'd do anything for him. "That sounds like a great idea, but maybe I can give you a massage first. Work out all those kinks from stress," she offered.

"Hell yeah," he said, giving her one amazing kiss before he started the truck.

The twenty-minute drive couldn't go fast enough.

21

REMY

The weeks passed slowly. Remy was careful what she brought up to Mikel. His moods were erratic. She supposed that was what she should expect if he was staying clean despite the urges. She tried to make his life as easy as possible wherever she could, not asking for too much, being there for him day and night. She blew off Emma and even Jasmine to hang out with him, which usually involved Mikel and her naked and panting. He didn't always respond to her texts or calls, but she figured he was busy with work or tired from the long hours and overtime he was putting in as the cold weather drew nearer.

"I'm gonna go shower and then we can get some dinner," he said, stripping naked before grabbing the towel from his dresser. He wrapped it around his waist and headed along the hall to the bathroom.

Her phone rang. She answered it. "Hello?"

"Hello. Is this Miss Remy Stone?"

"Yes, this is she."

"This is Monica from Doctor Amir's office. She wanted

me to call you and let you know there has been a recall on the new birth control she prescribed you. I see that your old one was giving you headaches. Would you mind coming in this week and talking through other options with her?"

"Sure, I can do that."

"Friday at noon work for you?" she asked.

"Yes, that's fine."

"Great. See you then."

She glanced around the room, deciding to tidy while she waited. She picked up the scattered clothing and placed it in the empty basket. Suspicion pulled, tugging her towards the bed. She lifted the mattress. Relief splashed across her chest at finding it bare of bags or pills. Shame that she had been snooping crashed over her.

Shouldn't she trust him? He had trusted her with so many of his secrets. She walked around to the other side of the bed, her shoulders a million pounds lighter. Making herself useful, she lifted his dirty clothes from the floor.

Smack!

Her heart plummeted at the sight of the white pills, mocking her temporary celebration from the floor. She dropped the clothes in the basket before reaching a shaky hand to pick the offending item up.

He is still using. He'd promised her he was done. *Mikel lied to me.* Her stomach knotted with indecision. Should she get rid of it and see if he brought it up? Should she put them back and act like she didn't know? Should she confront him?

"Remy."

She startled.

Her name was like a plea.

Mikel leaned in the doorway. Rivulets of water dripped down his corded chest, disappearing into the towel hanging low on his hips.

Her whole body trembled. Conflicting desires spun inside her. Confusion. Love. Disappointment. Betrayal. Fear. Hope. Doubt. It all came crashing down, sending her reeling. His presence was potent and powerful. She became hazy and lost, knocked off her axis as the ground beneath her quaked. What was she supposed to believe? How could she help him? Would she hurt him further by standing up for herself? "Y-you told me you were done. You told me that you stopped," she said, her voice trembling as her eyes burned with unshed tears.

"I did stop—I swear I did." He shut the bedroom door before sitting on the bed beside her.

"How long have you been using again?" she asked.

"Not long. I just . . . I needed it to make the nightmares stop. It helps me. I just take a little bit. Just enough to calm my mind down."

She shook her head. "Mikel, you lied to me. You promised me you were done."

His hands pressed into her skin, clinging to her as if he was afraid she would walk away and leave him. "Remy, I *need* them. They help me function."

It had been easy for her to see someone labeled an addict before and make assumptions about them. They had a problem and needed help. But knowing one personally, seeing all the different layers of them, their potential, their pain, their loving, wholesome, good side, made it that much harder to figure out how to help. "You have to stop. Get rid of them," she pleaded, knowing it was the right thing to do.

His eyes snapped to her, focused and angry. "You said you would be what I needed. I need someone who will stand by me no matter what. I warned you this wasn't going to be easy with me. I'm trying to stop, but it's harder than I thought. I'm weaning myself off."

She swallowed, remembering the words she'd spoken. If

she didn't follow through, that made her a liar too. Guilt clung to her, wrapped in uncertainty and unease. Nothing about the situation was black and white. She had pored over pages of information online, trying to figure out the best way to help him. To ensure she was as knowledgeable about the issue as possible. She had all the facts and figures, but how did she apply them in real life? "You're trying to rationalize your addiction."

"And you're trying to control me," he snapped. His cold eyes flashed, the barriers reinforced and guarded.

"I love you, Mikel. I want to help you, but I need you to help yourself too. Maybe if you went to rehab, or talked to a counselor—"

He shot to his feet and grabbed her face, his chocolate eyes now soft and pleading. "Please, Remy? Don't leave me. I swear I don't have an addiction. You're making this out to be bigger than it is. I don't need rehab. That's for addicts. I'm just a guy who uses a prescription to help with my sleep and stress, just like countless others do. Honey, I don't know what you have been reading, but you're blowing this way out of proportion," he said, scattering seeds of doubt.

"You don't think you're addicted?" she asked.

He shook his head, grabbing the bag of pills from her hands. "Could an addict do this?" He took her hand and pulled her into the bathroom. Dumping the pills in the toilet, he flushed the empty bag with it.

"Come on, Remy. If I needed rehab, if I was an addict or some shit like that, I wouldn't be able to do that." He pointed towards the swirling water. "I've seen addicts. I've lived with them. Believe me, I'm not one. You're so smart, baby, but also naive. I don't know who or what put that idea in your head, but it's not fact."

What he said seemed to make sense. She wanted to believe

him, but that nagging feeling that gnawed at her inside was getting louder. He had gotten rid of the pills though. That meant this was over, for now.

"You promise you won't do it again?" she asked, searching his expression for any sign of dishonesty.

"I fucking swear on my love for you. I'm done."

"Do you have any more?" She searched his eyes.

"No."

Could she believe him? She wanted to, and so she did.

22

REMY

Slowly, Friday came and Emma covered her shift at the bakery so she could go to her appointment.

She settled into the chair of the exam room, eyeing the cold metal stirrups. *Thank heavens I won't need those today.*

Ding!

She dug her phone out of her bag.

Emma: *Dolly wants to know where the sugar flowers are that you finished decorating yesterday.*

Remy: *Top shelf in the back room labeled "Johnson Wedding."*

Emma: *Thanks!*

Remy struggled with whether or not to open up to Emma, or her mother for that matter, about the issues she and Mikel were facing. She'd always been able to turn to her mom for advice before. But would that be betraying Mikel's trust in this situation?

She clicked his name, finding the last message he'd sent.

Mikel: *Working overtime this week, finishing up a project. Won't be available for a while.*

That was five days ago. The all-too-familiar worry that niggled at the back of her mind was getting louder. She couldn't ignore the alarm bells going off, nor the fear that rattled in her bones.

Distance. Again. While part of her was upset he was shutting her out, she was glad for the space to clear her own mind. Being with Mikel was emotionally draining sometimes. Guilt weighed heavily on her shoulders. *He's been through hell, Remy. He deserves a little understanding.*

There was so much to figure out. The more she read up on addiction, the more she was convinced that her gut feeling was right. The consensus was that an addict couldn't begin their journey of recovery until they could admit they had a problem. But Mikel was adamant that she was making this out to be a bigger deal than it was. Was she? Her head swam; she was so mixed up.

"Good afternoon. Didn't expect to see you again here so soon." The friendly nurse smiled as she greeted her.

"Me either."

"Well, I'm sure you remember the routine. Pee in this cup, leave it sealed in the window, and the doctor will be in soon." She handed the sterile plastic container to her.

Remy accepted it and headed to the empty bathroom. She did her business, and walked back to the patient room before sitting in one of the empty chairs.

Time ticked by slowly as she waited for Doctor Amir to come in. Should she text Mikel? She'd check in on him. He'd be off for the weekend for sure.

Knock, knock.

"Remy, good to see you again." The doctor entered.

"You too."

"I'm sorry about the recall, but I guess it was a good thing you came back in after all," she said, reading over the chart.

"What do you mean?" Remy asked, a tinge of worry bubbling in her belly.

Doctor Amir set the iPad down. There was caution in her kind eyes. "The pregnancy test we always run before prescribing your birth control turned out positive. When was your last menstrual cycle?"

Pregnant.

Panic and fear seized her, sucking the air from her lungs. *How? Oh, god.* Mikel had freaked when he'd realized he'd come without a condom.

"But…I had a period…last month." Surely the test wasn't accurate.

"Some women experience what is called implantation bleeding. It can mimic a light period. Other women still have a cycle for several months into their pregnancy. I'm guessing this is a surprise."

Pregnant.

Excitement and hope bubbled under the shock and fear. Sure, this wasn't what she'd planned, but a baby?

Mikel.

What was he going to think? Would this cause him to spiral and use again? She burst into a sob, her body shaking and trembling. She was pregnant and the father of her baby was an addict.

Doctor Amir put her arms around her. "I know it can be a lot to take in. You have plenty of time to digest this and make the decision that's right for you. I want you to know you have several options."

Remy tried to pull herself together, taking the tissue the doctor kindly offered her.

The nurse came in to draw blood once she'd calmed down and then made another appointment farther out.

Remy walked back to her car in a haze, uncertain and drained. *Six weeks pregnant.* She just wanted Mikel to hold her and tell her everything was going to be alright. She texted him.

Remy: *I need you. Can we talk? Pick me up at my house when you get done with work.*

She went home, thankful both her parents were gone, and texted Emma to let her know she would be out the rest of the day. There was no way she could face her friend and not tell her everything. She was going to fall apart and she didn't need an audience.

The hours trickled by slowly. She cried and sobbed in a flurry of emotions as she accepted the news. Remy laid her hand against her flat belly, in awe that an actual human being was growing inside her. A piece of Mikel. A symbol of their love. What kind of family could they make for their child? Would the baby be light-skinned, closer to its father's, or darker like hers?

The door opened and she looked up, hoping to see the man she loved walk through it. Instead her mother's kind face peeked in. Her smile quickly faded when she locked eyes with Remy.

Wiping her tear-stained cheeks, Remy sat.

"What's wrong?" her mother asked worriedly as she settled next to her.

Remy couldn't say anything for a while. She sobbed into her mother's chest, taking the comfort she was offered. Sniffing, she finally got a hold of her emotions.

"You're worrying me," her mother said. "I'm sure nothing can be that bad. Tell Mama what's troubling you," she soothed.

Oh, how she wished she was a little girl again and that her

mother would be able to wipe her tears and fix her problems. "I-I'm p-pregnant."

Her mother's body froze before she hugged Remy harder. "Does Mikel know?"

Remy shook her head.

"Sometimes these things happen. I know it's a lot to take in."

There was no reproach, no disappointment in her mother's voice. Tilda was simply there for her.

"Mama, what am I going to do?"

"That's a decision only you can make. I'm sure Mikel will support you no matter what you choose. A good man would."

Remy trembled.

"Is there something you're not telling me?" her mother asked.

"I promised I would keep his secrets. I don't think I can tell you without betraying his trust. I don't know what to do, and I'm afraid he is going to be mad at me." Remy shook her head. Her swollen eyes felt like sandpaper from all the crying she had done.

Her mother was quiet for a few moments before replying, "You don't think he'd help you if you chose to carry this pregnancy to term?"

"I honestly can't say." Did she even know Mikel at all? She'd thought she had before. Maybe she was naïve, like he'd said.

Her mother lovingly wiped the matted hair from her forehead. "Whatever you decide, I'm here to support you. You are not alone, whether Mikel is happy about the news or not. I know his opinion is a factor, but you'll be the one having to live with whatever you choose for the rest of your life. You should take some time to reflect on it. The answer will become clear in your heart and you'll know. Talk to Mikel. I'm sure everything will work out. After all, it takes two to make a child." Her mother kissed her forehead.

"Thank you, Mama."

"Always, baby. I'm always here for you. Now, you rest. This isn't the end. It's just a fork in the road. Sometimes the best things in the world are unexpected."

Her mother always knew what to say to put her mind at ease.

As her mom exited, Remy was able to breathe a little lighter. The room grew hazy as her eyes fluttered closed, dreaming of the face of the child that grew within her. The thought of her womb being emptied brought her a hollow ache. She would keep their child. Maybe a baby would give Mikel even more reason to get clean.

* * *

Remy woke to a dark room. She switched on the lamp by her bed. Her phone showed several texts from Emma, and one from Mikel.

Mikel: *Not tonight. I'm too tired. Just gonna go to bed.*

Her heart sank.

He needed to have a clear head when she told him anyways. She could wait until the morning.

* * *

The sun rose and she sent him a text first thing.

Remy: *Can you come over? Or I can come to you? I really need to talk to you.*

Hours passed with no reply. He was probably sleeping in. She texted Jasmine.

Remy: *Hey, do you know if Mikel is still sleeping?*

Jasmine: *Snoring loud enough to wake the neighbors.*

* * *

It was three in the afternoon. When she'd been staring at the same page of her book for an hour, she gave up. She was crawling out of her skin, unable to sit still any longer. She got in her car and drove to his house.

She didn't bother knocking. Turning the knob, she pushed the door open the same moment someone on the other side pulled, causing her to stumble. A large body bumped into her, arms shooting out to steady her before she fell. She gasped.

"Mikel, I—" She covered her mouth in shock at the black bruise around his eye: angry red marks fading into purple where the skin had split open. His mouth was cut and swollen too.

"What happened?" she asked, concern and fear rooting in her belly.

"You should see the other guy." The joke wasn't light, but forced.

"When?" she asked.

"Last night."

"I thought you came home and went to bed after work?" she asked, her tone more accusatory than she'd intended.

His expression hardened. "I was planning on it, and then Isaiah texted me. I went out to have a fucking drink with my friend. I've been neglecting him, spending every waking minute with you."

She winced as his words shredded her. *Am I too clingy?* "I needed to talk to you."

He sighed. "Fine, you can come with me." He walked off the porch towards his truck. She hurried to catch up.

She didn't like this version of Mikel. He was unpredictable. *Withdrawals? Is he going to buy from Isaiah?* He had sworn on his love for her that he wouldn't use again. Once they got through this period, he should be back to normal. *I hope.*

She climbed into the cab and buckled up. He drove down the road, turning the music up loud. Linkin Park drowned out any chance of having a conversation.

He parked in front of the house she had come to know as Isaiah's, and her hope plummeted. He shut the car off as she sucked in a breath. Confusion and uncertainty violently twisted inside her.

"Do you really think it's a good idea to hang around with Isaiah since he always has drugs?" she asked, disbelief and fear coiling inside her and latching on to what little control she had left. *Not to mention your history with June.*

He turned his gaze to her, every muscle in his expression angry and rigid. "Are you gonna try and tell me who I can hang out with now too? Clingy *and* controlling," he scoffed before fleeing the truck, slamming the door, and stalking over to the house.

Surrounded by empty silence, she tried to take slow, even breaths. It was clear he needed help. He was only lashing out at her because of the drugs—picking a fight to push her away. This wasn't the real Mikel.

She had known this wasn't going to be easy. Now, they had more than just their lives to think about. Maybe after he found out about the pregnancy, it would give him the final push of courage to seek help.

She drew in a hopeful breath and swallowed the tears that threatened to spill. Courage welled in her chest, her stomach an anxious ball of nerves. She had a little more left of herself she could give.

Remy's hand trembled as she reached for the door latch.

She could do this for her baby.
She could do this for Mikel.
She would do this for *herself*.

23

MIKEL

Mikel took the beer Isaiah readily offered as he walked towards the large lounge chair. Was this all a dream? Was it his hand accepting the joint from his friend, sucking on the paper, filling his lungs with smoke? Music played in the background. The man's voice echoed how he felt. Paralyzed. Where was the real him? Who was the real him? He didn't know, but had he ever? The man he'd thought he was would have never snapped at Remy like that, nor left her alone in the car. Anger and disgust roiled in his gut. Hatred for himself clawed his insides. Guilt and shame kept him glued to the spot where he sat.

You're nothing.

You should kill yourself and put us all out of our misery.

You failed her.

Weak.

Selfish.

Fuckup.

Pain laced his every breath. Living was a punishment. He was tired of pushing through, and just getting by. He was filled with an empty loneliness and impending darkness that only seemed to get worse by the minute. Why did he even bother trying to keep his promises to Remy? He was a failure. Always would be.

Isaiah snorted a line and offered him one. Mikel's hands clenched, his whole body itching for a high to forget the fact that he'd just gotten beat up by Joe Canoby and his buddy. That they had threatened his life and that of anyone he loved if he didn't behave like the well-trained lapdog he'd been in the past. *That fucker mentioned Remy by name. He knows her address.* It was better if he pushed her away. She needed to stay far from him for her own safety.

"Maybe you need a better reminder of who owns you." Joe's last words still possessed him. Sick motherfucker wanted to remind Mikel just how powerless he really was. He'd never be free. He never should have given in to his selfishness. He should have ended it all before it began, taken himself out of the equation. *I should just kill myself and everyone will be better off.*

You'll never amount to anything.

You're just like me; you're nothing.

Murderer.

You don't do anything right.

You belong to me.

You are nothing but a failure.

Worthless piece of shit.

Dirty bastard.

I hate you.

I hate me.

Torment lit his rib cage. Shame was a crushing weight on his chest. He would do anything to feel light and free, just for a stolen minute—escape this world and all his regrets.

June sauntered her way over to him before sitting on his lap with a glass pipe. Her perfume was strong and sickly sweet.

She licked her lips seductively before saying, "I've missed you. Haven't seen you around in a while."

"I've been busy."

"Well, I'm glad you came home where you belong."

She had no idea how her words cut to his bone, sunk into his marrow. She was right; this was all he was ever gonna be. He was starving for a fix, to feel something besides this internal agony and skin that burned with a million tiny paper cuts. He took what she had to offer, giving in to temptation. Remy was better off without him.

She lit the pipe, sucking in and blowing the smoke of the crystal meth in his face. He inhaled, seeking the dark escape. His painkiller. Her hand rested on his chest and she laughed. The noise echoed as the beginning effects of the drug seeped into his cells and poisoned his veins. She did it again, and again until he was floating in warmth—lying on a sandy beach with the sun shining down on him. His body relaxed, like he was floating in the water without a care in the world.

Hands unbuttoned his shirt . . . a hot mouth licking his nipples.

Remy was here in this dream.

Her face was shocked, tears welling and spilling down her face like sad blue paint leaking from the anger and betrayal in her eyes. "You promised. You swore on . . ."

"Well, I lied." It sounded like his voice, but rougher.

No, Remy. Don't leave. That wasn't me.

Joe's ugly face lit up his vision, the threats he'd spewed before punching his ribs one more time.

"Go, Remy. Run. Go!" he shouted. Someday she would see it was for her own good.

She turned, her body shaking and trembling as she stumbled away from him. His chest tightened, pain lacing through his heart. Somewhere in the distance his body was being ravaged, brutally being ripped apart by his choices. But he would deal with that later. Right now, June had another hit waiting for him. He was going to choose that escape for a little longer and deal with his regrets another time. He always did.

June lowered her mouth to his. She tasted like a bad decision and self-loathing, nothing like Remy's sweet mouth. He floated high above, watching the scene before him. His body was moving without his permission, doing anything he had to avoid the pain plaguing him, the shadow that followed him, drowning him in a dark sea and sucking him under to hell on earth.

His lip stung from the pain of her bite; he relished it. Anything to help him not feel numb. Her hands moved quickly to unbutton his pants. The tang of iron filled his mouth, sending him plummeting back to his body. He shoved her away roughly, standing up and running out the door, not caring that his pants were still unzipped.

Blood. He lifted his hand to the doorknob. They were red, dripping with *blood.* His father's life force. Crimson handprints taunted him as he ripped open the door, needing escape from the chaos raging inside him. He had to get air.

Mikel stumbled onto the porch, every sense heightened, every color sharper. Remy's sobs echoed in his head; she was still sitting in the truck. Of course she was. He had brought her here and abandoned her with no way to get home. He pulled the keys from his pocket. He would drive her, make sure she was safe. He could still fix this. She couldn't leave him. He couldn't live without her.

The sound of an engine approaching wrenched his thoughts from her. A truck he recognized came barreling down the road towards them.

"Remy—"

24

REMY

Remy shook as her tears threatened to drown her. Mikel had become someone she didn't recognize. Or maybe she'd just had her eyes opened to who he'd been the whole time. He had done things she had never imagined him doing. That woman was wrapped around him, and he'd *let* her. He was getting high after he had promised *on his love for her* that he wouldn't. *It was all a lie.*

Now, she was pregnant and alone. Anger roiled in her stomach. She bent over and vomited. Wiping her mouth, she stood and climbed into his truck. *How dare he.* She'd given him everything she had and then some and he'd thrown it back in her face. *I am done.*

She clutched her phone. Mikel had left her no choice. As much as the heartbreak from losing him was tearing her up inside, as much as she wanted to smash his truck to smithereens, he needed help—even if she wasn't the one who could do it anymore. This wasn't the life she wanted for herself, or her child. She would have to do this alone.

The rumble of an engine came closer and she spotted

Bently's truck speeding around the corner. He parked in front of her before hopping out and eyeing her with concern.

Bently started shouting to someone. Remy turned. Mikel stood by the window, staring in at her. His face twisted with a vacant expression she hadn't seen flashing in his eyes before. Betrayal. Hatred. Anger. Pain. So much regret.

Remy got out of the truck. She just needed to go home. Half of her didn't even want to look at the man who had taken her heart. She'd given it so freely, just to have it ripped to shreds and stomped on. The other half still loved him and worried for him, and she hated herself for being so weak.

"What the fuck is this?" Bently snapped. She had never seen him so angry with Mikel before. "Are you high? What are you on?"

"Nothing, man. We just got in a fight." Mikel hid his hands behind his back and eyed Remy as if he expected her to back him up in the facade.

No more. "It was something in a glass pipe," she answered for him.

Bently glanced at her, and then back to Mikel. He reached behind Mikel and pulled out a set of keys that Mikel must have had in hand before tossing them to Remy. "Take his truck and get home safe, Remy. I'll take care of this."

She caught them and nodded, her heart pounding. There was so much she wanted to say, but all of it would be lost to deaf ears.

"Remy! Wait! I'm sorry, baby! *Please,* just wait. I promise I won't do it again. I swear!" Mikel pleaded as she continued to walk to his truck. It was her turn to put some distance between them.

She whirled around to face him, anger seeping from every pore. "No! We're done. Don't call me. Don't text me. Stay away from me. I'm done with your lies. I gave you everything and you—you fucking used me!" Her knees knocked and her body trembled, fueled with adrenaline and heartbreak. Confusion blurred her vision. Every breath hurt. Tiny remnants of her shattered heart pierced her rib cage.

"Baby, please," he begged.

She climbed back into the truck, ignoring his cries as Bently pushed Mikel into the passenger side of his pickup. She took a deep breath and started the engine with her shaking hand before pulling out onto the road and heading towards the only place she felt safe. *Home.*

At the stop sign, she turned onto the empty country road. Bently's car followed not too far behind. She focused on the pavement in front of her, a single car waiting at the next crossroad. She stopped and waited, but they waved her along. Pressing the gas pedal, she drove through the intersection the moment another car sped into her line of vision. It all happened in slow motion: the crash of bending metal and smash of broken glass as she surged forward. The air bag being deployed, and the breath-stealing force of the steering wheel striking her chest. Her lungs burned. Everything turned upside down as shattered glass rained across her skin. She was whipped around like a rag doll as the car screeched and tumbled upside down. Something hard hit her skull and then red filled her vision.

Only one thing captured her focus.

The baby!

Shouting and gunfire filled her ringing ears as she struggled to find the release for the seat belt that was keeping her hanging. Smoke and something sour filled the air as she pressed the button. Glass imbedded into her hands and knees as she protected her stomach as much as she could during the fall to the roof of the car, which was now below her.

She scrambled towards the broken window of the passenger's side, as hers was too bent to crawl out of. She peered out, hesitating a moment as Bently crept around the truck before tackling a man she didn't recognize who was firing his weapon towards her left. The gun flew to the ground in the struggle, and Remy dragged herself out of the crushed opening. Adrenaline numbed the pain, her child's survival her only concern. Her leg caught and she started to panic. *Trapped.*

Bently had the man zip-tied as he glanced over to her, seemingly hesitating as he made a choice before he disappeared behind the car.

Where is he going? Help me!

Bently and Mikel came back into her line of vision, dragging a bloody zip-tied Joe.

Mikel dropped the man's legs and ran over to her.

"Remy! Baby! Oh my god. What have I done?" he screamed, pulling at his hair like a madman.

"Help me," she croaked.

Mikel climbed in the window as much as he could, his hands moving her leg around. Her sneaker loosened and she pulled her leg out, freeing herself. She wrapped her arms around her body as pain ached and throbbed in her abdomen. Tears streamed down her face as panic surged.

"The baby. The baby."

25

MIKEL

Mikel's mind registered what she said as bile rose in his throat.

"The baby. The baby." Remy shivered and rocked, holding her arms against herself. He reached out, afraid to touch her, but needing to with every cell in his body.

"What are you talking about?" he asked, praying this was all just a part of a really bad trip.

"I tried to tell you." Tears streaked down her face as her eyes grew vacant.

What had he done?

Bently came rushing over. "Are you okay, Remy? The ambulance is on its way. Where are you hurt?"

"The baby. The baby," she kept repeating. She had never looked this forlorn before. She seemed . . . broken. He'd done this.

You ruin everything.

You destroy everything you touch.

Killer.

Murderer.

Remy was loaded into an ambulance as he watched help-lessly, having to stay with his brother. Bently fielded questions from the other officers, promising to bring him down to the station to answer them after they had gone to check on Remy. Joe and the same guy who had held him down while he was beaten were led to the back of a patrol car.

Mikel climbed into Bently's truck and his brother drove him towards the hospital.

"Did you know she was pregnant?" Bently asked.

"No."

"How long have you been using?"

"Since high school." It didn't matter now. His secret was out.

Bently was silent for a moment before asking, "After all we saw growing up, you turned to the same thing. Why?"

Because it's the only escape. The only way to feel something besides pain and emptiness. "Sometimes it's the only way to get through the day."

Bently slammed his fist against the dashboard. "How the fuck could I not see? My own brother!"

Mikel focused outside the window, daring to hope that Remy would be okay, that he hadn't ruined her life too.

He was a murderer with blood on his hands. How could he not expect that to taint anything else good in his life? Because of his decisions, he had hurt one of the people he loved most in this world in the worst way.

He balled his hands into fists, knuckles split and bleeding from fighting Joe. He would have killed him if Bently hadn't pulled him off the scum. Remy had almost died because of him. *I didn't protect her.*

* * *

Mikel sat in the waiting room, his leg bouncing up and down anxiously as he bit his nails until they bled. Remy's parents rushed in before being quickly escorted away with a nurse.

Andre arrived just minutes behind them. "What happened?" he demanded, eyeing the bruises and blood on his face.

"It's all my fault," Mikel admitted.

"What?" Andre blinked in disbelief.

"A man ran into Mikel's truck and Remy was driving. We're waiting on the news from the doctor," Bently explained.

Tilda came out, tears rolling down her brown cheeks.

"What is it? Is she okay, Mom?" Andre asked as the three men stood.

Mikel held his breath and searched her face for any sign that he hadn't fucked this up for her.

Tilda eyed him, flames of righteous anger in her gaze as she nodded. "She will be okay."

"And the baby?" Mikel asked, terrified of the answer. *Shit, has Remy told her mom?*

Andre's gaze hardened as he stared at him. "What baby?"

"Andre, now is not the time." Tilda put her hand on her son's arm. "Remy wants to talk with you, Mikel," she gritted out.

He nodded, putting one shaky foot in front of the other. The heavy weight knowing that whatever was said when he walked into her room would change his life forever descended on him.

Tilda led him to a room partitioned off with curtains. Mathew, Remy's father, sat holding his daughter's hand. Mikel avoided his eyes. There were only two things he would find in them: disappointment and anger. What nobody knew was that no matter how much rage they had for him, it would be nothing compared to the hatred he carried in his tattered black heart for himself.

"Can we have some privacy?" Remy asked quietly. Mathew tensed as his stare bored into Mikel. "Please, Daddy. Just a few minutes."

Mathew leaned and kissed her forehead, his expression softening. Her father walked over and stood in front of Mikel, forcing him to face him as he placed his arm around Tilda's shoulders. "I trusted you with one of the most precious people in my life and this is how you treated her?"

Mikel looked down, ashamed.

Tilda spoke to Remy. "We'll be right outside if you need us."

Mikel took in the sight of Remy, hooked up to lines and tubes. The wound on her head was bandaged. She was curled up into a ball on her side, staring at nothing on the wall.

He moved to the empty seat. Her expression was drawn, empty, as silent tears poured from her eyes. He knew it then. *She lost the baby.*

"Remy," he said, wet streaks pouring down his face. He was at the bottom of the barrel, lower than he had ever been. Seeing the light dim in those deep brown eyes was his biggest torment.

"Just hold me for a little while." Her voice seemed so small and distant.

He climbed in next to her, wrapping his arms around her.

She gripped his shirt, taking a deep breath. "If I close my eyes, I can pretend we're under the stars that night at the Black Cliffs. I wished for you on every star I could find that night. I wished for your happiness, for you to mend and heal —for your secrets not to eat you alive. I wished that you would feel my love, and see yourself the way I saw you."

He trembled, the saltiness of his tears dripping into his mouth. "Why would you waste that on me?"

She nuzzled closer into his chest, against his heart. "Because you are worth it. I thought maybe someday you would see that, see the good you have to offer. I told you I would do anything, be anything for you. I guess . . . I'm a liar."

Remaining silent, he let her say her piece. She believed her words, but there was no way she was in his league. Seeing her question her worth was just another nail in the coffin. She was perfect just the way she was; the realization that she'd been changing and trying to mold into what she thought he needed made his stomach roil. He'd known this day was coming. He'd sensed the end before they began.

"I have nothing left to give you. I can't keep doing this. The lies, the broken promises. The sight of her in your arms. I can still smell her on you." She pushed him away and pulled him closer all at once.

He clung to her, knowing this was the last time he would ever get to hold her like this. *This is our goodbye.* "I know I fucked everything up, baby. Loving you was the only honest, the only good thing I've ever done in my life. I'm sorry I was too selfish to leave you alone. If I could take it all back, I would. I would trade every moment with you to save you one ounce of this pain."

She shuddered and looked up at him, her bloodshot eyes lit with a spark of hope amidst the chaos of loss and grief, and his betrayal. "Go to rehab. *Please.* Come back when you're done. I'll wait for you."

His chest tightened, emotion clutching at his heart. Her words sent daggers piercing through his flimsy armor.

I believe in you.

Failure.

You have good in you.

Murderer.

"You'd be waiting a long time. I've done things, Remy, that are unforgivable. Things no one knows about." He took a deep breath. "I became what I hated most—but I can't change that, baby." If he did, the pain of reality would eat him alive. His penance was living, and the only way he could do that, to get through the day, was his addiction.

She looked up, tears and hope and everything bright still filtering through those damaged brown spheres. "You admit you have a problem?"

A humorless laugh rumbled from him. "I have a lot more than *one*. But I'm done making you a victim of my self-destruction. I'm gonna do what I should have done a long time ago. I'm gonna leave."

She clutched him tighter, delaying the inevitable.

"I want you to open that bakery, and find a man who's better than me. A man who will take care of you. A man who I want to be, but can't. Someone who can give you everything. I want you to be happy." He kissed her forehead, jealousy raging in his belly for the man who would come and take his place. His stomach twisted as his breathing became ragged. "I'm so sorry about the baby."

She reached her hands to his face, searching his eyes. Remaining silent, she bit her lip as if holding back. "I may be young. I may be naive about a lot of things, but my love for you isn't one of them. I know now that I can't be the reason you get clean, that you must do it for yourself. It was wrong of me to believe I could save you."

She took a deep breath, as if seeking the remaining courage deep down in her soul.

"When you get sober, and find the real Mikel, the one I see when I look at you, come back to me. Let me know that you're okay, that you're happy. Maybe we weren't meant for each other—maybe you're right about that. All I know is that you will always have a piece of my heart. Promise me you'll find me when that day comes?"

He kissed her, melding his mouth to hers for the last time. Pain and heartache and sorrow mixed with the connection and burning embers of lust. Why did love have to hurt so much?

Their tears fell, blending and mixing, saturating his skin. Sparks of light glowed in the dark empty recesses of his heart, tempting him with false hope. The burn of penance and retribution slammed into him. He slipped his tongue inside her mouth, needing one more taste. It would never be enough, just a parting memory to hold on to and remind him of all that he had lost. Trembles rocked through her body as pieces of her weaved and blurred into his DNA with a mix of loss and love. She whimpered. Clinging to him, she dug her finger-nails into his scalp, holding him captive. He was a prisoner to her touch.

He wanted to give in, to beg her forgiveness, and try his best to make it all better. But for once in his life he was going to do what was right. He would walk away so that she could live. Leave her before he could destroy her and everything he'd spent his whole life building, his family and friends. Hopefully Andre would understand.

He pulled out of her embrace, severing their connection for the last time. He walked out the door, not turning to look back as he left her room far more broken than when he'd entered it.

He didn't look back.

26

REMY

The fall rain drizzled outside her window in the silence—Mother Nature crying for her pain when she no longer could. She tucked her hand to her belly, thankful. *At least my child is safe.*

Remy snuggled closer to the pillow that smelled of home. Her eyes burned, dry and swollen from emptying all her hopes and dreams for her and Mikel's future one tear at a time until she was nothing but a hollow, dried-up well. Her body ached. Every muscle was sore and bruised. But nothing compared to the internal bleeding of her heart.

When Mikel had walked out of her hospital room only yesterday, she'd loved him and hated him at the same time. He needed help. She'd learned the hard way that he had to find that himself. He needed to want to be helped.

She was still at risk for a miscarriage, but for now, her baby was alive. She had pled with her parents to keep it a secret. Mikel was in no place to be a father. She wanted more for both him and their baby. He needed to be sober, and she would continue to hold on to the hope that one day, he would.

She just prayed he wouldn't hate her. She was doing what was right for her unborn child.

Her mother came in, preceded by the smell of coffee. She sat across from Remy, taking a sip of the paper cup before setting it on the bedside table.

Her mother's anger had faded, worry and disappointment taking its place.

"I just want to know why you didn't tell me he had a problem?" she asked.

Remy sighed. "I thought I was protecting him by keeping his secrets, like I had since we were kids. I stupidly assumed I could help him heal if I loved him enough."

Her mother nodded, seemingly deep in thought. "Real love doesn't require you to be someone you're not, Remy. It doesn't make you isolate yourself from your support system. Love isn't selfish. I know you care deeply for him, but what you two had seems more like codependency."

Remy remained silent, letting her mother speak.

"Do you realize the risks involved for the baby if the person who fathers the child is doing drugs?"

"I would never have my child around that, Mama." Remy defended herself.

Her mother shook her head. "No, sweetie. I'm talking about fetal addiction. The very DNA is altered. The man's sperm can be affected directly by the drug use, causing abnormalities. The baby may not even make it to term. If the child does thrive, they are at a high risk for congenital defects of the heart and other cognitive issues."

Remy struggled for a breath, like the air had been sucked out of the room. "But I never did any drugs."

"It's a possibility when either parent uses. But what's done is done. I'll be here with you every step of the way."

Remy's head was reeling. Hadn't she just been thankful

that at least her child was safe in her belly? The knowledge that her precious baby was still in danger nearly swallowed her whole with preemptive grief. "I'm sorry, Mama." Tears streamed down her chapped face once more. "I'm so sorry."

"Shhhh. I'm here, baby. Get some rest. No sense worrying about what we cannot change. We'll hope for the best, but prepare ourselves for every outcome."

Remy cried as her mother softly rubbed her head and hummed a soothing melody. She drifted into sleep—her only refuge from the pain.

* * *

Sometime later, there was a knock, waking her.

"Can I come in?" Bently peered through her doorway.

"Yes," she said, her voice hoarse as she rubbed her eyes, adjusting to the light.

He looked sympathetically towards her as he walked over to the empty chair beside the bed. He had his deputy uniform on, his hat in his hand. Bently was so much like Mikel it hurt to look at him. Bently's eyes were bright blue instead of the warm chocolate color of his brother's, so she focused on them.

"How are you feeling?" he asked tentatively.

"I've been better." She forced an empty laugh. Everything was one overwhelming mess of emotions. Her baby could have birth defects. Would she be able to make her dreams come true? Would the man she loved ever get clean? Would he come back? Could she ever get over him if he didn't? Could she be a single mother? At least the baby was safe for now in her womb.

He stared at her in silence for a moment, as if gathering the courage to say something. "Remy, I'm sorry I didn't see he had a problem. I should have noticed the signs. He's always been moody and slept when he was off work. I should have suspected it was something more."

She shook her head. "He was good at hiding it. Sometimes it's the people closest that miss it because we don't want to believe the ones we love are capable of something like that."

He nodded. "Yeah, but I was supposed to take care of him and Jasmine."

"You did your best. Mikel is a grown man making his own decisions. He's sick. I tried to help, but . . ."

"You've helped, Remy. More than you know." Bently reached his hand out to cover hers, the warm connection in his touch offering her some comfort.

"The people that ran you off the road, Joe Canoby and Jim Fisher, are in jail. Joe's looking at a decade behind bars, and his accomplice much longer for having the weapon. *You're safe.*"

She nodded, glad to hear she wouldn't have to keep looking over her shoulder. "How is he?" she asked, not able to say Mikel's name yet.

Bently sat back in his chair, clenching his fists in his lap.

"Tell me," she prodded.

"I don't know. He took off. Can't locate him." He sighed, the worry written across his face.

"He said he was leaving."

"He left knowing you're pregnant?" he asked, anger simmering just beneath the surface of the question. He assumed Mikel had abandoned her.

She shook her head. "He believes I lost the baby, and I didn't tell him otherwise. I love him, Bently, with every cell in my body, but he's in no place to be a father. He can't take care of himself. I made him promise to come back once he gets clean for good."

"You . . . he doesn't know?" he asked in disbelief.

"Promise me you won't tell him," she begged.

"That's a big ask, Remy. When he finds out I knew and didn't tell him, it could destroy any progress he's made."

"Don't put him in the position to choose his addiction over his child, because I could never forgive him for that." Her voice trembled as the words cut like glass from her mouth.

"If he asks . . . I can't lie to him. I won't do that," Bently said, standing and pacing the short room.

"My child almost died because of him, and it still might. I can't endanger this baby further. He promised me he would never touch the stuff again and then I walked in and found him with that junkie on his lap with her hands all over him while he got high. He told me to go, to stay away from him. I'm finally listening."

Bently tugged the hair on his head and grit his teeth. "I'll try to get him into rehab when he picks up my call."

"Thank you," she said. She closed her eyes, exhausted. She just needed to sleep again, escape her reality for a little while. Maybe when she woke up, this would all be a bad dream.

Her hand rested against her belly as she imagined a life where her baby would get to grow up with two parents who loved her, like she had. Would she have her father's eyes? Would he have Mikel's love for astronomy?

Remy slipped into a peaceful dream of the fictional family she'd created in her mind.

27

REMY
EIGHT MONTHS LATER

"Push, Remy. You got this!" her mother said as Remy bore down with every bit of remaining strength she had left. Sweat trickled from her forehead, and she ground her molars as the force of another contraction rolled through her.

Emma wiped a cool cloth over her skin as she offered encouraging words. "You got this. You're a badass."

"I can't." Remy cried from exhaustion. The one person she needed wasn't here with her. "I can't do this on my own."

Tilda firmly took her face, forcing Remy to meet her mother's eyes. "You are doing this. There's no turning back now. You're not alone. You have me, you have your family, and you have your friends. Remy, you come from a long line of strong women, and their blood runs through your veins. You. Can. Do. This. Now, take a deep breath, and help me meet my grandchild."

Remy gulped in air as the strength of another contraction increased. Tears still escaped the corners of her eyes. Determination filled her. She would do this for the sweet little girl who had captured her heart before she'd even drawn breath.

Remy pushed with everything in her, until the slippery burning release of her child entering the world erupted between her bloody thighs.

Sweet little cries filled the room.

"Oh my god!" Emma gasped.

"You did it, baby," her mother said.

Remy reached out, instinctively taking the slimy newborn from her mother's hands as the midwife checked her baby girl without being too intrusive.

Tears burned her eyes as she clutched her newborn to her bare breast. The infant rooted, finding what she was searching for and suckling. *I did it.* She was a mother now. This tiny girl was the most beautiful person she'd ever seen. Her heart nearly burst with the mixture of awe and love, and fear for the unknown.

A while later, Emma had gone home and her mother lay sleeping next to her on the pullout chair in her room at the birthing center.

Remy kissed her daughter's sleeping nose and whispered, "Baby girl, I promise I'll never let anything happen to you. I'll keep you safe. I'll be strong for you. You'll always come first. Someday, you'll meet your daddy." Remy choked back the tears as she continued, "But, until then, I'll love you enough for the both of us, Lyra. More than all the stars in the sky."

Mikel

Mikel woke with a pounding head and a mouth as dry as the desert. Squinting at the light coming from the dirty motel room curtains, he groaned in pain. Everything hurt.

Memories from the previous night came in flashes. The blonde he'd followed home, hoping to finally rid himself of Remy's memories. He'd just wanted to forget for a little while. Punish himself.

He hadn't gotten far. The sight of those blue eyes looking up at him as she'd unbuttoned his pants had only made him more disgusted with himself. He'd stopped her and stormed out without an explanation. The next thing he remembered was the entire bottle of the pills he'd bought from the dealer he'd run into on the corner. Why was he still alive? How was it possible? He'd taken more than enough to get the job done. Mixing it with whiskey should have been a sure thing.

He was alive—the ache throbbing through his entire body was a painful reminder. Apparently, he was such a failure, he couldn't even kill himself properly.

Maybe you're still alive for a reason.

The voice came from somewhere in the distance of his mind. He needed to get out of here, do something different.

Mikel found himself at the airport two hours later. He was tempted to call back home, see how his brother and sister were doing—how Remy was. If he did, he'd probably go back, and there was nothing they needed less than his burden.

He had to get far away. Living like this wasn't working anymore, but rehab had never helped his mother, or his father. He was doomed to deal with his addiction for the rest of his life. The least he could do was keep his loved ones out of it.

"Can I help you, sir?" the woman at the ticket counter asked.

"I need a ticket on the next international flight out of here," he said, setting his worn duffle bag on the counter. He'd sold his truck and he had nothing left to lose.

The woman eyed him curiously as she typed the keys on the keyboard. "The next flight is heading to Africa with a connecting flight in Heathrow."

"I'll take it."

The farther away from Remy he was, the safer she would be.

28

REMY

PART 2 - FIVE YEARS LATER

R emy handed an iced latte to a customer when a familiar face greeted her through the door. Happiness spread through her.

"Hey, gorgeous."

"Hey, Aaron. What can I get for you today?" she asked, not bothering to hide her smile.

"How about a date this Friday?"

She took a deep breath, steadying the swirl of emotions in her belly. The man knew how to flirt, and she enjoyed being reminded that she was a woman as much as a mother.

"What time?" she asked. Uncle Andre would be more than happy to babysit Lyra.

His smile widened. "Pick you up at six? Does that work with Lyra?"

Another flutter danced in her belly. "Yes, that works," she answered.

"Now all I need is a black coffee." He smirked.

She grabbed the paper cup and filled it before handing it to him.

His warm hand wrapped around hers, lingering as he leaned in and spoke. "I'll plan something special." He kissed her cheek. The tender caress caused embers of heat to blossom like a flower over her skin—years of celibacy sparked alive with his careful touch. Not scorching heat, but it was something.

"I look forward to our date," she said, almost as if instructing herself.

"Me too." Aaron backed away, waving as he left.

She locked up behind him and wiped down the appliances before going to the back room to check on the baked goods saturating the café with their sweet aroma.

She pulled a fresh sheet pan of muffins from the oven and set them on the cooling rack.

Emma walked in the back door, holding the tiny hand of the most beautiful little girl in the whole world.

"Mommy!"

Remy opened her arms wide to catch her smiling daughter. "Hey, baby. Did you have fun with Auntie Emma?"

Lyra nodded, her chubby cheeks dimpled as her curls bounced with her excitement. "Yes! Can I have a cookie?"

"Go pick one out." She released her daughter, and the little girl ran towards the shelf of freshly decorated sugar cookies.

"I want a mermaid one!" she squealed, taking one from the assortment.

Remy turned to Emma. "Thank you for watching her while I got these done. Now I can relax the rest of the day."

Emma smiled. "You know I love time with my favorite girl. We played our very own rock show today."

"You did, huh?" Remy teased.

"Lyra just might be my newest member of my band when I go back on tour next month."

"Can I peeeease, Mommy?" Lyra begged with a mouthful of half-eaten mermaid cookie.

"I think I would miss you too much."

"Well, maybe you could come with us?" Her daughter, always the problem solver.

"Who would run my café?" Remy held out her arms.

Lyra scrunched her forehead in concentration. "How about when I'm older?"

"It's a deal, kid," Emma answered. "I gotta get to the studio. You two have fun today." She hugged Remy and then Lyra.

"We will. We're going to Bently's for a cookout. Andre will be there," Remy said, handing a box of cupcakes to her friend as payment.

"Oh, I hope he isn't bringing you-know-who." Emma rolled her eyes.

"Who?" Lyra asked, wide-eyed.

"Baby, why don't you go grab a juice from the fridge and then we'll get going?" Remy distracted her with a smile.

When her daughter was out of earshot, she addressed Emma. "Listen, Tiffany may be a bitch, but my brother loves her, so we just have to deal with it."

"And hope he comes to his senses. That woman just rubs me the wrong way." Emma shivered.

"And you have such great taste in the people you've dated?" Remy smirked.

Emma held out her hands. "Hey now. The men and women I've dated were definitely bitches—some of them. Okay, most of them. But that's how I know one when I see one."

Remy laughed. "I don't disagree with you, but we can't help who we fall in love with, can we?"

Heaviness descended upon Remy as chocolate eyes and

Mikel's handsome face flashed in her mind. Five long years had turned the unbearable pain into a dull ache. No one had heard a word from him since he'd left. He could have been dead for all they knew.

No. Surely if he was gone, she would feel it in her heart. She would know. What was clear though was, despite everything they'd shared, he hadn't come back for her.

Emma's eyes dimmed as she turned her attention to the little girl skipping through the double doors of the café. "Well, looks like that's my cue to leave. I'll see you later, Lyra."

"My name is not Lyra anymore. It's Princess Mermaid Rock Star," her daughter said, matter-of-factly.

"Alright then, Princess Mermaid Rock Star. You have a good day with your family." Emma saluted them and exited.

Remy shut off the lights and took her daughter's hand, grabbing a box of cupcakes for the barbecue with the other. They went out the back screen door. Warm June air billowed around them.

Lyra buckled herself in her car seat as Remy rolled down the windows.

"Ready to go, baby girl?"

"Yes, Mommy."

"Pull your chest clip up a little bit," she directed, peering at her daughter in the rearview mirror.

"Is this good?" Lyra asked, pushing the plastic clip higher.

"Perfect."

"Can you tell me the story of my daddy again?" Lyra asked.

Not again. Remy's heart twisted as her little girl pulled a worn photo from her pocket.

"How about we listen to some music instead?" She put the radio on, stopping on one of Lyra's favorite songs by Katy Perry. She just needed a break from thoughts of Mikel today.

"Ro-o-o-o-oar!" Her daughter's sweet off-pitch voice sang as loud as she could. Remy smiled.

A weight settled over her shoulders as her stomach churned with anxiety. A thousand tiny needles prickled her skin in awareness. The energy in the car shifted, electrified like the atmosphere before a big storm. She checked her surroundings; only a few people milled about. No one that stood out to her. It was probably just the past that had seemed to creep up on her today. Changes were scary, and she was ready to move on.

Thunk! She jumped. *What the heck was that?*

"What happened, Mommy?" Lyra asked, fear tinging her little voice.

Black feathers danced limply on the hood of her car.

"Looks like a bird flew into the windshield." Remy's voice rattled with her own unease.

"Is it okay, Mommy?"

Remy unbuckled and opened her door. "I'll check."

A warm gust of wind blew through the trees, shutting her door with force. The sky was bright and sunny, nothing like the ominous feeling that bubbled up inside her. The black bird slid across to the other side of the car. The creature twitched and wobbled to its feet drunkenly, flapping its wings before flying off.

Remy searched around her one more time before she climbed back into the car and buckled.

"Did it fly away, Mommy?"

"Guess so. Must have just stunned it," Remy said, forcing a smile.

She couldn't shake the feeling in her gut that something was about to happen—and it was going to be bad.

29

MIKEL

Mikel climbed into the cab at the airport. It had been more than five years since he'd last been in the United States. For the first time in his life, he wasn't drowning in the urge to use whenever he had a bad day. He missed his family. He owed a lot of people apologies.

He had dialed his brother on several occasions, only to hang up. It would have hurt too much to ask about Remy. He didn't want to know if she had met someone else, or if she had a family of her own now. He'd ruined the only pure thing in his life because of his choices, his disease. He owed her so much, and the only way he knew how to repay her was to stay away.

She had asked him to come back when he was able to look at himself and see his life was worth fighting for. He would always be a work in progress, but if he waited any longer, it may have been too late to fulfill at least one promise he'd made to her.

"Where to?" the cab driver asked.

The truth was, he had never been more terrified in his life

about going back than he was now. This was a fork in the road. A small choice with a huge impact. He took a deep breath.

"Shattered Cove." *Home.*

* * *

An hour later, he stood across the street from the house he'd left all those years ago. Memories returned of stuffing the bare necessities he'd owned into the bag still at his side and rushing towards his truck; and of Jasmine's pleading voice, begging him to stay and think about what he was doing. He swallowed the lump of emotion rising in his throat.

The smell of barbecue lifted from the backyard where he could hear the unmistakable laughter of his brother and sister. He took a deep breath and crossed the road. His body trembled, and he forced his leaden feet forward.

What if they can't forgive me?

What if they reject me?

What if they pity me?

He walked past the two lilac trees, their sweet floral scent drawing him out of his head. Pressure settled in his chest as nervous knots twisted and wound his guts tight. A car door shut somewhere in the distance.

He kept his eyes trained ahead as his family came into view. Jasmine was not the teenager she'd been when he left. She was much more woman now, having grown into her curves. Her long hair was shaved on one side—an edgy look only she could pull off. Bently stood at the grill flipping the burgers, holding a beer. He seemed bigger, larger than life, a commanding presence as always.

A gasp from Jasmine directed Mikel's attention back to her. She was looking right at him, her hand covering her mouth. Bently turned to see what had alerted her, locking on to Mikel.

There was none of the expected anger. Shock turned into disbelief. Neither of his siblings moved, as if they were afraid to spook him, or end the mirage in front of them. He walked forward, dropping his bag in the grass and placing his hands in his pockets.

"Mikel?" The shocked sweet voice came from his left—the one he only heard in his dreams. *Remy.* All the same feelings he'd had for her came rushing back to the surface, threatening to drown him. His heart throbbed with the all-too-familiar ache that he had grown accustomed to in her absence.

She was now curves and glowing brown sun-kissed skin. His Dove was as beautiful and pure as he remembered, if not more so.

"Is that my daddy?" came a little voice.

Mikel spotted the little girl with chubby cheeks and tight curls hiding behind her mother's leg, her skin a few shades lighter than her mother's.

Daddy? What the fuck?

His world spun as the ground beneath him swayed and bucked. He staggered back before falling to his knees, the breath sucked from his lungs.

"Lyra, why don't you come with me?" Jasmine said, rushing to whisk the little girl into the house.

Lyra. The power in those four little letters would have knocked him to the ground again if he had been standing. If he'd had any doubt in his mind that she was his daughter, it was erased with that name.

"You came back," Bently said as he took a few steps closer.

"She's mine?" Mikel asked, hot anger burning his skin as he managed to consider the watery brown eyes staring back at him.

Remy nodded.

"I thought she was dead. You told me . . ."

Remy approached him on shaky legs as he stood. A current of electricity lit the air between them like a live wire.

"Where have you been?" Her voice wavered.

"Everywhere. Nowhere. What . . . why didn't you tell me at the hospital? Why did you let me believe she was dead?" Anger cut from his words as his fists clenched.

"What the fuck is this asshole doing here?" Andre's voice boomed from behind Remy as he rushed towards him, seething.

"Andre, calm down," Bently said.

Andre didn't slow, getting right in his face as Remy tried to push them apart. His world was spinning, tumbling into an abyss of confusion as he tried to make sense of everything.

"Fucker abandoned my pregnant sister, almost got her killed, and left me in the lurch with our business. I had to cancel contracts and work twice as hard to keep my reputation. And you want me to calm down? Nah, this has been a long time coming."

"Dre, he didn't know. I told you, he didn't know," Remy argued, but it was no use.

One minute he was looking into the angry snarl of the man who used to be his best friend, the next he was somehow facing the clouds. His eye burned and throbbed as Remy's scream erupted. Andre's blow had knocked him to the ground.

Bently was quick to drag Andre away, leaving Remy and Mikel alone in the backyard.

"Are you okay?" she asked, her soft fingers touching the tender spot that was sure to bruise. A jolt of energy shot from her hand—the overwhelming chemistry that was all too familiar with her. She dropped it as he sat.

"We have a lot to talk about." She bit her bottom lip.

"That sounds like the understatement of the fucking century," he growled.

* * *

Remy handed him the pack of frozen green beans as they sat in the kitchen. Bently leaned against the counter while Jasmine played in the grass outside with his daughter.

My daughter.

"I'm gonna take Lyra home," Remy said, getting to her feet.

"The hell you are. I want some answers," he snapped.

"You think I don't?" she yelled, her fierceness surprising him.

"Settle down," Bently warned.

Remy swallowed the tears forming in her eyes. His chest tightened. How could he love someone and be so angry all at the same time?

"Lyra is my first priority. I'm sure she has a lot of questions because of you just showing up like this. Let me get her settled. If you want to talk, you can meet me after work tomorrow," she said.

"Where?"

"The Stardust Café—used to be Dolly's." The name was like a trip back in time. She'd really done it—made all her dreams come true. She had everything, including his child. He had nothing.

"How did she know who I was?" he asked.

Her eyes fluttered closed momentarily. "I have pictures of you."

"What did you tell her about me? About why I wasn't here?" His voice trembled, fearing the answer.

Remy sighed and shook her head, crossing her arms across her chest protectively. "I told her that her daddy was sick and getting help. That someday when he was all better . . ." She swallowed, wiping away a stray tear that had rolled down her cheek, past the walls that she'd built in his wake. "He promised me he would come back. Then she could meet him."

His chest tightened as regrets filtered through him, snaking around him, masked in shame and guilt.

I abandoned them.

I should have been there.

Mikel halted the intrusive thoughts, changing them the way his therapist had suggested.

I needed to leave for my own mental health.

I did my best.

I can be here and help now.

He nodded, unsure of what to say.

Remy stepped forward, placing her hand on his shoulder tentatively. A spark ignited his skin.

"I'm glad you came back," she said.

His body ached to hold her in his arms. A magnetic pull raged between them. He wanted to lay his head against her belly and wrap his arms around her, get lost in those long legs and curves that offered him so much comfort. Another part of him roiled in anger at the betrayal. How could she not have told him?

Remy walked away to the backyard before leading the little girl with eyes full of questions out of sight.

Jasmine came back in and took the seat that Remy had occupied. "Long time, big brother," she said, crossing her arms across her chest.

"How . . . where have you been?" Bently asked.

Mikel filled them in on his life for the past five years, swallowing the burning questions only Remy could answer.

Bently whistled. "Wow. What made you come back now?"

"You guys are my family," Mikel answered.

"That didn't stop you from abandoning us before. Just like Mom," Jasmine said.

"Jasmine!" Bently shushed her.

"It's fine. I deserve it. I know you're angry with me and you have every right. I needed some time to get my head on straight, to kick this for good before I came back. I'm sorry I had to leave everyone to accomplish it. But I would do it all again if I knew it would help me get clean."

"Yeah, you're right. I am fucking angry. You should have been here." Jasmine huffed.

"He's here now," Bently argued.

"And how long will he stick around this time? Huh?" She rounded on Mikel with fire in her eyes. "Long enough to see Bently lose his hair from chemo? Long enough to help drive him to his appointments when he's too weak to do it himself?"

The room started spinning again. *Bently has cancer.* He'd wasted so much time. *What if I lose him?*

"Jasmine, stop!" Bently jumped to his feet, eyes angry.

"Cancer?" Mikel asked. Fear clutched his chest, making it impossible to breathe.

His older brother tore his hardened stare off Jasmine and turned to Mikel, his expression softening. "Yeah, but they caught it early. They're hopeful."

Mikel was at a loss for words. What did you say when the world as you knew it started crumbling to pieces? He stood and pulled his brother into a tight hug. Slapping Bently's back, he exhaled for the first time. He was home. Even though it was hard, and he had a lot of questions to ask and answers to give, he was glad he had come home.

"Since it's confession time here at the Evans household, you should both know that in seven months we will have a new roommate," Jasmine said, standing. Both men turned to look at her.

"What? Who?" Bently asked.

Jasmine rolled her eyes. "I'm pregnant."

Bently sat back in the chair, as if to steady himself. "Jaz." His worried gaze studied her. "Who's the father?"

Something flashed in Jasmine's eyes before they fell. Shame. Regret. Emotions Mikel knew well.

"Doesn't matter. He's not in the picture."

Mikel knew there was far more to the story than their sister was letting on, but who was he to demand answers now? They had been close once. He'd literally killed for her. That trust had been severed the moment he'd left.

"Welcome home, Mikel," Jasmine snarked as she walked out of the room.

And what a welcome it had been.

30

REMY

Sunday afternoon, Remy's hand trembled as she checked the clock one more time. Five minutes until closing. Mikel would be here to talk after that.

She finished cleaning the espresso machine, Remy opened the cupboard with the extra coffee. The jug of almond milk was on the shelf. *Crap.* She'd really been distracted today. She sniffed it, checking to make sure it wasn't spoiled before she moved it to the fridge where it belonged.

Ding!

She pulled her phone from her pocket. Lyra's smiling face greeted her, holding a painting in the image her mother had sent. Remy had left her daughter with her grandparents for the evening. The little girl had been shocked at seeing the man she'd idolized for so many years through his pictures in the flesh. She'd just wanted to know when she could meet him.

"Why didn't he want to talk to me?" she'd asked.

Remy had carefully explained that he did, but that Uncle Bently and Aunt Jasmine needed to talk to him about important things first. She'd seemed satisfied with the answer, but it would only hold the little girl back for so long.

The bells above the door jingled, signaling a customer. Her eyes caressed every inch of the man who seemed to swallow all the air in the room when he was around. His very presence commanded her attention. Strength and power emanated from him. New ink covered his arms, disappearing behind his short sleeves, only adding to his bad-boy aura that she'd always been drawn to. His muscles seemed larger than before, his shoulders in particular more massive than she remembered. He was the same, and yet different in so many ways.

His eyes wandered around the café before landing on her with an intensity that made her knees wobble and her secret places ache. Why did he have the ability to affect her so fiercely? The moment she had laid eyes on him, it was like a wave of rogue emotions rushed over her. A tsunami, drowning her with everything she'd stuffed down for the past five years.

"You really did it," he said, pride glowing from those bronze eyes. "Stardust Café."

She swallowed. A blush of self-conscious shyness seared her cheeks as her belly tumbled. "Just like we said." Her eyes conveyed thousands of unspoken messages as they locked with his.

I never gave up on you.

I hope you found your peace.

I'm glad you came back.

I waited for you.

I'm angry with you.

I'm sorry.

I hate you.

I love you.

She set the towel down and walked around him to the

front door to lock it and flip the sign to closed, breaking the trance. "Can I get you a coffee or anything?" she asked, careful not to touch him. The man was like gravity, pulling, tugging her towards him with an overpowering force.

"Sure. Coffee would be nice," he said, his gaze following her every move.

"You still take it black?" she asked.

"Some things never change," he said, his tone heady.

She ignored the flutter in her belly and tightness in her chest as she made his drink. Swallowing the emotion that surged, she denied herself hope.

After pouring hot water into a cup for herself, she added a tea bag. Remy didn't need the extra stimulation—she was jittery enough. She led him to the back room where she did all her baking and decorating, not wanting to draw any town gossip from anyone peering in through the windows.

They sat in silence for a moment. She was unsure if she should speak first. A million questions swirled around in her mind, mixing and tangling with confessions on her tongue.

He took a drink before scratching his overgrown stubble and running his hand through his coal-black hair that had grown longer since she'd seen him last.

What did you say to the man you loved who'd abandoned you when you needed him most? The man who'd betrayed you in the worst possible way?

"How about you start," she said, and then cleared her throat, setting her shaking hands on her bare thighs. "What happened after you left?"

He set the cup on the large stainless steel island before he took a deep breath and began.

"I just got in my truck and took off. I found work where I could. I was using pretty heavily. July eighth, I found the bottom of the darkest pit I'd ever been in. I tried to end it all

—just stop the pain and the memories. I swallowed a bunch of pills and went to sleep." He dropped his head, staring at the cup of coffee in front of him.

Remy's eyes stung almost as much as the pain in her heart. She was filled with sympathy for this man who was loved so fiercely and yet who had felt hopeless enough to try to end his life. He was being surprisingly open and honest.

"July ninth is Lyra's birthday," she said, amazed at the connection.

He blinked, clearly in awe himself. "Really?"

She nodded. "What happened?"

He was silent for a moment and then he said, "I woke up. I don't know how or why. But I took it as a sign. I sold my truck and bought a ticket on the next plane leaving. Turns out it was headed to a country called Ghana in Africa. From there, I found some people who needed an extra set of hands building schools and hospitals. They traveled around to different countries, and I tagged along with them. I met someone there who helped me."

A pang of jealousy seared her gut as she winced. Mikel was doing better, and that was all that mattered.

"He was a recovering alcoholic himself. He knew what I was going through, and what I needed."

Remy's body relaxed—the friend was another man. Her mind whittled with confusion and denial. She shouldn't care. She had a boyfriend and Mikel had obviously moved on.

"I got to work with these people who had seen wars and famine in different parts of Africa. They always had smiles on their faces. The kids laughed and played with sticks and rocks. Some had been child soldiers—seen and done things I can't begin to imagine. Yet, they found a reason to smile, to enjoy life. It just hit me, gave me some perspective on my own life. It took crossing an ocean and going to the other side of the world, but I found a reason to keep going."

She nodded, encouraging him to continue as tears slid down the corners of her eyes. A pang of hurt rippled across her aching heart. She hadn't been enough.

"If those kids could find a reason to smile, then so could I. I mean, yeah, I went through a lot, but I still was born with so much privilege. I was given the gift of life, and I was wasting it away when I could have been helping others like those kids in the villages."

Wiping her eyes with the back of her hand, she sniffed. "I'm sorry."

"For not telling me I had a kid? Sorry for letting me believe our child was dead and it was my fault?" His voice was hard, and his eyes cold.

Remy shook her head. "You don't get to do that. You can't come back here like this and treat me like this is all my fault. I'm not the same naive timid girl I was when you left."

"Remy, that's not—" He slammed his hand on the table as he stood abruptly, making her startle. "Fuck! I'm sorry."

She waited for him to bolt out of the room, or shut down and grow distant. He surprised her by taking several deep breaths and sitting back down.

"Please tell me what happened after I left." His eyes locked with hers, as if pleading for the impossible—for the last five years back.

"After the accident, the doctor told me that the baby was fine, but that I was at high risk of a miscarriage. After everything that happened . . . I knew you were not in a place to help me raise a child. I figured the extra stress might . . . I just . . . I couldn't trust you. I couldn't have my baby around the drugs and the danger. I was almost killed because of . . ."

"Me," he said.

She glanced down momentarily and nodded.

Mikel was silent. His gaze was a contradiction, both hard and soft. Unreadable.

"Say something." She stared at her tea.

"'I'm sorry' doesn't begin to cover the regret I feel for what I did and what happened. There are no words to make up for any of it."

"I never thought you would disappear for so long," she admitted.

"I never thought I would come back." His words sliced through her. The sting of rejection lacerated her insides into ribbons of regret. What they'd had was in the past, but she'd believed she meant more to him. She had been sure that once he got clean, he would return for her.

"Why did you?" she asked.

He shook his head. "Something . . . just pulled me back. I promised you I'd return . . . and if I could only keep that one promise . . . I at least owed you that."

Her belly fluttered and tumbled as her bottom lip quivered. She swallowed, reining in the hurricane of emotions hammering her insides. Hope and regret. Love and anger. Uncertainty tangled in a thousand memories of starry nights, ocean spray, her first time, and her first love. Pain and pleasure. Heartache and living life to the fullest. Desolation and restoration. All of it tumbled and weaved into the air, tangling and crossing between them in silvery webs of a life shared— forever connected by the creation of another human.

He reached out, placing his hand on hers. Magnetic energy jolted through their contact, stealing her air. The potent current radiated and vibrated down to her bones. She didn't pull away. She'd been starved of this man's embrace for more than five years; to be in Mikel's arms again and have him tell her everything would be okay would be her wish come true. If all she could have was his palm on hers, she'd take it.

"Baby, I'm so sorry you had to do all of this alone. I can't imagine how hard it was."

She nodded. "My parents helped, and our brothers. Andre gave me some money from the business profits that would have been yours. I only used it for Lyra." She hoped he wouldn't think she'd taken more from him.

"That's good." He sounded relieved. His thumb gently caressed the soft flesh of her hand. "You made your dream come true despite . . . everything."

"Yeah. I did." Because she'd had to learn some tough lessons and take the hard road.

"Remy." Mikel's voice was husky. Her name on his lips made her body tremble. The webbing tethering her and Mikel cinching, blurring, pulling her towards him.

"Can I get to know my daughter?" he asked, unshed tears shining in his eyes, fueling the ache in her heart.

She swallowed, pushing the swirling, growing feelings down and pulling her hand from his as she turned her attention back to the only thing they would ever share: their child.

"I-I want you to. But . . . if you do this, you can't leave again. You can't use again. She must be your priority. Above all else."

His eyes flashed before he nodded solemnly. "Absolutely. I'm not the man I used to be. I know I don't deserve it, but I'm asking for one chance to prove it to you."

She wanted to believe him wholeheartedly, hoped that he was telling the truth and he could remain sober. A lifeline. She owed him that much for keeping his child a secret from him.

She nodded. "Okay. One chance."

Relief and determination flashed in his dark brown eyes before he spoke. "When can I see her?"

31

MIKEL

Mikel leaned against Bently's truck as the sun blanketed him in warmth. The air was saturated with the sweet fragrance of summer flowers and fresh-cut grass. Children laughing in the distance mixed with the buzzing of insects. Bees darted in and out of the fresh blossoms, drinking their fill of the plants' nectar.

Green Park hadn't changed too much in the time he had been gone. Memories of that first night he'd rushed here to meet Remy descended upon him. She'd walked towards the back of her car in the same short floral sundress she'd had on at the café only an hour earlier. Her hair was shorter now than when he'd left, her dark tiny curls just reaching her shoulders.

Anxiety snaked around him as his stomach tied up into knots. He was a father. He was going to meet his daughter. He'd never thought this day would come. It was because of the pressure and responsibility of caring for a life—all the horrible things in this world he'd seen. What if he couldn't protect her? *Hopefully I don't screw this up.*

Remy unbuckled their daughter and took her hand,

leading the curious little girl towards him. She was beautiful. A mini Remy with a hint of him. His heart thudded faster with each step closer they took. It was time. He straightened, reaching for the teddy bear he'd picked up at the local drug store. He'd been unsure what he should bring the first time he officially met his four-year-old daughter.

They stopped in front of him and he bent down on his knee. Lyra's cheeks blushed just a little as she partially hid behind her mother's legs.

He struggled to find the right words as questions flooded him, his mind tangled in a million emotions.

What was her first word? What did she like? What was her favorite color? Was she happy?

Guilt for not being there hung heavy on his shoulders, sinking its claws in his mind. He was overrun with his feelings: anger at Remy, at himself, and his past; joy that he was getting this chance; awe that this was his daughter standing in front of him, waiting for him to say something.

"Hello." If one word could convey every emotion that welled up and overflowed in his chest, that was definitely not it. Nevertheless, it was a start.

"Hi." Lyra sucked in her bottom lip. Remy rubbed the girl's shoulder soothingly.

"Do you know who I am?" he asked.

She nodded. "You're my daddy."

Daddy. The word staggered him—a force to his already mangled guts. Never in a million years did he think that term of endearment would be used towards him.

"That's right," he managed to croak out.

She eyed the pink bear that he had forgotten all about. "Is that for me?"

Handing over the fluffy creature, he said, "Yes. I didn't know if you liked pink bears or not."

"Blue is my favorite, but I like pink too." She hugged the stuffed animal close, and he was instantly jealous of the inanimate object.

"Do you wanna hang out for a little while? We can swing, or whatever you want to do."

Remy added, "Lyra loves the swings. Don't you, sweetie?"

The girl nodded, still seeming hesitant and unsure. "Why didn't you come see me before?" she asked.

Of course the kid would ask the hardest question—one he didn't have the answer to.

"Remember I told you that your daddy didn't know about you? You were a surprise present."

That was certainly one way to put it.

"Like the teddy bear?" Lyra held out the pink animal.

Remy bit her lip and nodded. "Sort of."

"Daddy? Mommy said you were sick. Are you all better now?"

He drew a breath before replying, "I get a little better every day." The truth was the nagging need to use was always there. He had just learned how to drown out the voice more effectively.

"Why didn't you want to meet me yesterday? I'm impotant too."

Remy winced.

Pain surged through him, lacerating what was left of his heart. Guilt crashed over him as his legs trembled, struggling to keep him upright.

Mikel kneeled in front of her, grasping for the words to convey his true feelings despite the turmoil of emotions raging inside him. "You're right. You are the most important person to me in the whole universe. I hope you can give me a chance to show that to you."

Her eyes grew wide. "The whole universe? That's so big!"

She smiled, her eyes lighting up. "In the pictures Mommy has of you, and at Uncle Bently's, you didn't have any tattoos."

He smiled. "You're very observant. I got these after I left."

"Mommy has one too." She looked up to her mother the same instant Remy's body grew tense.

"Why don't we do some of that swinging now?" Remy asked before he could.

"Can you push me, Daddy?"

He swallowed. The name didn't get any less amazing coming from that little mouth each time she said it. "Of course, baby girl."

He followed her to the swing set where a few other kids were running around the play structure. She handed her bear off to her mother and waited, staring at him with her arms lifted.

He carefully picked her up and set her in the seat. The significance of this moment—the first time he was getting to touch his daughter—made his hands tremble.

"I like to go high!" She giggled, seeming unaware of the jumble of emotions rising inside him.

"Hang on with both hands," Remy warned before she backed away and sat on the bench, giving the two of them some privacy.

"So, Lyra, do you like this park?" *God.* Was there a lamer question he could ask? It was the kid version of "Do you come here often?"

"Yes. Sometimes Mommy brings me at nighttime and we look at the stars."

His breath caught as he pushed her swing forward. Remy had shared a piece of him with their little girl.

He cleared his throat and asked, "Do you like looking at the stars?"

"Yes. Mommy said I'm named after a con-sell-a-ton."

He smiled at her pronunciation. "Yes, you are." A pang of guilt hit his chest at the lie he'd told Remy about their daughter's namesake constellation all those years ago. "What do you like to do when you're not at the playground?" he asked.

"I like watching *Paw Patrol*. My favorite is Everest, and Skye. They are both girls. But there is also Chase, Rumble, Marshall, Zuma, and Rocky," she continued her banter, talking a mile a minute. Sometimes he had a little trouble understanding her words, but he got the overall gist of what she was trying to say.

She moved on from the swings, deserting him for a new friend she made on the slide. Mikel turned back to Remy. She gave him an encouraging smile as he walked towards her. The golden rays of the sun broke through the green trees that swayed above them in the warm breeze. Dapples of sunlight glittered over her, making her glow. She was radiant. The sight made his chest tighten. They still had so much to uncover between them.

"That went well," she said.

He sat beside her, wanting more than anything to wrap his arm around her and have her snuggle into his chest as their daughter played. "She's got a lot of energy," he said.

Light, honest laughter tumbled out of Remy's mouth as she smiled. "She sure does."

"You bring her here to see the stars?" he asked.

She blinked and avoided his eyes, focusing on their daughter and her new friend piling wood chips and leaves together.

"I tried to share you with her the only way I could."

He swallowed.

"You named her . . ." He let the question hang.

"Lyra Jane Evans."

"I lied to you," he admitted.

"About what?" she asked hesitantly as her shoulders tensed.

"About the myth, Lyra. How it ended. Orpheus went to the underworld to get his wife. The deal was neither one of them were supposed to look behind until they crossed over to the land of the living. He forgot that tiny detail. As soon as he arrived, he turned to look at her. She was sent back to the underworld and they were never reunited. He fucked it all up," he explained.

"I know," she said, surprising him.

"Then, why?"

"The thing was, even though they didn't get their happy ending, Orpheus left something behind that brought joy to others through beauty and music. His lyre was forever immortalized in the stars by the Muses. I looked it up."

He swallowed at her confession. The tension thickened between them. Her interest, loyalty, and everything they had shared added kindling to the long-suppressed need that spun through him. He wished upon invisible stars that he could get another chance.

He reached out his hand to cover hers, needing to touch her. She grounded him like no other, and he'd missed her.

She turned to face him. Even through the pain in her eyes, desire glowed. She still felt something for him too. But the flash of worry told him that they were on a precarious ledge, one she had worked hard to avoid. She had picked up the pieces he'd left her in and molded herself into who she was now as a woman. Fragility and strength beamed from her. Goodness and light poured out, just as he'd remembered. Only this time, she seemed more guarded.

"You've really done an amazing job with her."

She blinked a few times as she took a deep breath. "Thank you. I wish I could make this easier for you and Lyra."

"You already have. What you told her about me was the truth, but it painted me in such a better light than the reality."

"You were never a bad person, Mikel. You just made some bad decisions."

Her words were a punch to the chest. After all he'd put her through, she still saw him as a good person, worthy. Why had he been so selfish all those years ago? He'd ruined the best thing in his life.

"Remy." His voice was husky.

Her gaze locked with his. So much was being said without words. The internal struggle of past hurt and current hope played across her expression.

Fear won out. She pulled her hand from under his before settling it on her lap.

He'd do anything to fix this, to earn back her trust. He'd travel to the moon if it meant he could hold her in his arms again. He'd have to take it slow. "When can I see Lyra again?" he asked, staying in safer waters.

She turned to where their daughter waved goodbye to her friend before heading towards them. "Friday, Bently was going to babysit for me. You can be there if you want."

That was five days from now. *Too long.* "Can I see her sooner?"

Remy took a deep breath. Her body trembled slightly as she rubbed her palms on her knees, making the soft fabric of her dress ride up a little more.

He needed to be patient. "I'm sorry. I just feel like I missed out on so much. I don't want to waste another minute."

She nodded. "I have dinner at my parents' tomorrow. You're welcome to come. But if you'd rather not, we could meet on Wednesday after I get done at the bakery. We usually do dinner around six. She goes to bed by eight."

He wasn't quite ready to face her parents. He had a lot to

make up for with her whole family, but he was going to start with his daughter and Remy. "Can I bring dinner to you guys on Wednesday?"

"Sure. You should know, she's celiac like me." Remy opened her arms to Lyra as she approached.

"Mommy, I'm hungry."

"We were just talking about food. How about we go get some ice cream?" he asked, not ready to let their time together end.

Remy's body stiffened.

Shit. He should have checked with her first.

Lyra jumped up and down excitedly. "Can we, Mommy?"

Remy's expression softened when she looked at their daughter. "Sure. We can do that."

"Yay!" Remy clapped her hands before grabbing on to one of his. "Can I ride with you, Daddy?"

Mikel pulled his gaze from his daughter's pleading brown eyes and glanced to Remy for permission. "There's a car seat in Bently's truck?"

She hesitated, wringing her hands together. "Let's go, then."

She didn't trust him with their daughter's safety yet. He got that. She had no idea how far he had come from the man she used to know. The idea of having his two girls with him for another hour sent tingles of anticipation through him.

He would do whatever he could to draw out their stolen moments.

32

REMY

Wednesday evening, Mikel showed up at the bakery right on time. Lyra ran to greet him with a hug as the force of one thousand galloping horses stampeded her defenses. Her heart squeezed and her ovaries ached at her fantasy come to life. All those tear-filled sleepless nights, she'd imagined this scene, dreamed of it.

"Hey, princess. Are you guys ready for dinner?" Mikel spoke to Lyra. Their little girl looked up to him like he was her hero. God, she hoped he could be.

"Thanks for being flexible about the change of plans. We're just in the mood to go out." The truth was, inviting Mikel into hers and Lyra's home felt like too much at once. She needed to keep the personal space between them—co-parent without any more . . . entanglements.

"Of course. Anything you guys need, I'm your man." He winked at her.

Was he flirting?

"You guys can ride with me and I'll bring you back here afterwards."

So much for personal space. "Oh. Okay. Let me grab my purse." She went to the back room to steady her trembling hands. *Get it together.*

"Mommy, come on! I'm hungry," Lyra called.

Steeling herself, she drew in a gulp of air and grabbed her purse before heading back out.

"Ready," she lied.

Mikel didn't bother ordering a regular pizza for himself, but decided to share a large gluten-free one with them. He talked to Lyra, asking her questions about her life, hobbies, and interests. Remy was glad to sit on the sidelines, as the two interacted.

"I checked out those *Paw Patrol* characters you talked about last time, Lyra."

Their daughter lit up like she was full of twinkle lights. "Which one is your favorite?"

"Hmmm. I think I'd have to say Skye is pretty cool."

He's putting in the time, making an effort to connect with her. She sipped her iced tea, trying to swallow the ache that bubbled up. She needed to keep her past feelings separate from now. It was the only way she would survive this.

"I thought you would pick Chase because boys are better at saving people," Lyra said, reaching for a crayon to color the children's menu.

Remy's voice clogged in her throat. Why would her little girl think that?

"Who told you that?" Mikel asked, voicing her concerns. His brow furrowed.

"Max from school. He says boys are better than girls at everything."

"Boys are not better than girls. In fact, girls are usually better at stuff."

"But you're a boy," Lyra said, glancing up with her lips pursed.

"That's how I know. Trust me, Max probably feels jealous that you're so smart and kind."

"Does that mean Mommy is better at stuff than you?"

He chuckled and shot her a look. "Your mommy is better at everything that matters."

Good god. How did he know the perfect thing to say? "Boys and girls are equal, baby. The truth is, everyone is different and we're all good at various things, and need more practice on others."

"But women have superpowers," Mikel said, like it was a secret.

Lyra's eyes grew wide. "They do?"

Mikel nodded his head. "They can grow a human being inside them, and then birth that baby into the world. No man can do that."

"Whoa! Mommy has that superpower," Lyra said excitedly.

"She sure does. She's a goddess." He swiped the dark hair from Lyra's little face, tucking it behind her small ear.

The way he tenderly cared for her and showered her with his attention made Remy feel like her heart was about to burst. This was what she'd wanted for her daughter: a daddy who would love and care for her. This was the family she'd imagined all those years ago as she cried herself to sleep.

Lyra yawned, leaning into his arm. He pulled her against his chest and then held her as her little hand rested over his heart. It was past her bedtime, but Remy didn't have it in her to stop their animated conversations.

"I just can't believe this is real." He looked down at Lyra

as her eyelids fluttered closed. The way his muscular, tattooed arms held their child was reverent. "You made a dream come true I didn't even know I had," he said as she met his gaze.

Flutters filled her belly as tears prickled her eyes. She wiped them away before they fell. He reached out his open palm for hers. She placed her hand in his.

"I'm truly sorry I caused you so much pain back then, and all these years since. I wasn't right in my mind and I acted so selfishly."

"I appreciate that. I'm sorry I couldn't . . . that I didn't . . ." She struggled to find the right words to convey the mountain of pent-up emotions and regrets.

His thumb gently caressed her hand. "I had a lot of fun tonight. I love that she's so full of questions."

Remy chuckled, thankful for his change of subject.

She studied his face, now rimmed with a short beard. He seemed older not only in looks, but in his eyes. They seemed softer somehow.

"I better get her home to bed."

He nodded, reaching into his back pocket for his wallet.

"I can pay," she offered.

He shook his head and pulled out a few twenties before placing them on the table. "I got it. You and Lyra are mine to take care of. I haven't been able to before, but that changes now."

How could that statement make her feel loved and angry at the same time? "I can take care of myself, and Lyra."

He stood, their daughter not even stirring from the movement. "Never said you couldn't, darlin'. You've been doing it all this time and rocking it like the queen you are. But now you don't have to. Now I'm here to share the responsibility and pick up the slack."

She felt exposed. Like his words had swooped in and wrecked all her defenses. Was Mikel really the man she always knew he could be? Was it too late?

33

MIKEL

Mikel walked into his old bedroom, fresh out of the shower. He opened the drawer and picked one of the neatly folded T-shirts that smelled like pine. The scent transported him to the last time he'd lived here. Memories, both good and bad, brought on by one of the most underrated senses in the human body.

He finished getting dressed, pulling on the fresh tee and black cargo shorts. He ran a hand across his now-smooth chin; he'd put in a little extra effort for his two guests. His black hair hung low on one side over his eye. He was overdue for a haircut. Delicately, he pressed his cheek and winced. It was still a little discolored and sore from the sucker punch Andre had delivered.

Mikel took a few calming breaths before settling into a meditative pose. He reflected on how the week had gone so far. Having Remy in his space had given him a glimpse of what could be—of all he'd left behind. Maybe this was his second chance to be a good father and to take care of the woman he loved. His chest expanded, full and warm as images of Remy filtered in. She was the most beautiful woman he had ever known. Different now, and more grown up, but he could tell she was an amazing mother. She had done everything she'd wanted despite the curveball of the unplanned pregnancy and all the shit he'd put her through.

Was it too much to hope she still harbored feelings for him? Had he destroyed any chance they had to be together? He had to earn his way into their lives, and he would.

Mikel checked his phone. They should be here any minute. Nervous excitement tumbled in his belly. He slipped on his black boots and headed downstairs just as the front door opened.

The little face he had been waiting all day to see appeared. "Daddy!"

He opened his arms wide, catching the wild ball of energy. He was still getting used to the fact that he was her father. Apparently, she was much faster to forgive his absence than her mother.

Brown Timberlands walked through the door, stopping in front of him. Instead of the beautiful Remy, he was met with Andre's hard glare.

"You gonna hit me again?" Mikel asked, standing tall.

"We don't hit. Hands are not for hitting. Right, Mommy?" Lyra chimed in, her little voice reminding him of their audience.

Remy came in, setting down a bag before crossing her arms and glaring at her brother. She too had dressed up. A short yellow floral sundress showed off her long legs. Her smoky eyes were darkened and her lips painted with something pink and shiny. He swallowed, fighting the urge to get her alone and dive into that tight little body—feel those curves wrapped around him as she shuddered and pulsed. To take her and remind her how he'd been the one to show her the stars.

"That's right, honey. Sometimes big boys need a reminder that things cannot be resolved with violence," she said.

"And sometimes big girls need to be reminded that there are some exceptions," Andre growled.

"Come on, baby. Let's get your dinner ready before I go," Remy said, reaching her hand out for her daughter.

"Go?" Mikel asked, confused.

Remy chewed on her bottom lip as she avoided his eyes. "Yeah, I'll be back by eight."

She disappeared into the kitchen with Lyra. Dishes clinked as Andre stepped closer into his space. Mikel turned to face him. "I let you hit me once, and I deserved it. Won't let it happen twice."

Andre smirked. "You asshole. Always were a righteous motherfucker."

"Hey, watch your language near my daughter," Mikel clipped.

"Oh, *now* she's your daughter? Who do you think has been here the whole time watching over this little family?" Andre asked, crossing his arms.

The accusation stung. "I would have been here had I known."

Andre wiped a hand over his face. "I know. I don't agree with how she handled everything back then. But you disappeared, man. You could have come to me. I could have helped you. Instead, you ran and I was left to run the business by myself, and deal with all the shit that came out."

Mikel nodded. "I shouldn't have gone without taking care of everything. I'm sorry I left you in the lurch with the company. I can sign whatever you need now stating I give up my half of control to you."

Andre shook his head and laughed. "You're back. You can pick up the slack. It's time. I've earned one hell of a vacation."

Mikel sucked in a staggered breath. "What are you sayin'?"

"I'm saying, Seaview Construction is still half yours. And you're gonna need a way to support this little family. Your portion of the profits have been put aside in an account while you've been gone, all except what I gave to Remy for Lyra."

"What? Why?" Mikel demanded.

"Remy wouldn't take it. She knew you'd be back and she wanted you to have something. She agreed to come to me if she ever needed some extra help. I figured I'd keep it for my niece if you didn't return," Andre explained.

Mikel sat on the stairs as Andre shut the front door. His thoughts tumbled and tangled, along with his emotions. She'd believed he would be back. Andre had kept his half of the profits for him and was offering him his position again. Remy had refused taking all the money, choosing the harder road to achieve her dreams—all while taking care of their daughter. "I don't know what to say. You trust me to return to the business? Why are you doing this for me after everything?" Mikel asked, searching his friend's face for answers.

Andre pointed to the kitchen. "I'm doing it for them, first and foremost. Look, you needed help and we all failed you by not recognizing the signs. But you're here now. You have Lyra to take care of. My sister could use a break. I know you have been through a lot of shit. Just because the abuse stops happening doesn't mean the trauma disappears."

The breath was sucked from his lungs at the power in his friend's statement. He forced a chuckle, pretending he wasn't affected. "You been watching *Dr. Phil?*"

"Nah. Been doing some reading." Andre smirked again.

Mikel shook his head. "You're too fucking much."

"Hey! Language." Andre laughed.

Mikel stood and Andre pulled him into a hug, slapping his back harder than necessary as he spoke into his ear. "I'm glad you're back, brother. I'd love to have you by my side at the company. I'm happy Lyra finally gets to meet her dad. But you run away, put them in danger again, or hurt my sister, and I will hunt you down and kill you myself. Are we understood?" Andre backed up, locking his dark brown eyes on Mikel's.

Mikel nodded. "Yeah."

Bently walked in the door, followed by Jasmine.

"What is this? A party?" Jasmine said, heading straight to Remy and Lyra in the kitchen.

"Yeah! Auntie Jasmine, it's a party! Mommy brought cupcakes," Lyra screamed excitedly.

"After your dinner," Remy gently reminded.

Bently hesitated, looking between Andre and Mikel. "You two finally kiss and make up or should I go get the handcuffs?"

"Does that line really work on women?" Andre scoffed, unimpressed.

Bently smirked. "It has once or twice."

"You haven't changed at all," Mikel said.

His brother's eyes clouded over, his smile fading.

"Alright, now that all the mighty knights have assembled, we can keep the princess safe while the queen is out having some adult time." Andre changed the subject, walking back into the kitchen. Mikel followed, shooting a questioning glance towards Bently before searching out Remy. His stomach twisted in a sickly knot. *Maybe she is just going to have some time by herself . . . all dressed up . . . smelling like heaven and looking like an angel.*

"Don't forget Aunty Jasmine. She's a princess too." Lyra smiled, her face covered in chocolate frosting.

"I'm a goddamned queen." Jasmine winked.

"Language!" Andre and Mikel said in unison.

Jasmine rolled her eyes. "One of the most empowering things a woman can do is learn to not give a . . . duck. Right, Lyra?"

Lyra nodded, licking her fingers. "Yup. Auntie Jasmine said not to give any ducks. But I don't have any ducks to give anyways."

The adults burst out laughing as Lyra finished her frosting, blissfully unaware.

"You still hang out with Emma?" Mikel asked, fishing.

Remy finally glanced his way. "Yeah. She's here for another month before she goes back on tour."

"You going to meet up with her tonight?" he pressed. She averted her eyes to the sink, getting a wet paper towel and cleaning Lyra up as she shook her head.

Bently opened the fridge and pulled out a bottle of water before opening a cabinet that was littered with orange prescription bottles.

"Okay. Her foods are marked in the fridge. Snacks in the bag with her toothbrush and pajamas. I'll be back by eight," Remy said, kissing Lyra.

"Bye, Mommy. Have fun."

"I love you more than all the stars in the sky." Remy hugged the little girl before walking towards the door.

"You can stay out all night. Lyra can come with me. Tiffany is on a business trip again, so I could use the company," Andre offered.

Green hot flames of jealousy burned his insides. He was too late. Remy had found someone. He had no right, no claim on her, but every cell in his body protested.

Remy glanced his way shyly for a moment before shaking her head. "I'll be back by eight."

"Have fun with Aaron," Andre said, driving the knife in deeper.

She waved goodbye to Lyra, carefully avoiding his gaze before she turned and left the room. Pulled like a magnet in her direction, he wanted to grab her arm and stop her—push her against the car and remind her that she was his, that he had known every part of her first. He clenched his jaw, fisting his hands as he tried to get control of himself.

"Daddy, can we play *Candy Land?*" The sweet little voice interrupted the war going on in his mind and body. Those big brown eyes and that cute face grounded him in the present moment, reminding him why he was here.

My daughter.

REMY

There had been a shift in Mikel since the night she'd left their daughter at Bently's for her date with Aaron. She had spent most of the time distracted.

Being out with Aaron was always fun. He was a great guy and he could make her laugh. But she found herself wishing he was Mikel more than once and that wasn't fair to Aaron.

She'd tried for a month, juggling a weekly date with Aaron and meeting up with Mikel for playdates with their daughter. Watching him with Lyra was always bittersweet. With so many moments missed, it made her cherish those they shared even more now.

Her whole body reacted like a furnace when he was around. Memories of intimate touches resurfaced with his presence. His gaze always lingered longer than necessary, and she tried to ignore the ache that throbbed in proximity to him. A drawer full of vibrators, courtesy of Jasmine, couldn't give her the release she craved so much.

She wiped one of the tables clean in the empty café. The hair on the back of her neck stood on end. An awareness prickled across her body, gooseflesh rising on her arms. Was she being watched? She glanced out at the busy street beyond the large window. She gasped. Gone were the cold blue eyes she'd seen only for a second. She searched desperately for confirmation that this was just her imagination and not the nightmare that had haunted her since the accident. *Joe Canoby is in prison. You're safe.*

It was probably just someone that looked like him. After two minutes of scanning the street, she let out a sigh of relief. *It wasn't him.*

Remy flipped the sign to closed. The morning rush was done, and Aaron should be arriving soon. He was always on time. One thing she admired about him was his dependability.

The bells above the door rang as he walked in, all six feet of muscled perfection. He had been an athlete in college, and now, thanks to some government grants and his college earnings, he worked with underprivileged kids in the seedy part of the neighboring city as a philanthropist. He could easily be someone she imagined having a future with, or at least she used to think so. It was hard to see your future when your past was blocking your view. Especially when said past was wrapped in such a god-like package, with golden brown eyes and jet-black hair.

"Hey, beautiful. How's your day going?" Aaron asked, holding his arms out to her, jarring her to the present.

"Hey, Aaron. Good." She hugged him. "Yours?"

"Pretty good. I was assigned a new kid who just got kicked out of his house after coming out to his parents. So after this, I'm gonna go find him a room at the facility."

She gestured towards the empty chair as she sat across from him and said, "I'm sorry to hear that. Do you have the room?"

The building he had bought as a shelter for teens was

always full—a symptom of the effect of drugs, broken homes, and closed-minded parents.

"Yeah, we just opened the new dorms."

"Oh, Andre told me he almost had them finished." She smiled, happy that more kids would get a safe place to stay. Mikel had been working with Andre on Aaron's project. She'd expected Mikel's jealousy to ruin everything, but that hadn't happened. Maybe he was different. *Or maybe he doesn't care about you that way anymore.*

Lies. His gaze lingered on her with more than friendly appreciation.

"You didn't call me here to talk about the Hope Facility though," Aaron said.

"I'm happy for you and those kids, but you're right. I just don't know where to start." She sighed. A part of her was sad to end the relationship with Aaron. She really liked him, but it was more of a friendship than anything else.

"How about you just be blunt? Don't bother to sugarcoat it. I think I have a pretty good idea what you're gonna say anyways," he said.

"You do?" she asked.

He nodded. "We've been seeing each other for three months and you have never tried to move beyond a casual, almost platonic relationship with me. At first I figured you just wanted to go slow, but then Andre's business partner showed up and you pulled away. You stopped being present with me when we did spend time together."

She bit her lip. "We have a history."

"Dre told me he's Lyra's father," he said.

"I'm sorry. I should have mentioned it. I swear I really wanted to try to make this work," she said.

"I know. I guess we're better as friends, as clichéd as that sounds." He chuckled, clearly having expected this.

"I would like that." She smiled.

He stood as the bells behind them signaling a customer. Aaron leaned and kissed her cheek before giving her a final nod. "I'll see you around."

He left as she slipped behind the counter to remind the patron they were closed. "What can I get for—?"

Before her stood the man who'd occupied all her thoughts as of late: *Mikel.*

His jaw was clenched and his shoulders tense as his golden eyes flamed with jealousy. He shook his head and scowled. "Never mind. I've lost my appetite." Mikel spun around and stalked towards the door.

Remy turned and went to the back room as the bells chimed, announcing his exit. Anger welled inside her. He had no right to behave that way. The ache in her chest throbbed, her heartbreak still as fresh as it had been the day he'd left. It was like everything she had felt for him before came rushing back a hundred times stronger than when he left. Her wounds were still raw and bleeding. Love still tangled and wove between their two souls.

A set of hands roughly grabbed her and she gasped. Remy was spun around. Mikel stared at her, through her, as his chest heaved against her own. Fear was quickly mixed with lust at his nearness. She panted as his eyes raked over her, possessive and hungry. It was like she was eighteen again, and ready to bend to his will. *No.* She wouldn't get caught up in him, leaving her own needs by the wayside.

"I know I don't have the right," he began, his voice deep and heady. "But you have no idea what it's like to see you with another man."

She shivered as his deep voice reverberated through her, igniting every nerve ending with yearning.

"I hate the fact that some other guy has touched you." He

gripped her waist. Mikel's voice sent shivers through her bones, sinking into her marrow. "It makes it worse that he's a better man than me. You fucking deserve someone like him."

Something flickered in his eyes as her heart squeezed. She saw through him, finding the lost boy she'd once loved in the body of the man she worshipped.

"I'm just the selfish bastard who wants another chance," he finished.

A thousand moths of hope woke from their five-year slumber, fluttering in her belly. She looked at his mouth, licking her lips. Anticipation pricked her skin in a million tiny needles. She wanted to taste him again, feel his lips move against hers. But fear of letting down the walls she had worked so hard to build over the years froze any further action from her. No words would come.

He leaned forward, touching his forehead to hers, nose to nose, as he drew in a ragged breath. How could something that was wrong feel so right? His darkness was alluring. Every cell in her body screamed at her to take what he offered.

"Remy?" His voice pleaded as his exhale danced across her lips, teasing her, tempting her. "Dove."

The endearment on his mouth cut the last thread of her self-control. Her body moved without her consent, hands gripping his shoulders as her lips hungrily met his—crashing together for the first time since they had been reunited.

Fireworks and explosions of memories assaulted her as her long-held wishes came true. Mikel swiped his tongue into her mouth. She tasted him. His arms wrapped around her, locking her in his embrace. A captive and a willing prisoner, she moaned, a tiny erotic sound betraying her want. Raking her teeth against his bottom lip, she seized control through the onslaught of emotions spinning her from the inside out. Gravity moved, no longer around her, but embodied in a man.

Mikel had always been a magnet, and now the force pulling them together made it seem like any resistance on her part would rip her to shreds.

He squeezed her ass as he lifted her onto the counter, stepping between her thighs. It had been so long since she had been held like this, years since she had been satisfied by him.

She pulled at his shirt, ready to strip him bare and let him take her right there in the back room of the bakery. Damn the consequences. Her body was burning alive and she needed release. She craved him inside her. Remy could regret it later, because right now, resisting whatever this was between them was impossible.

His hand grabbed hers, stopping her as he pulled back from their kiss.

She searched his eyes, confused.

He was out of breath, every muscle rigid as he shook his head. "Not like this."

Hurt and rejection lacerated her heart as she swallowed her tears. She pushed him away and stood on her own. *What did I almost do?*

"Remy," he said, as she averted her gaze to the floor and stormed past him. He grabbed her arm, pulling her back against his chest as he locked her in with his embrace. "Remy," he said, this time with more authority.

"What?" she snapped.

"Dove, I want you more than anything, more than my next breath. But we need to talk first. There's a lot about me you have to know before we do this again."

She relaxed in his arms, turning to face him. He'd called her Dove, just like he had the first time they'd made love. Back when he had made sure she was making the decision for herself, assuring her he would wait. Was he doing the same thing now? Ensuring she had all the important information before making such a huge decision?

This was the Mikel she'd fallen in love with. This was the man who'd stolen her heart and starred in her dreams. This was the one she'd wished would return to her. "When?"

35

REMY

Remy kissed Lyra's cheek before she pulled the covers above her shoulders. Glancing around her childhood room, the memories settled over her. She and Mikel had so many obstacles between them. Their history was cloaked in darkness, regret, and heartache. Was she making the right choice for her daughter? Was she delusional to entertain the idea of a second chance with the father of her child?

He hadn't been the only one to make mistakes. She had knowingly hidden their child and kept Lyra a secret from him, and he hadn't held it over her head. They needed to talk it all out. *Tonight.*

She crept out of the room, leaving the door cracked as she made her way to the dining table where her parents were enjoying a glass of wine together.

"That was fast," her mother said.

"It was all that swimming at the beach today." Her father laughed.

Remi nodded and took a seat.

"I'll bring Lyra to your house tomorrow afternoon. What time will *he* be here?" Her mother's kind eyes met hers as she asked.

"Eight fifteen."

"You be careful, baby girl," her father said, reaching out to pat her hand on the table.

"I will." She swallowed the emotions that bubbled, her belly twisted with uncertainty. She just wanted to get this over with.

"Are you sure about this?" her mother asked, worry evident in her voice.

"I hurt him too, Mama. I kept his child from him. We have a lot of things to figure out now that he's back," she defended. Her parents gave each other a concerned look.

A knock at the door ended the conversation as her stomach fluttered with a mix of excitement and unease. Remy stood and walked over to let him in.

Mikel towered over her wearing low-cut jeans and a black T-shirt that gripped his muscles like it was made for him. His hands rested in his pockets as he leaned in to kiss her cheek and whisper, "You look beautiful."

His hot breath sent shivers down her spine. *Good god.* One inhale of his woodsy scent and she was a puddle.

He backed away, a nervous smile playing at his lips. "Can I say hello to your parents before we leave?"

Surprise stole her voice as she nodded and stepped back from the door to let him in.

He walked in and greeted her parents. "Mr. and Mrs. Stone, I just wanted to tell you how thankful I am that you took such great care of Remy and Lyra after I left. I know I disappointed you both. 'I'm sorry' doesn't seem like enough. Just know I'm gonna do everything in my power to make this right and keep my girls safe and cared for now that I'm back."

Remy's eyes stung with tears as her chest tightened. The old Mikel wouldn't have faced her parents and admitted his failures. The way he'd said *my girls* made her heart leap into her throat. She was the farthest thing from being safe with Mikel Evans. Because this man still owned every part of her, body and soul.

Her mother stood and walked over to him, her father following suit. Tilda gave him a tight hug as a tear fell down each of her brown cheeks.

"You know you always have had a special place in our hearts, Mikel. When you left, it was like losing a son. We just want you to be healthy and happy." She squeezed him tighter before releasing him.

Her father offered to shake Mikel's hand as he spoke. "Glad to see you're back and doing better. Lyra's a special little lady, and she deserves the world. They both do."

"Yes, sir," Mikel agreed.

Her father continued, "But if you ever put Remy or Lyra in danger again, if you hurt them . . ." Both men seemed to be having a silent conversation with their eyes.

"I'd deserve whatever you intended," Mikel stated simply.

Her father nodded before he released Mikel's hand.

"Well, you two kids have fun. Be safe," her mother said.

Remy turned towards the door with Mikel right behind her. They walked to a black truck she didn't recognize in silence. The humid night air was as heavy as the anticipation that wound between them. Flashes of fireflies blinked as the rise and fall of the melody of summer bugs became background noise. He started the truck.

"Is this yours?" she asked, buckling her seat belt.

"Yeah. Got it yesterday."

She nodded, glancing at the car seat set up in the back. That warm fullness blossomed again in her chest at his efforts. Looking out the window, she asked, "Where are we going?"

"It's a surprise." He smirked.

Her belly flipped as memories of riding shotgun in his truck, going on adventures late at night with him, came rushing back.

He reached his hand to cover hers as if sensing her need to be grounded. His touch was tender and warm as yet again his calloused thumb rubbed circles on the fleshy part of her hand, soothing her worries and igniting a fire in her belly.

Large pines and massive cedar trees lined the road on either side of the mountain path. The scenery was familiar as they drove towards the Black Cliffs—the very place she had given her virginity to him.

She hadn't been back there since. The memories were too painful. It had been easier to focus on the bad rather than the good times when she'd missed him.

"Is this okay?" he asked, studying her.

"I haven't been here since the first time we . . ."

"Really?"

She nodded.

"We can go somewhere else if you want," he offered. The fact that he seemed to care so much about her feelings was a testament to how much he'd changed.

"No, this is fine." She opened her door and climbed down. The salty breeze mingled with the scent of the evergreens. The parking lot was empty. They were truly alone up here.

Mikel handed her a blanket and a basket from his trunk, as he picked up a bulky case. She followed him towards the same spot they had camped so long ago that it seemed like another lifetime.

He laid the blanket down before she sat. Her eyes stayed glued to his sure movements as he started a fire. The waves crashed in the distance, the almost cloudless sky enabling the moonlight to reflect on the black water below. Once the fire was roaring, he opened the long case and pulled out a telescope.

"Just like old times, huh?" he asked as he sat next to her. "Except this time, I brought stuff for s'mores. Even got gluten-free graham crackers." He gestured to the basket.

Everything was perfect. *He* was perfect. It was surreal.

"What are we doing?" she asked hesitantly.

He wrapped his arm around her and let out a long breath. "We're starting over."

Hope surged, rippling and radiating in her chest at his words. Uncertainty and fear welled up, blocking her lungs from getting enough air. How long had she waited for Mikel to come stumbling back into her life? She'd wanted more than anything to hear him speak those words. But now she had so much more to lose. How could she trust him? How could she make sure she didn't fall into her old role of enabling him? Panic set in and she trembled.

"We have a lot to work through between us. We're different people now, and it's like we gotta get to know each other all over again. But you need to understand I never stopped loving you. I just had to learn how to forgive myself before I was capable of showing you what it truly means to be loved. I'm ready to do that now, if you'll let me."

Her heart raced as his words sunk in. His body was so close, fueling the lust tangling and blurring inside her. An avalanche of sensations swirled within. Everything spun as what he'd said hit her. The cleansing rain of tears streamed down her face, removing the old anger and making room for a new start.

He wiped her cheeks. "Baby, I'm so fucking sorry." His voice broke as he pulled her into his lap, against his chest. He cradled her as she came apart, letting go of everything she had held inside for so long, purging the bad and allowing herself to remember the good, leaving only the lessons learned.

"I'm sorry too," she finally said, wiping her eyes on her sleeve as she took a few calming breaths.

He was silent for a few moments, and then he asked, "Why did you let me think she was dead?"

His question wasn't a surprise, nor was it asked in anger. They were both being open and honest, and she needed to take ownership of her choices.

Remy sat up in his lap to face him and drew a deep breath before admitting what she'd held in her heart for so long. "I knew we couldn't survive if you found out about her and you continued down that path. If you chose your addiction over your child."

His expression changed. "I can't say if it was the right or wrong thing to do. Fact is, it's done. We just need to decide if we're willing to pick up the pieces we have left and start again."

"I'd like that," she said without hesitation, speaking from her heart, her choice suddenly clear.

"Me too. But . . . there are some things you must know before you can make that decision. I never fully opened up to you before, and I'm man enough to do that now."

"Okay." She encouraged him, giving him her full attention.

"I stayed away from you thinking you'd be safer without me, better off. I still managed to fuck everything up by not being here. I want to be in our daughter's life and yours—more than anything—but I'll respect whatever you choose after hearing what I have to tell you."

He leaned down, his lips meeting hers, soft and slow, as if

he was savoring this moment too. Her heart ached for him as her body begged for more.

He broke the kiss, resting his forehead against hers as he spoke. "I've never told a living soul my secret. I can't give you all the details because they are not mine alone to tell. I know you're gonna look at me differently after this. But you must know who I truly am and what I'm capable of before you decide. You have to see all my darkness."

Her body trembled alive with his touch and the mystery of his foreboding words. Her chest tightened as her heart raced, his confession could change everything. She searched his bronze eyes, now seeming darker as he cleared his throat and locked his gaze to hers.

"I killed my father."

36

REMY

Mikel's voice rang in her ears. Surely, she'd misheard him.

She swallowed, unsure of how to respond to his statement, waiting for him to explain.

"Paul Evans was a mean-ass drunk. Our mother was always his biggest target. When she was gone, he focused his rage on us kids, specifically Jasmine, since she wasn't his." He swallowed, his face grimacing in disgust.

"He'd hit us with anything he could find—belts, shoes, wires, electrical cords, his fists, or kick us with his steel-toe boots. He never needed a reason. We just happened to be in the wrong place at the wrong time."

She reached her hand out to his thigh in comfort. Bile rose in her throat. She knew their home hadn't been safe, but she'd had no idea it was that bad. The details of his past helped her see him in a different light.

"One day . . . I came home and . . . his door was closed. I could hear Jasmine inside, begging for him to stop. I was frozen there, paralyzed with fear. I swung open the door and .

. . I flew at him. I just started beating him and it felt so fucking good to let that rage take control and release it on him."

Remy's mouth had opened in shock as tears blurred her vision. This beautiful boy, having to face such horrific things his whole life. *Poor Jasmine.*

"You beat him to death? I thought he overdosed," she said.

"Nah, the fucker was bigger than me. He beat me within an inch of my life."

Remy gasped, tears falling freely for the pain that Mikel had endured. Guilt weighed heavily on her shoulders for not having tried to do more to help. "He almost killed you?"

He pulled her closer to him with his arm around her. "Jasmine got away and that's all that mattered."

She understood the dynamic between the siblings now better than ever. Bently, always the protector on the straight and narrow. Jasmine, who wore a mask of indifference and anger to hide how vulnerable and fragile she really was, seeking out love the only way she knew how in all the wrong places. "What happened next?" she asked, pushing him to give her as much as he was willing. Was it murder if the victim was a sadistic monster?

"I woke up on the floor in a pile of my own blood. Bently was there. I'll never forget his face. He was white as a ghost. After he assured me Jasmine was safe—at your house, actually—he helped me get cleaned up."

Shock squeezed the air from her lungs. "I remember a day Jasmine showed up crying, but she wouldn't tell us what was wrong. My mother cared for her, got her some soup and a shower, before holding her until she fell asleep."

Mikel focused his gaze towards the fire, going silent for a moment.

Did Paul sexually abuse her? She guessed that was part of

the secret that wasn't his to tell, so she didn't press it further. She and Jasmine had been friends for years, and she'd never mentioned it.

"Bently moved us out. We lived in the old factory warehouse that was condemned for a couple weeks while I healed. Bently managed to get us some food. I'm guessing your parents had something to do with that too."

"I don't know," she said. She'd been so blind back then, living in her bubble where the world was mostly good and everyone got happy endings.

"Once I was healed enough, I went down to find Joe Canoby at the corner to get some heroin."

She gasped. *The man who tried to kill me.*

"I had planned it the whole time we were scraping by in that dump. The easiest way to take down a man twice my size and keep the suspicion off my back. I honestly didn't care if I was sent to jail, as long as it kept Jasmine safe."

Her chest tightened as she closed her eyes. Pain lacerated her insides at the thought.

"I snuck into the house when I knew he would be sleeping. The one thing I had going for me was that when he finally passed out, not even a train going by could wake him. I picked up his arm and injected the poison—four times the amount Joe told me to use for myself."

She laid her head on his shoulder, wrapping her arms tightly around him, holding him as he bared his deepest, darkest secrets to her.

"I didn't even hesitate. I did it and watched as the seizure started. He reached out for me at one point, and I just let him die." Mikel's eyes glistened and fluttered with anguish as he frowned.

Her stomach knotted tight at the confession, and her heart ached for him. She wished she could take the pain from him, carry the burden herself, even for a little while. *I can't save him. He's got to do that himself.*

She placed a hand on his wildly beating heart, letting him know she was still listening, that she was there for him as he faced the demons of his past.

He continued, "I turned around and walked out of the house. I felt relieved and then . . . nothing. Any ounce of emotion was killed that day by the blood on my hands. Until you . . . and now . . . now you know I'm a monster. I'm a killer." Mikel stiffened, turning to look at her, searching her eyes as if he was looking for fear and judgment from her.

How could she blame him? If Paul Evans did what she thought he'd done to Jasmine, if he'd nearly beat his own child to death, he deserved to be punished for his crimes. Mikel had protected his sister. Jasmine would have been eight years old. Mikel had done what he'd thought was right, made the only choice he had when the system had failed him and his family.

He relaxed into her arms and started shaking. The sob broke free, letting out a lifetime of trauma as she held on to him, keeping him grounded as he had for her. Their truths were breaking them down before they could restore who they were piece by piece.

"I'm so sorry."

He sat, wiping the tears from his cheeks before bracing his hands on either side of her face. "That's your response after I tell you I'm a cold-blooded murderer?"

"I can't say if it was the right or wrong thing to do. But it's done. We just need to decide if we're willing to pick up the pieces we have left and start again," she said, throwing his own words back at him. "You were a child—an abused and traumatized boy who protected himself and his siblings the only way you knew how. Sometimes the lines between right and wrong are not so black and white. Sometimes they get blurred into different shades of grey. I can imagine wanting to do the same if someone had hurt Lyra like that. I just don't know if I would be brave enough."

His grip tightened, nearly bruising her as she continued, "I know you just showed me what you think is the ugliest part of you, but you're so blinded by the darkness that you don't see the light. You're not the villain of this story, but the hero. A fallen star is still a star."

He trembled as he looked at her with his heated gaze, fierce and powerful, commanding every cell in her body merely by his presence.

"How can you believe that? After everything I put you through? After everything you know about me?"

"Because I never stopped loving you either, Mikel. You've always had my heart and you always will. You're so much more than you realize."

Pure adoration shone from his eyes. She had never felt so emotionally connected to him in all her years of knowing him. Mikel Evans had opened up and exposed every piece of himself, not bothering to hide what he thought was the ugliest, all so that she could make a decision that was best for her and her daughter. True sacrifice. Any doubt in her heart had been wiped away by his transparency. *We will do it right this time.*

She leaned her head towards him, parting her lips in invitation, needing to connect with him intimately, wanting to comfort him the way she used to. His mouth descended on hers, soft and slow, savoring her. His hot tongue traced the seam of her lips before flicking inside. Mikel's hands moved to cradle her neck as she straddled him. A fire raged inside her— an inferno of true unselfish and unadulterated love. It ran much deeper than any feeling she had known before. Not the kind that fairy tales were made of, but the real, raw, painful love that comes from life and true sacrifice when two people come together and commit to growing and changing for the better.

She broke their kiss long enough to pull her blouse over her head, yearning to show him that she was there for him without words. His eyes hungrily admired her exposed flesh. Would he see her tattoo? His hands cupped her breasts over her white lace bra as she unsnapped the back. He pulled it off before setting it in the growing pile of her clothing as he expertly stripped her bare. She tugged his shirt off his shoulders, the firelight glowing against the contours of his muscled tattooed form—a body she once knew intimately, now so foreign to her. She gasped, tracing the ink across his heart. A constellation she knew so well. One she had on her own body. *Lyra.*

"You carried her on your heart all this time, and you didn't even know," she said, exploring his tanned skin.

He finished stripping, something flashing in his eyes like he wanted to say more, but this wasn't the time. He picked her up and she wrapped her legs around him as he lowered her to the blanket. He hovered above her, his kisses melting her insides. She shivered with anticipation while he explored her body—cherishing her, worshipping her.

Her hands wandered, reacquainting herself with him as she burned from his closeness, sparked alive by his touch.

It had been so long since she'd been held like this, worshipped as a woman. Desire swam, pooling in her center. He trailed kisses down her neck, his teeth grazing her shoulder. The pain sent a bolt of pleasure to her core.

He growled. "You're so goddamned perfect. Every inch of you." He kissed and nipped her chest before lazily taking turns grasping and sucking her breasts. She dug her fingernails into his scalp as she writhed from the sensations building in her womb. Every nerve was alight with erotic anticipation.

She spread her thighs. "Please, Mikel. I need to feel you."

He shook his head, his mouth moving farther south across her belly. He licked the white ink on her rib cage, tracing the stars of the constellation. She covered the sides of her stomach, self-conscious of the marks left from carrying their child: nature's tattoos.

"Don't you dare try to hide from me." His deep voice vibrated against her, sending a shot of heat and wetness to her center. She had forgotten how dominant he could be when they made love. He gripped her hands, binding them at her sides while he traced each line with his tongue before leaving a kiss on every mark.

Her body lit with a fever, impatient and unable to wait another second. "Please, Mikel. I just need you inside me," she begged, completely at his mercy.

"I know, but it's been a long time since I've been with you. I wanna taste you when you come."

He still held her hands in place as he lowered his face to the junction between her thighs and slipped his hot tongue between her folds. She gasped, eyes widening. Pleasure jolted though her as he lapped up her wetness.

"Oh! Oh, yes!" she moaned as her back arched.

He released her hands, hooking her legs over his shoulders as he used his fingers and tongue ruthlessly, seeking out her orgasm.

The pressure built and compounded until she shattered into a million pieces. White spots flashed in her vision as her body quaked and shuddered her release.

He climbed over and settled his weight on top of Remy, grounding her as she came back to earth. His mouth crashed onto hers. The taste of her essence on his tongue made the kiss even more erotic.

"Remy. Baby, I love you so much."

She reached her hand out and slid his hardness into her slick entrance without hesitation. She wasn't the unsure eighteen-year-old girl anymore. She was a woman and what she wanted—what she needed was *Mikel.*

He thrust, stretching her as she adjusted to him. Five years without having him or any other man inside her was like losing her virginity again. The burning pleasure overpowered every other thought as her impending need to come overrode all else. "I love the way you feel inside me," she said, her voice breathy.

He pounded harder and faster. His eyes locked on her—glowing golden orbs in the firelight. His body tensed as his features grew serious. "You're so tight, baby. So wet for me."

"Only for you," she panted.

"You're mine, all of you," he demanded.

"I've only ever been yours," she admitted. The emotional intimacy they shared was unlike anything she imagined, and far deeper than she'd ever thought possible. This was a turning point. This was why she'd give him another chance. This was the Mikel she'd known he could be—the man she'd held out hope for.

The mixture of his intense gaze and the whirlwind of spinning desire dancing along her every nerve ending as he thrust inside her, propelling her off the cliff. Her orgasm crashed over her at the same moment his body tensed and pulsed. They came together, eyes locked, only compounding and magnifying their connection as their souls left their bodies, reuniting for the first time in five years. Completion. Connection. The stars were aligned. Death of the old, rebirth of the new. The end and the beginning. Life and death.

A second chance.

37

MIKEL

The next morning, Remy led Mikel into her small house. Joy overwhelmed him that she was finally letting him all the way into their lives. A decent-sized kitchen immediately opened up to his left, everything clean and organized. The place smelled of cinnamon and sugar, like her.

She turned to face him, a timid smile quirking the side of her face. Telling her the worst parts of him had been the hardest and yet most rewarding thing in his life. Where he'd fully expected her to cower in fear, or hate him for eternity, she had shown him compassion and understanding. *Love.*

Remy Stone still loved him. That was something to celebrate.

"So, this is the kitchen, where most of the magic happens. We usually eat at the bar on the stools unless we have company for dinner." She pointed out the small circular table.

He nodded, taking it all in. How many family dinners had he missed? What had been Lyra's first food? Had she made a silly face when she tried solids?

"The living room is through here." She walked to the opposite end of the room and motioned to her right. He followed, glancing at the grey overstuffed couch with multicolored pillows. A heaping basket of toys sat in one corner. He entered the room, touching his finger to the profile of one of the dolls on the coffee table wrapped carefully on a makeshift bed of blankets. *She needs a cradle for her doll.*

"Cozy," he said.

"I'll show you the upstairs. I need to shower. I smell like campfire."

He approached her, threading his hands in her hair as he leaned and breathed her in. He would never take touching her for granted again. "You smell like toasted marshmallows. I like it." Sleeping in the bed of his truck wasn't what he'd planned, but the ache in his back was worth it.

She smiled, reaching on her tiptoes to peck the corner of his mouth. *God, she feels good.* He ran a hand over the scruff of his beard. "Lead the way."

She turned, lacing her fingers between his—a reminder that they fit together so well, like two pieces of the same puzzle. His eyes were glued to the curve of her hips swaying as she led him back to the kitchen, up the stairs, and through the white hallway.

"The door on the left is my office. The next one is the bathroom, on the right. Then the last two are Lyra's bedroom and mine, although she typically ends up sleeping with me still."

Mikel froze, staring at the pictures hung on the wall. Lyra as a baby. Lyra as a toddler. His daughter's first birthday, pictures of her and Remy at the beach, and with her grandparents. All moments he'd lost.

Remy wrapped her arms around him and sighed. He still held a little resentment that she'd hidden their daughter from him, but the logical side of his brain understood why. She had been a mama bear protecting her baby. She was the type of mother he wished he'd had growing up. Mikel couldn't fault her for that.

"I have some photo books if you want to look. I also uploaded everything to the cloud. I can share the files with you so you can glance through them whenever you want," she said.

He swallowed the ball of emotions building in his throat. "That would be nice." He ran his palms up her sides, squeezing her closer to him as he swayed slightly. He leaned down, hungry for a taste of her. Her lips were soft and sweet. She was like fresh cinnamon rolls with extra icing on a cold day. Remy moaned as he deepened the kiss, gripping his shoulders and digging her nails into his flesh. Gone was the timid girl he'd left, replaced by a woman who seemed far surer of herself. It only made him love her more. She reached down, unbuttoning his pants.

"Baby," he groaned, peppering kisses down her neck.

"Let's take a shower together," she said, her voice breathy and dripping with need.

"I know it's kinda late, but are you on the pill?" he asked.

She stepped away enough to look in his eyes. "No. I haven't been . . . I mean, there hasn't been anyone, so I didn't need to."

Fuck. He hadn't used a condom last night.

She seemed to read his mind. "I just finished my period two days ago, so we should be safe, but condoms would be a good idea from here on out. I should have asked . . . are you clean?" Insecurity flashed in her eyes.

He brought his thumb up to trace her bottom lip. "Yeah. Remy, I haven't been with anyone since you either."

Pure shock lit her features, replaced by a smile she tried to hide. "Really?"

He nodded. "Came close a few times before I got sober. I just couldn't do it."

She swallowed, her sexy neck begging him to suck and bite it. But he needed to be responsible this time. "I don't have any condoms. I wasn't expecting anything to happen last night."

She nodded. "We could just shower."

He smiled. "There are other ways to make you come."

She trembled in his arms. So responsive. This was going to be heaven on earth.

Remy tossed him his shirt before pulling her hair into a poufy ponytail. The glow on her face was mesmerizing. Pride filled his chest at the knowledge that he had put it there.

"My mom is on her way here with Lyra," she said, interrupting his salacious memories.

"I'll run to Bently's and change into some clean clothes and then be back to have some dinner with you guys around five. Should I bring something?" he asked, pulling his shirt on.

She shook her head. "I'll cook. Don't forget to stop and get some condoms. I have a feeling we might need them later."

He smirked before kissing her forehead, her cheeks, and then her lips. "Can't get enough of me, huh?"

"Never." She nipped his bottom lip.

Mikel parked his truck at the local pharmacy. He found the family-planning aisle and grabbed a large box of condoms before heading to the front to check out. The cashier was a young teenage girl whose cheeks blushed bright red, scanning his one item.

"Nineteen ninety-nine," she said.

"Debit." He swiped his card.

"As I live and breathe. Is that you, Mick?"

Mikel turned around, coming face-to-face with his past: June and Isaiah Sampson.

"Hey. Long time, man. How are you doing?" Mikel asked, taking the box from the cashier and moving out of line. The bags under his old friend's eyes were deep-set and dark. He had aged ten years at least, and he was far too skinny.

"Pretty good. Can't complain." He itched his left arm, drawing Mikel's attention to the purple needle marks mixed among the bruises.

"Happy to hear."

"How long have you been back?" June asked, her blue eyes hungrily watching his every move, studying him far too closely.

"A little while."

"And you didn't stop by and say hello?" She stuck out her bottom lip and pouted.

"I've been busy," Mikel said.

"Certainly looks like you have." She eyed the box of condoms in his hands. "Make sure you stop by sometime. We can all hang out for old time's sake." She winked.

His stomach roiled at the thought. The last place he would go was to a drug den with a woman he used to screw.

"Joe's out. I'm sure he'd love to know you're back in town," June said.

Panic seized his chest, anxiety constricting his rib cage. *Joe is here?* Last he'd heard, the guy was doing ten years.

Maybe he'd stay on his side of town and not do anything

to risk being sent back. *Wishful thinking.* The last thing Remy needed was a reminder of how he'd failed to protect her in the past. This was a chance for him to do it now.

"Yeah, we can have a celebration party. The gang's all back together again," Isaiah said.

"I appreciate the offer, but that's not really my scene anymore. I'm sober now."

Isaiah and June shared a look of surprise. "Oh, so you're too good for us, huh?" June chided.

"Good for you, man. Don't worry. We won't hold it against you. Stop by sometime and we can catch up," Isaiah said.

Mikel nodded as he headed out of the store. "Can you not mention to Joe that you saw me?"

June's eyes narrowed.

"Sure, man," Isaiah agreed.

"Thanks. I'll see you around." *Or never.* Except for passing encounters in town, he had no intention of meeting them again.

His sobriety was like walking a tightrope most days. He didn't need the extra temptation. He wished he could help Isaiah, but Mikel had learned the hard way that the desire for change had to come from within, not others. He had to be willing to do whatever it took to get clean and stay that way because every day was a fucking battle.

Remy didn't need any reason to doubt him. He had the woman of his dreams and the daughter he ached to know and provide for. Nothing would get in his way. It was time he took his happiness in his own hands, letting go of the past. If Remy could see beyond his failures, so could he. He would do anything to be the man she deserved and the father Lyra needed.

If only fate would agree.

* * *

Later that week, Mikel walked into Bently's house. He'd spent the last few days getting reacquainted with their company, and reorganizing the books. It had always been Andre's least favorite task, and unfortunately, it showed.

"Jaz?" Bently called from the living room.

Mikel turned and headed towards his brother. "It's just me."

Bently lay on the couch, covered in sweat and paler than a ghost.

"You okay?" Seeing his brother in this position was like having the wind knocked out of him every time he laid eyes on him. Each day this week he'd come home from his treatments weaker than he'd been the day before.

"Just peachy," Bently joked.

"You had another treatment today?"

"Yeah, they're being aggressive. Gives me a better chance."

Of not dying. Mikel couldn't help his morbid thoughts. His big brother had always been a rock, an unbreakable figure he could look up to in life. *This isn't fair.* After everything they'd been through, Bently was the last person who deserved this. "You want something to eat or drink?"

Bently closed his eyes and grimaced. "Nah. Too nauseous to eat."

"Weed might help that," Mikel joked.

Bently's eyes shot open. "You better be joking."

Mikel chuckled. "I'm not saying I'm above using my connections in this town to get you a little herbal relief. But your doctor could give you a medical marijuana card. So even you, Mister Sheriff, wouldn't be breaking the law."

Bently relaxed into the pillow. "The last thing I need is you near that world again. I mean it, Mikel. You got a fresh start and a chance with a good woman who's been to hell and back because of your screw-ups. Don't fuck this up."

Don't I know it. "I won't. I'm not that guy anymore."

Bently nodded and closed his eyes.

Mikel walked into the kitchen, searching the cupboards for a can of soup. While the food heated on the stove, he grabbed a bottle of water and a tray.

After setting the steaming bowl of chicken noodle soup in the center, he added a napkin and a spoon along with the water.

His brother's eyes were still closed when he returned. Placing the tray on the coffee table beside him, Mikel said, "Here. You need to keep up your strength. Try to eat some."

Bently's eyes flickered open as Mikel sat on the table next to the meal he'd prepared. Taking the warm bowl in his hands, he dipped the spoon in and offered it to his brother.

Bently growled and pushed off the couch so that he could sit, holding his head for a few moments as if the movement had been too jarring. Mikel waited patiently. Bently reached out and grabbed the bowl and spoon. "I can feed myself. I'm not an invalid."

"Didn't say you were."

Bently sighed. "Thanks for this."

"Anytime." Mikel flicked the television on. "Wanna watch a game?"

Bently would never admit it, but he was too full of pride to ask for what he needed, or appear weak. Bently had taken care of Mikel and Jasmine when they were too young to do it themselves. Now it was Mikel's turn to repay the kindness.

Mikel wouldn't burden his brother with his problems anymore.

The door burst open. Mikel turned in time to see Jasmine

run inside to the bathroom. He stood and went to check on her before Bently could try to get up.

Retching came from behind the wooden door.

"You okay?" Mikel knocked.

The toilet flushed and then the water in the sink squeaked on. Jasmine opened the door, looking green. "Guess you missed this part of Remy's pregnancy. It's all par for the course. At least, that's what she tells me. This little bean doesn't want me to keep anything down."

Her insult hit its intended target. If only he could figure out how to fix his relationship with his sister. "I made some soup. There's some on the stove if you want it."

She glanced towards the kitchen and then to Bently, who held up his bowl and smiled at her.

"I guess it wouldn't hurt to try," she mumbled, heading into the kitchen.

Mikel followed her. "Weren't you working with Remy today at the bakery?"

She poured the remaining contents of the soup in a bowl as she nodded. "Yeah, she sent me home because I wasn't feeling so good. All the different smells were just too much. It's not even the bakery stuff; it's the customers' perfumes."

"Oh."

"I felt bad because she's totally slammed and shorthand-ed." Jasmine carried her bowl into the living room and sat next to Bently.

He picked up his phone and messaged Remy.

Mikel: *Hey, baby. Just wanted to let you know I'm thinking about you. Miss you.*

It was time he took care of his family.

38

——————

REMY

The café was slammed. Emma was out of state for the day, her college student employee had class until three, and Jasmine had been so sick Remy had had to send her home.

She flicked another glance towards the ever-growing long line at the door—good for business, but bad for her sanity on a day like this. She just needed to get through this rush and then she could breathe. *Oh, to put my aching feet up.* She'd been here since five this morning and it was only noon now.

"So sorry about the wait. What can I get you?" she asked the next customer.

"A venti latte with half the foam. Can you make that with half two percent milk and half skim milk? Oh, and a shot of caramel."

Remy smiled and wrote the picky customer's order on the cup as the door jingled, signaling yet another customer. She was drowning here. People were going to start walking away soon and she would lose business.

"Hey, beautiful." His voice was like a breath of fresh air.

She made the woman's coffee as she turned and smiled at him. "Hey yourself. I'm a little busy right now."

"I can see that. That's why I'm here. Put me to work." He smiled.

"Don't you have to help Andre today?"

"I took the rest of the day off. It's just paperwork that I can do this weekend instead. Jasmine told me you were slammed."

She wiped the steamer off and placed the lid on the latte as his firm fingers kneaded her stiff neck. Sure, he'd have no idea what he was doing, but any help would be better than no help. Mikel had always been a fast learner. A weight lifted from her shoulders as she handed the woman her drink.

"Okay, can you ring her up?"

Mikel stepped in front of the register as she walked him through the touch screen.

"I'm going to give everyone a ten percent discount for waiting so long today," Remy said, loud enough for all the patrons to hear.

"Oh, I really appreciate it," the first customer said.

Mikel got to work, bagging baked goods and ringing up customers as she filled the drink orders. The line moved along much quicker, to her delight, and every customer left with a smile.

Remy let out a sigh of relief as she wiped the counter down. His warm arms embraced her from behind as he breathed in at the base of her neck.

"Thank you," she said.

"Remember what I said: I'm gonna take care of you. Next time you get like this here, just give me a call."

She nodded, her heart full, nearly bursting—a feeling she'd had so much of lately. This was too good to be true.

Mikel was beginning to be the partner in her life that she'd always dreamed about.

"Why don't you have a seat and eat something while I clean the tables?" Mikel asked.

"I gave Jasmine my lunch, hoping it would help settle her stomach."

"Then it's a good thing I ordered you Thai food that should be delivered in about two minutes."

"You . . . when?" She turned around to face him.

He held up his phone. "They make apps for that now."

The urge to kiss this man was too strong for a place of business. She grabbed his hand and dragged him into the back room before plastering a kiss on his mouth. He tightened his grip around her, pulling her closer. All the things she wanted to do to him required privacy and time—two things they didn't have in that moment.

"Wow." He chuckled. "Is that my thank you?"

"That's just the preview." She winked.

His mouth curved up into a smirk as his eyes darkened. "I'm just taking care of my woman."

"Your woman, huh?"

The door chimed from the café.

"Mm-hmm." He placed his palms on both sides of her face and kissed her forehead before walking back out to the front counter.

She couldn't stop the smile that bloomed. She wasn't alone in this anymore.

* * *

At three thirty, Remy waved goodbye to her closing staff and walked to her car.

"I'll meet you at home?" Mikel asked, pulling his truck keys from his pocket.

"Yeah. I'll get Lyra from my parents and then head over."

"Drive safe." He gave her a quick peck on the lips.

By the time Remy unbuckled Lyra and got her inside, her feet and her back were throbbing.

"We're home, Daddy!" Lyra said, running up as Remy shut and locked the door.

He picked her up and swung her around as she giggled. "How was your day at school?"

"It was sooo good. Miss Piper said I could be the next one to feed our pet turtle."

"That's awesome, princess," Mikel said, kissing her cheek before he set her down.

"What smells so delicious? Did you order something?" Remy searched the empty counters, focusing on the sink of soapy dishes that were half done.

"Nope, I made it. It's baking in the oven. Which means you have exactly forty-five minutes to soak in the tub I ran for you upstairs before we need to eat." Mikel came over and kissed her neck.

He made dinner? He . . . ran a bath for her? He was doing dishes?

Mikel laughed. Her shock must have been written across her forehead.

"You go and relax. Lyra and I are gonna watch some *Paw Patrol*."

Lyra jumped up and down. "Just you and me, Daddy?"

He tucked her stray curl behind her ear. "Just us."

Remy was left utterly speechless as they made their way into the living room.

"Go before your bath gets cold," Mikel called.

* * *

Remy studied her pruney hands. Suds gathered around her arms and breasts. The foam had left a milky sheen on top of the once hot, now tepid water. Lyra's giggles could be heard every now and then. This was pure heaven. She could definitely get used to it. She hadn't felt cherished since the day he'd gone out and bought all the baking flours she'd wanted to experiment with. That was a memory she'd replayed several times in the past when she'd wanted to remember what it was like to feel special.

"Knock, knock," Mikel said, opening the door. "The lasagna just came out of the oven. Do you want us to wait for you?"

"I'm coming." She smiled, sitting to pull out the plug.

He walked in and leaned down, cupping one of her soapy breasts in his hand. Remy gasped and checked the doorway for a possible little girl sighting.

"I hope to hear that a few times tonight." He pinched her nipple and kissed her shoulder. Her breathing became ragged as her arousal bloomed. Need and desire tightened like a coil ready to snap. Ringing filled her ears as her blood rushed to her aching center.

Mikel got to his feet abruptly and turned towards the door just as Lyra came bounding inside. Remy had been too out of it to hear her daughter approaching.

"Come on. Let's set the table. Mommy's gonna get dressed and meet us down there," Mikel said, steering Lyra out of the room.

Remy swallowed as she tried to rein in her demanding libido.

* * *

After dinner, they played a game with Lyra before getting her in the bath. At bedtime, Mikel read her a story and kissed her good night. Remy did the same. Lyra was out like a light.

Remy sighed as she sat on her bed. The man she craved walked through the door, shedding his shirt until he was only in a pair of black sweatpants. As exhausted and sore as she was, there was still energy to lick every ridge and line on that perfectly sculpted torso. The *V* at his hips was especially enticing.

Mikel grabbed a bottle of lotion and sat at the end of the bed, placing one of her feet in his lap.

"You don't wanna sit up here next to me?" She furrowed her brow.

"Patience, woman." He smirked, squirting some of the lotion in his hand before he got to work kneading and rubbing her feet.

She moaned. "Oh my god. That feels so good."

"Do you think I can make you come from a foot massage?" He chuckled.

"If it can be done, I'm sure you'd be the one to make it happen." She closed her eyes and enjoyed the way his strong hands worked out every last bit of tension in her feet before moving up her legs. She was soaking wet by the time he told her to get naked and flip over to her stomach.

His hard cock grazed her side as he moved along her sore back, rubbing all the kinks out. Her body was limp and boneless as he moved to her neck and scalp, leaving no spot untouched—pure bliss saturated her every cell.

His warm hands moved slowly down her spine, almost light enough to tickle her sensitive flesh, curving over her bottom before diving into her pussy. "You're so wet." He spread her thighs as she whimpered. "Time to fulfill my promise and make you come."

"Yes, please," she begged.

The bed bounced as he moved. A moment later, his bare thighs were between hers. "Put that beautiful ass in the air."

She did as he said, eager for the pleasure and connection.

His newly grown beard scratched the back of her thighs as he licked across her hot folds. She bit her lip to hold back the moan.

"I'm gonna take care of you," he said, before repeating the action.

If this was how Mikel Evans wanted to take care of her, she'd let him. This was so much more than she'd ever thought possible. He'd proven to her he was all in, that he loved her and their daughter. She loved him with every fiber of her being.

Mikel was her forever.

39

REMY

Remy carried out a freshly decorated set of unicorn cookies and slid them into the glass display case. The café was filled with happy customers enjoying their beverages while reading, working, or chatting at the several tables spread throughout the room—her dream come true.

Emma wiped down the steamer before holding the white paper cup towards Remy. "Here. Looks like you need a little caffeine in your life today."

Remy stifled a yawn before she wrapped her fingers around the warm concoction. Bringing it to her nose, she inhaled the earthy roast with a hint of sweetness. "Mmm, thank you. Is it that obvious that I was up half the night?"

Emma smirked with a knowing glint in her eye. "Only for those of us who know how to read you. Now, tell me, how has this last week of sneaky sleepovers been? How much rest are you actually getting?"

Remy's cheeks burned as she tried to hide her smile.

Deciding the conversation was best had in private, she nodded towards the back room.

Emma followed her, not waiting until the door had swung closed to remark, "Good god, I'm surprised you're not limping after such a hiatus and then going at it like rabbits."

"Emma! Do you have to say that *so* loud?" Remy cringed.

The smile on her friend's face only widened. "Well, you need to spill. I want every sordid detail. The dirtier, the fucking better."

Remy rolled her eyes and sipped the hot coffee, buying herself some time. "We've had a lot of catching up to do." She played coy.

"Five years is a lot of fucking to make up for." Emma laughed.

"Why are you so crude?"

"All I want to know is, does he make you happy? You were wrecked after everything. I know he seems good now, but with addicts . . . you never know what will send them over the deep end." The glint in Emma's eyes faded.

Remy touched her friend's arm. "Hey, I promise if it turns into anything unsafe or if I find out he's using again, I will end it. But some addicts do turn everything around. They are not all like . . . *her*."

Emma sniffed and nodded. "You can say *my mother*. She's not Voldemort. He who must not be named." They laughed together and Remy pulled her friend in for a hug.

"Okay, enough of this emotional crap. You have somewhere to be and I have a café to run while you're gone," Emma said, moving away.

Remy's heart ached for her best friend. She admired how far Emma had come with such a difficult past. "You're right. Take care of my Stardust Café and she'll take care of you."

Remy winked and kissed her friend's cheek before grabbing her purse and keys.

"Drive safe," Emma said.

"I always do."

* * *

Remy walked along the front path to Bently's house. The summer sun was already beating steadily, forming a sheen of sweat on her body. *Thank god for summer dresses.*

A rustling in the bushes at the side of the house caught her attention. She froze, searching the mass of green. *Is it an animal?*

A low, deep growl emanated from the shrubbery. She gasped.

"That's right, baby, it's the big, bad wolf," Mikel said as he climbed out from behind the leaves.

Remy placed a hand over her thumping heart. "You scared me to death."

"You should fear me." Mikel stalked towards her, a predatorial gleam in his eyes. He was still wearing his clothes from work: steel-toe boots, torn jeans, and an orange T-shirt with Seaview Construction written across his broad chest.

"You look mighty hungry, Mister Wolf." She played along.

He leaned in, inches from her, and sniffed her neck before nipping it with his teeth. "I'm starving. Do you think you have something that could appease my appetite? It's very specific," he said, staring into her eyes.

She shivered at the intensity. This felt too real. She swallowed as her legs wobbled. "Th-that depends. W-what do you like to eat?"

He traced the shell of her ear with his hot tongue before whispering, "I'd like to eat you."

Oh, Jesus, lord in heaven. Her panties were soaked. How did the heat rise ten degrees in the last minute? A flicker of movement in the window of the house caught her attention. A small head with curly hair bobbed behind the glass pane, staring at them. Lyra was excitedly bouncing up and down, pointing towards Mikel. They had an audience.

Remy turned her face, kissing the scruff of his beard, and placed her mouth by his ear. "You'll have to do one thing for me first." She backed away slowly.

"And what's that?" He smirked.

"Catch me!" She ran towards the front door of the house just as his strong arms encircled her waist, pinning her backside against his erection.

The door opened and a vivacious little girl came bounding towards them, wrapping herself around Remy's leg. "Mommy! Did Daddy scare you? He's the big, bad wolf trying to catch little girls!"

"He did. Oh no!"

"That's right. I see a little girl right now who would be a tasty treat." Mikel licked his lips in show and reached his hands out.

Lyra squealed, releasing Remy's leg and running away.

Mikel leaned in to her ear, speaking in a low voice so only she could hear, "Tonight we get to finish this and I get to feast on my favorite."

Her body heated with his dirty promises and electric touch. The man surely knew how to set her on fire.

"I forgot how gross you two can be together," Jasmine's voice teased from the kitchen.

Remy walked in and took a seat next to her. "Well, I think it's payback for the time I walked in on you having sex in the stockroom with a customer."

Jasmine cringed. "I'm really sorry about that. I know I've

fucked up a lot of stuff. I appreciate you giving me a second chance."

"Of course. How are you feeling?"

Jasmine sipped the peppermint tea in front of her. "Okay. The morning sickness isn't too bad today yet. I've been able to pick up a few more shifts at the hotel. Miss Jenson, who owns the big house on Shattered Cove beach, agreed to sell it to me as soon as I get the loan approved. I've got a big chunk saved for the down payment and then some for the remodel." Excitement and determination painted her expression.

"That's great. You've worked so hard to save. You're finally getting your dream to come true. You're making it happen." Remy smiled.

"Yeah, well, this baby has thrown a wrench into things, but I'll figure it out."

"They usually do. I've found they're totally worth the extra struggle they cause," Remy said, as Lyra's giggles erupted from the other room.

"Mommy! I caught the big bad wolf!" her little voice yelled.

"Awesome, baby! Way to go." Remy cheered her on.

"Girl power! That's ducking awesome, Lyra," Jasmine said, winking at Remy.

"You may have to work on that before the baby comes. Or else you'll have a tiny human that swears like a sailor." Remy laughed.

"Ducking is not a curse word. Besides, I do it more to drive your boyfriend crazy," Jasmine said.

Boyfriend. She still wasn't used to hearing that yet.

"Well, I hope the loan gets approved fast. You've wanted to own a bed-and-breakfast for as long as I can remember." Remy drove the conversation back to Jasmine.

"Yeah. Let's just hope the bank thinks I'm worth the risk," Jasmine said.

"What risk?" Bently said, walking into the kitchen. His face was pale, and his steps labored. The dark rings around his bloodshot eyes caused a wave of worry to wash over her. He was always such a force in their lives, full of life and jokes. This new Bently seemed like a shadow of his former self.

Jasmine shot out of her chair and grabbed a bottle of water from the fridge before handing it to him as he sat across from them.

"The risk to invest in my bed-and-breakfast," Jasmine explained.

Bently nodded. "Ahh, yes. Well, if they don't, they're crazy. Most people see that house as a big money pit though. It's a good thing one of your brothers knows his way around construction."

Jasmine sat back down, placing a bowl of soup in front of him. "I was going to ask Andre. I'm sure he'd be more than willing to help and give me a deal."

"Ask Andre what?" Mikel said, carrying Lyra in on his shoulders. She was all smiles.

Jasmine huffed. "To help me remodel the Jensons' beach house for my inn."

"I can do it," Mikel said, without hesitation.

"Are you gonna give me a better deal than Dre?" Jasmine asked, crossing her arms.

"Sure. You buy the supplies and I'll do the work for free. Can't beat free labor." Mikel smiled.

Jasmine was quiet for a moment before nodding. "I would appreciate that. Thank you."

"*Anything* for my little sister." Mikel seemed to send an unspoken message with his eyes towards Jasmine. Hope filled

Remy at the sight of them starting to make amends. If she and Mikel could find a way back to each other, anything was possible.

"Now, I seem to have misplaced my daughter," Mikel said, making a show of searching the room.

Lyra giggled above him.

"Has anyone seen her? I can hear her, but I can't find her."

"No, we haven't seen her." Remy played along.

"I guess she won't be able to look at the stars with us tonight, then." Mikel sighed.

"I want to go! I'm up here, Daddy!" Lyra yelled and pulled his face to look at her.

He chuckled. "There you are!" He swung her around and kissed her cheeks.

Remy's heart was bursting at the seams as the man she loved fit so perfectly into his role as Lyra's father as well as her boyfriend once again.

"I've got a surprise for you, princess," Mikel said.

"A surprise for me?" Lyra's eyes widened and her mouth opened in awe. "It's not even my birthday!"

"I know. But I saw your dolly didn't have a proper bed and I made one for her." He crouched down and opened the closet door before pulling out a beautifully carved, intricate cradle painted white.

"Oh, Daddy! This is beautiful. It has my name on it so everyone will know it's mine and my daddy made it for me." She ran into his arms, nearly knocking him over. Mikel caught her as tears welled in Remy's eyes. The well of joy spilled within her, soaking her in the warm sunlight of gratitude. Life couldn't get any better than this.

"Thank you," she said.

Mikel's eyes locked on to her, saying everything she had wished so long to hear. *I'm here for you. I love you.*

"Anything for my girls."

40

___

MIKEL

ang. Bang. Bang. It felt so good to be back in his element, hammering away with his best friend by his side. Not everything was completely resolved between them, but Andre was giving him the chance and that was all that Mikel cared about.

"That's quitting time," Tom, Andre's right-hand man, said, slapping his shoulder.

"See you tomorrow. Have a good night." Mikel nodded as he started to clean up his workspace.

"We're right on schedule to finish this rec room on time," Andre said.

Mikel glanced around the space—one long addition to the already big complex of the Hope Facility. Knowing Remy hadn't actually slept with the owner, Aaron, made it easier to see the guy was a genuine, good person. Every day they worked, he could hear the kids' laughter and joking around. They'd finished the new dorms, and within a week, Aaron had said they were full. How much better would his life have been

261

if a place like this had existed for him and his siblings when they were younger? "That's awesome."

"How you holding up?" Andre asked, stepping closer.

"I'm good. It's not like I was out of practice. All I did was build overseas."

His friend nodded. "I meant staying sober, acclimating to life being a father."

Mikel guessed he wasn't going to pull any punches. "Some days are easier than others. The voice is always there, tempting me to use. But each time I refuse, it gets quieter and quieter."

Andre crossed his arms and nodded.

"Being a dad is terrifying and the most exciting thing I've ever done all at the same time. I'm in a constant state of pure amazement that this is my life now."

"If you are ever tempted, promise me you'll get help. You can call me. I'd be there in a heartbeat." His friend's eyes shone with sincerity.

"I know. I appreciate it."

"All right, now let's clean up and get to the beach for that cookout." Dre slapped him on the back.

"You bringing your girl?"

Andre sighed. "If she's up for it."

Their relationship seemed like it was more work than it was worth, but who was he to lecture his friend about healthy relationships?

He packed his stuff into his toolbox and headed out through the main room towards the lobby. A group of kids were sitting in a circle listening to a man sharing about the struggles of his life as a gay homeless teen, and what had saved him from suicide. Mikel entered the lobby, feeling like an intruder on something personal.

Aaron came in the room at the same moment as him. "Heading home for the day?"

"Yeah."

"You guys work fast. I really appreciate it," Aaron said with a friendly smile.

"Is he one of the staff here?" Mikel nodded toward the older man.

"Nah, just a volunteer. Gary wanted to share his story with the kids and offer them hope. He runs a successful Fortune 500 company now, but he came from a pretty bad home and he was on the streets when he was fourteen."

"Wow." He turned back towards the room where Gary was hugging a young girl as he wiped at his eyes.

The man was talking about all the worst parts of his life in an effort to relate to the teens. If they came from a home like his, he'd hazard a guess they didn't have anyone else telling them that they could do something with their lives, that they were special. Because of Aaron, they did now.

"You ever need more people to come and speak?"

Aaron's smile grew. "Always."

Maybe it was time he gave back to his community. He could share his demons and possibly something good could come from it.

41

REMY

few weeks later, Remy shut off the car and rushed through the summer rain. Andre had texted her that it was urgent that she get over to the Hope Facility where they were working. Her texts asking if Mikel was okay went unanswered. Her stomach knotted with nerves as she opened the front doors, escaping the rain. Wiping the droplets from her face, she walked inside to the main room as a familiar voice spoke.

"I grew up a lot like you guys. My mom committed suicide when I was a kid. My dad was a mean drunk who was abusive . . . in every sense of the word."

The man she loved stood in front of a large group of kids, his life story pouring from his lips. His eyes met hers, surprise painting his features. He cleared his throat. "After he was gone, I got hooked in with some bad people. I became a runner in high school for a drug dealer."

She shivered at the reminder of Joe Canoby. He was a monster, and she was glad he was safely locked away from society; from her family.

Mikel shifted his gaze down. "I did a lot of things I'm not proud of to survive. Eventually, I started using myself. Just a little something to numb the pain and make life a little more tolerable."

Remy took a seat in one of the empty chairs in the back, listening intently as her boyfriend continued.

"I met this amazing girl. I fell in love, but because of my addiction, I ruined that too."

Her heart squeezed as she wiped away a tear.

"I abandoned her when she needed me most, and I went on a bender. I tried to kill myself. For some reason, I woke up. Then I spent the next five years volunteering in third world countries, building schools and hospitals. I met someone there who helped me see life as a gift rather than a curse. I learned I wasn't too broken and damaged to be loved. Everything I have been through in life shaped me in some way." Mikel took a breath as his gaze swept the crowd of teens.

"Sure, I was bruised and dented. Chipped at the edges and cracked. But, that didn't mean I was broken. I wasn't unfixable if I was still breathing."

Remy inhaled as his words stirred an aching gratitude in her chest.

"Coming from the life I lived gave me a unique under-standing of people and pain. I had a choice, just as you all do. I could let it consume me, and remain someone who spread that pain. Or, I could choose empathy and gratitude. I have a lot of privilege to be thankful for that most people in the world don't have." Mikel tapped his heart with his finger. "I needed to work on myself. First and foremost, I had to learn to forgive myself and then love me."

Remy wiped away the tears streaming down her face. Pure adoration and pride exploded in her chest like fireworks.

"Did you get the girl back?" one of the kids asked.

Mikel met her eyes as he smiled. "I did, and I'm working my ass off every day to be a man who's worthy of her so I can keep her."

He was so vulnerable now, nothing like the guarded man who'd kept everything to himself and been closed off from everyone. There was no more distance, only connection. No more doubt, only hope and belief. *Only forever.*

42

MIKEL

Mikel wrapped his arm around the love of his life as their daughter snuggled between them. The well of his heart overflowed with completion and gratitude. His girls watched him with rapt attention as he explained the myth of the Phoenix constellation. Remy's eyes brimmed with adoration for him, and joy. She had a spark in them that she hadn't had when he'd first arrived. Remy was an amazing woman, and an even better mother. *How did I get so damn lucky as to be loved by her?*

The last two months had gone by in the blink of an eye with ice cream dates, nights like this with his telescope, dinner together, and too many sleepovers to count. Lyra's fifth birthday had come and gone with a huge family party—the first of many to come.

Lyra's eyes drooped closed as his story came to an end. Remy's hand tenderly stroked her brown curls away from her forehead. "I think she's out," she said.

"She's so peaceful when she sleeps," he said.

Sweet laughter tumbled from Remy, lighting up the moonless night. "The only time she ever sits still. I can't believe she'll be starting school soon."

"I'm just glad I'll get to be here for it."

She moved her hand to his face, her touch soothing. "I am too."

"Remy?"

"Yeah?"

"I wanted to ask you what you thought about moving in together? I mean, I'm basically with you guys every night anyways."

Remy hesitated, taking a few deep breaths. His stomach knotted in worry. *Doesn't she trust me?*

"I think I would like that," she said finally.

Relief flooded his body with an overwhelming urge to celebrate. Feeling this good was almost unnatural. "You're sure? I don't want you to be pressured at all. I'm fine waiting until you're ready."

Remy smiled. "I'm sure. I love you, Mikel, and these last few months you have proven to me just how much you have changed. You are an awesome father to Lyra, and things with you and I have been everything I'd hoped now that you've opened up to me. I'm ready. I'd love for you to move in with us."

"Thank you." He kissed her forehead. "We'd better get her *home*, and maybe then we can celebrate."

"What did you have in mind?" she asked, a sly smile spreading across her lips.

"It involves you naked and screaming my name."

"Well, not too loudly I hope. We wouldn't want to wake the princess," she teased.

"So much pleasure you can't speak. Understood." He smirked as he lifted Lyra in his arms and gently placed her against his chest. Carrying his daughter to the car while Remy packed up the blanket, he inhaled deeply. Sweet summer flowers and hot August air filled his lungs. He was floating, on top of the world.

Mikel buckled Lyra into her car seat as she stirred. "Sshh-hhh, go back to sleep, baby." He waited until she dozed off and placed a kiss on her chubby cheek.

After quietly closing the door to his truck, he climbed in the front to start the ignition and get the air conditioner running. A piece of paper on the windshield caught his attention. He stepped out of the car, retrieving the note.

Time to pay for your sins.

A chill skittered across his spine as the hair on the back of his neck stood up. He searched the parking lot in the darkness, awareness prickling his skin. Was this some sort of sick joke? Who knew he'd be here, with his family no less?

Joe.

Anger rose as he clenched his fist, crumpling the scrap of paper.

Remy approached him with her hands full. He stuck the note in his pocket. She didn't need to worry. He would keep them safe.

Mikel took a few steps forward to grab the basket out of her arms. "I'll get the telescope. Lock the doors and roll up the window when you get inside," he said, trying to sound more put together than he felt.

"Why?" She turned her head to look around as she climbed in the truck.

"For safety." He put the basket in the bed of the truck and ran down to retrieve the equipment before jogging back.

Remy unlocked the doors when he got to the truck and he climbed in and drove them home where they would be safe.

Why did he have to borrow fifty thousand dollars from a drug dealer? *Pride.* He'd needed that money to invest in Andre's and his construction company and the bank had turned him down. If it was only the money, he'd get him the cash right now. He'd pay anything for Remy and Lyra's safety. But Joe was the one who'd sold him the heroin that Paul Evans had overdosed on. Joe had been his father's dealer, and he knew that heroin wasn't Paul's drug of choice. He knew what Mikel had done. Too many years had passed for there to be any real proof. But if Bently found out what Mikel had done, he'd lose his brother for good.

"Is everything okay?" Remy asked, watching him warily.

He reached out his hand and wove his fingers between hers. "Of course. I've got my baby girl sleeping in the back, and her sexy-ass mama by my side."

She smiled, blissfully unaware of the panic that seized his chest. He needed to talk to Bently and figure out why Joe Canoby was not behind bars still serving out the last half of his ten-year sentence.

When they pulled in to Remy's driveway, Mikel checked his mirrors one more time. As far as he could tell, no one had followed them.

He carried Lyra in before tucking her into bed and turning the baby monitor on. He'd need all the reassurance he could get. Mikel walked out to Remy's bedroom, *their bedroom,* as of tonight. He should be celebrating, like he'd said. But a nagging feeling was pulling him in another direction.

"Does this party involve you naked too?" Remy asked as she walked in the room wearing nothing but a white lace thong and matching bra.

He swallowed hard and clutched his chest. "Damn, woman. Are you tryin' to kill me?"

Her smile was confident.

He walked forward, hating himself for having to do this. "I need to go check on Bently really quick. And grab a few things from his place. Maybe we can move the party to tomorrow morning?"

Her face transformed with worry. "Is everything okay? Did something happen to Bently?"

"Nah, I just need to make sure he's doing fine. He's been tired and too sick to eat much lately. And you know him; he's too stubborn to ask for help. His treatments have been taking a lot out of him. I just want to check in."

"Oh. Okay. Yeah, I get it," she said.

He ran his hand over her cheek and then her bottom lip before kissing her, stealing goodness and comfort like a thief. With everything this woman had done for him, and after all these years, he was still taking. This would be it—the last time. He'd shoulder the responsibility for his mess and take care of it himself. She didn't need to be involved in this again. He couldn't risk hers or Lyra's safety.

"I love you," he said, pulling away.

"I love you too."

"Get some sleep," he said, kissing her forehead before making sure the baby monitor was turned on in her room. It was, so he left, not looking back at the lips he wanted to get lost in, or the thighs he wanted to part and dive between, or the white lace he would swipe aside surely to find her slick with arousal. No, he would not be selfish for once. He'd be the man she needed.

Mikel parked his truck and ran to the door of Bently's house before using his key to enter. All the lights were off downstairs, so he went up to his brother's room. *Empty.* His truck was in the driveway, so where was he? Light peeked out from the bathroom door as the toilet flushed, followed by a heaving noise.

Mikel knocked on the door. "Bent? Are you in there? You okay?"

There was a groan and then more heaving. Mikel turned the knob and entered. His brother was hunched over the porcelain bowl, white as a ghost without his shirt on. He was covered in a sheen of sweat, so much thinner than he had been when Mikel had first returned to Shattered Cove.

"I'm fine. Just go," Bently managed, out of breath.

Mikel grabbed a towel, and a glass which he filled with water. He bent and wiped the vomit from his brother's mouth and chin.

Bently groaned and clutched his stomach, shaking his head. "Just go."

"Here, rinse your mouth out with this."

Bently just stared at him.

"Goddamn it, Bently. You're so stubborn. Just take the fucking water."

Bently did as he said, rinsing and spitting into the toilet. Mikel flushed and then got him fresh water to drink. "You gotta stay hydrated."

"I never thought I'd see the day when my little brother had to take care of me," Bently said, handing him back the glass.

Mikel placed it on the sink. "We all need help sometimes. There is no shame in it. It doesn't make you less of a man."

Bently had always been the strong one, the rock in their lives. He couldn't remember a time when his brother had asked for help.

"Thanks, but I'm good now." He stood on shaky legs.

Mikel grabbed his arm to steady him. "I've learned a lot since I've been gone. You know it takes a real man to admit when he needs help. You've been there for me my whole life, even when I abandoned you. Let me help you now."

Bently grimaced. "I'll be okay. It's just . . . this chemo is kicking my ass. But today was my last day."

"Really?"

Bently nodded. "Last scan said I'm cancer-free. I'm in remission and today was my last maintenance chemo session."

Excitement pounded in his chest as Mikel digested the news. Bently had kept the details of his disease mostly to himself, remaining private about the whole thing. "You're in remission?"

A smile broke out on Bently's face as his blue eyes grew glassy. "Fucking free and clear."

"That's amazing. Truly awesome news."

Bently nodded. "I need to get to bed."

Mikel moved out of the small bathroom, giving his brother the room to leave. "Are you going into work tomorrow?"

"Nah, I got someone to cover my shift," Bently said.

He couldn't ask his brother for help now. He needed to rest, not worry. If Mikel told him about the note, the stubborn bastard would put on his shirt and drive down to the station right then. He'd probably collapse and end up hospitalized.

Mikel could wait a few days. "Okay, good. You need your rest," he said.

Bently made his way to his room, using the wall for stability. Mikel gave him some distance, while also making sure his brother got safely into his bed. He brought in a glass of water and set it on Bently's bedside table.

"Mick?" Bently said quietly.

Mikel turned to face his brother. "Yeah?"

"Thank you."

"Of course. I'd do anything for you."

Mikel turned and left the room, heading into his own,

stress and worry heavy on his shoulders. His chest constricted. There was so much going on in his life. He needed an escape. His fingers traced the edge of his mattress as he sat down. How many times had he done the same thing before he'd reached for the small bag of pills underneath?

Mikel could almost taste the bitter drug on his tongue. His fix was just a short drive and exchange away—a well-known ritual between him and his old friend. *Just one,* that little voice said, getting louder as his craving increased. *Just one. It would be so easy. No one would have to know.*

Old habits died hard, if they died at all.

REMY

Remy woke to an empty bed. Giggles came through from the baby monitor. She sat, adjusting the silk scarf on her head as she grabbed her bathrobe from the floor. A quick trip to the bathroom to relieve herself and then brush her teeth was in order.

As she did, she got lost in her thoughts. Mikel had seemed off last night. Maybe he was just worried about his brother. Bently had always seemed like an infallible giant. But the last several times she'd seen him, he'd appeared so weak and exhausted. His thick black hair had been shaved. She hadn't asked, but assumed it was because he had begun to lose it.

The deep rumble of a voice she recognized cut through her thoughts. She quickly finished up and walked down the hall to Lyra's room. Opening the door quietly, her daughter pranced around Mikel. Fairy wings adorned Lyra's back and her chubby little hand held tightly to a wand.

"Princess Daddy, your wishes will now come true!" Lyra said, dramatically waving the glittering wand.

Mikel was on his knees with his eyes closed and a pink sparkly crown on his head with several beaded necklaces around his neck. He opened his eyes, lovingly playing along with their daughter. "Awesome! I always wanted my wishes to come true. Thank you, magical fairy."

Remy covered her mouth, trying to suppress her giggle. Seeing the big, tough tattooed man at the mercy of a glitter-loving five-year-old was quite the sight.

His eyes snapped to hers as he smiled. "Oh, looks like we have a visitor to our kingdom."

Lyra turned and jumped up and down excitedly. "Yay! Mommy's awake. Now can we have breakfast?" She dropped her wand on the bed.

"I think breakfast is a great idea," he said, pulling off the layers of jewels.

"What do you want? Eggs? Muffins? Waffles?" Remy asked.

"Daddy said he was going to cook." Lyra skipped out of the room.

Remy turned her attention back to Mikel as his arms wrapped around her. "I bought some groceries and I'm gonna make a feast. Part one of our celebration." He kissed her neck, trailing his mouth closer to hers.

"Oh, I like the sound of that. What's part two?" She laughed.

"You and me, going out to The Shipwreck to dance the night away. Your mother already said she'd be more than happy to have a sleepover with Lyra."

"You talked to my mother?" she asked.

He kissed her lips, once, twice, and then a third time. "That's okay, right?"

She'd thought he was pulling away last night. Sure, he'd

been the one to bring up moving in together, but then he'd started acting distant. Maybe going home to check on his brother was all he'd needed.

"It's perfect. How was Bently?" she asked.

He sighed and her gut clenched in worry. "He was sick from the treatments, but he got good news. He's in remission." Mikel smiled with his whole face.

Joy filled her—a happiness overload. "He's all clear?"

"Yup."

"Oh, that's great news! Once he's feeling a little better, I'll make him a cake and we can have a party," she offered.

"I'm sure he'd love that. Now, go get dressed because I have another surprise for both of you." He slapped her ass playfully.

"You sure are full of them today." She laughed.

"I don't hear any complaints."

* * *

An hour later, she relaxed into the leather chair with Lyra seated in between her and Mikel.

"That tickles!" Lyra said, giggling as the woman scrubbed her little feet in the pedicure lounge.

"I gotta say, this is a first for me, but I can see why women love it so much," Mikel said, shooting her a smile.

He'd arranged for them all to get pedicures, and then she and Lyra were going to get manicures as well.

"We have many male clients come in. Sometimes even couples for dates, and we provide wine or beer," one of the women said.

"What do you think, baby? Should we make it a date next time?" Mikel asked.

"Sounds good to me." She'd take any chance to be pampered like this.

"My daddy is the best daddy in the whole universe," Lyra said.

"I bet he is," the woman working on Lyra's feet answered.

"He had to go away for a long time because he was sick, but now he's better," Lyra rambled on.

Remy winced and glanced at Mikel. The same regret and pain she felt was reflected on his expression.

"Now he's going to stay forever. Right, Daddy?"

Mikel nodded. "Sure am, princess."

* * *

Later that night, Remy held Mikel's hand as he guided her through the doors to The Shipwreck. A tall burly man was stationed outside. Remy recognized him as the quiet ex-Navy SEAL who sometimes came in for her lavender cupcakes.

"Hi, Mason," she said.

Mason nodded and half his mouth turned up in a smile. The other half of his face was badly scarred. As big and tough as this man looked, he always chose the most delicate concoctions from the bakery.

"Hello, Remy. Nice to see you out and about."

Mikel's grip tightened on her hand.

"Mason, this is my boyfriend, Mikel."

The men eyed each other warily before Mason stuck out his palm to shake Mikel's.

"Nice to meet you."

A line was beginning to form behind them.

"You too. It's gonna be busy in there tonight—band's playing," Mason said.

"Thanks for the heads-up." Remy smiled as she led Mikel inside. She tugged the bright blue fabric of her dress lower on her legs. It was much shorter than she was used to, but tonight she had a reason to wear it. She wanted to look and feel good as she danced with Mikel. Memories of the night he'd rescued her on this very dance floor came crashing back.

"This place hasn't changed one bit," Mikel said.

"Why fix what isn't broken?" she yelled over the crowd.

"Let's get a drink at the bar. Is that Charli? She still works here?" he asked.

Remy nodded before he led her to the wooden slab of the bar. A nervous knot formed in her belly, a nagging feeling that continued to grow. As far as she knew, Mikel hadn't had a drop of alcohol since he'd come back. Did he drink anymore? Would she be comfortable with him having a drink? Alcohol hadn't been as much of a problem for him as the harder drugs.

"You want a drink?" he asked.

"Pepsi, please."

Remy stood closely by him as the room began to fill. The band started playing, their music drowning out most of the conversation Mikel yelled to Charli.

Alternative rock blasted through the speakers while they waited. Remy searched the crowd for any faces she might know. Too bad Emma wasn't playing tonight. Her best friend was states away, touring with her band.

"Which one would you like? They're both the same," Mikel asked.

She turned to the two colas he held out to her. The nervous butterflies calmed with the knowledge they would both be sans alcohol tonight. She smiled and reached her fingers around one glass, sipping the cool bubbly liquid.

"Dre just texted me and said he was here too. He's got a table in the corner." Mikel led her through the jostling crowd as she tried not to spill her drink. They made it to the only open chair by Andre. Setting their drinks on the small circular table, Mikel sat and pulled Remy into his lap.

"Hey," Dre said.

"Hey yourself. Where's Tiffany?" Mikel asked as Remy took a sip of her soda.

Dre shook his head slightly, staring at his drink. "Pregnant."

Soda bubbles burned her nose as Remy choked on her drink. "What?"

"Congratulations?" Mikel said it more like a question.

"It's not mine," Andre said, deadpan.

Mikel and Remy gasped in unison.

"All those business trips came with the added bonus of seeing her man on the side, apparently," Dre continued.

"I'm sorry, Dre. I don't know what to say." Mikel sighed.

Remy reached her hand out over her brother's. The reason why he had chosen Tiffany, out of all the women in the world, was beyond her. Now that bitch had gone and broken her brother's heart. Andre was the most loyal, caring partner she'd ever seen. "You deserve someone better. I know it doesn't seem like it now, but there's a woman out there who will be willing to give where Tiffany only took from you."

"Nah, I'm done with women—at least for a while. I'm gonna go home and find the bottom of a bottle, and get this all out of my system," Andre gritted out.

"Take a few days off. I got you covered," Mikel offered.

"Thanks, man." Dre stood, slightly off balance.

"You okay to drive?" Remy asked.

"Nah. Ordered a Lyft."

Remy slid off Mikel's lap and wrapped her arms around her big brother.

Andre patted her back and released her before saying, "Stay out of trouble, you two."

"Won't do anything you wouldn't do." Mikel chuckled.

"Better not do that either." Dre smirked and disappeared through the crowd.

"You should text Bently and let him know that Dre may need a friend tonight. I know my brother, and he's gonna pull away for a while. He needs someone who's willing to just sit with him."

Mikel nodded and pulled out his phone. "Wanna dance?" Mikel asked when he was finished, grabbing her hand and pulling her close.

"Absolutely. Let me run to the bathroom really quick."

Mikel glanced at the line in front of the ladies' room. "I doubt that's gonna be quick."

"I'm worth the wait." She smiled and kissed him, nipping his bottom lip playfully.

He growled, barely audible over the music. "You certainly are."

She walked to the back of the line, smiling so big it almost hurt. How much had they overcome? Here they were, years later, two people who'd been through hell and come out stronger. Together they would be unbreakable.

Once she was done using the facilities and washing up, she headed to their table.

Her gut clenched tight as the air was stolen from her chest. A blonde with a face that had been burned into her memory was smiling and laughing with her hands on Mikel. Her stomach burned, bile rising in her throat. Jealousy and fear gripped her like a vise. What was that bitch doing laying her paws on her man? Why wasn't he pulling away?

Remy stood witnessing the scene unfold, her feet too leaden to move. Mikel shook his head and leaned in to say something in June's ear. Why was he so close to her?

June's painted claws slipped into the back of Mikel's pants pocket. He backed away from her, grabbing her arm and moving to put some distance between them. Remy forced her feet forward; she needed to hear what they were saying. She needed to confront the matter head-on.

Her belly flip-flopped as she got closer. June's lips moved and then she glared at Remy. A vindictive smile twisted her face before she said, "Well, I better go. It was so nice running into you *again*, Mikel. We seem to be doing a lot of that lately." June turned and left, swinging her hips and turning more heads than one.

Remy's blood boiled.

Mikel ran a hand through his hair, tugging at the ends, turning as his hesitant eyes met hers. "Hey, baby."

Ask him. "What was that all about?"

Mikel shook his head. "Nothing. She just wanted to stir up some trouble."

"What did she mean that this wasn't the first time she'd run into you?"

His eyes glanced around the room as he gripped her hand. "I ran into her and Isaiah at the pharmacy a while ago. That's it. She's just trying to twist shit and start something."

She sought his eyes, searching for any sign of dishonesty. She found none.

"Look, please don't let this ruin our night. I swear I've put them in my past. The reality is, she lives in this town and we may run into her from time to time. You just gotta ignore June. And I'll avoid her."

Remy's anger subsided some. He was being truthful. Mikel was right. Shattered Cove was a small town and the likelihood of seeing people they had a past with was unavoidable. He was committed to her, and that was all that mattered.

She nodded. Mikel kissed the top of her forehead and led her into the crowd of dancing bodies. The band's playing drowned out any hope of further conversation.

Mikel pulled her close, sliding his knee between her thighs as the tempo changed to a slower song. His arms wrapped around her tightly, drawing her to him like he was the one who needed support. Kissing her neck, he swayed his body.

Did she trust Mikel? She'd asked him if he was all in, and he'd sworn he was. Now it was up to her to decide. He'd shared his deepest, darkest secrets with her. Guilt clouded over her. She hadn't given him the same trust.

She relaxed as the song played and his body melded against hers.

Mikel's hands traveled down her backside, and squeezed. She kissed his lips, taking her time to explore his mouth in slow, languid strokes. Her hands wandered across his muscles, desire building as they swayed together, no longer moving as two individuals, but one entity. He ground his leg against her center as heat gathered. *Yes.* That was the spot.

"More," she breathed in his ear.

He moved harder, faster against her as she began to pant. Pleasure sparked each time he hit the swollen juncture just right. He was basically humping her in the middle of a crowd, but she didn't care. All that mattered was how close she was to diving off that cliff and coming undone. And . . . she . . . was there! White spots filled her vision as the music drowned out her cries of ecstasy. Mikel gripped her tighter against him, holding her as she came down. Limbless, she rested in his arms, yearning for more, needing to connect with him.

"Take me home," she said.

He nodded, his lust-filled gaze locked on her.

She wouldn't let anything ruin her night. For once, she was going to shut out that nagging feeling and live in the moment. Tomorrow was going to come whether she wanted it to or not. She'd take a leaf from Emma's book and make the most of the only thing she could count on—*tonight*.

44

REMY

Naked and panting, Remy moaned as Mikel sucked her clit into his mouth. "Harder," she commanded. His beard scruff scratched her thighs, the sensation only adding to the building pleasure. "You're so bossy in bed. I like it," he said before he did just as she'd asked.

He was her only. Aching need zapped her body.

"Oh, god. Yes!" she screamed, taking advantage of the fact that they were home alone—their first night officially living together.

He flicked his tongue, circling around the pearl that throbbed for more of his touch, teasing her. She whimpered and wiggled, every nerve ending alive and seeking the raw euphoria his body promised.

"Please," she begged.

He inserted two fingers inside, curving them upwards to her G-spot while he sucked her clit. Overwhelming ecstasy pierced through her, transporting her to the heavens. Stars filled her vision as she arched her back off the bed.

"Holy fuck!" she cried.

"I wanna make you come all night," Mikel said, his deep voice against her tender sex sending another wave of pleasure echoing through her body.

Her heart beat wildly in her chest. The hollow ache between her slick thighs begged for Mikel to fill it. "I need to feel you inside me."

He smirked and pushed his fingers into her. "Like this?"

"No, *you*. I need *you* inside me." She grunted in frustration.

"You need to be more specific. Do you mean my tongue?" He licked and lapped her swollen folds.

"Your cock," she said, her body heating from lingering shyness. He was pushing her boundaries.

He chuckled. "What my baby wants, she gets." He spread her thighs, wedging in between them. "I want to feel you so bad."

"I'm on the pill," she said.

"You sure?"

"I want to feel you without anything between us."

Mikel nudged the tip of his cock past her entrance, slowly sinking into her. He groaned, as her eyes fluttered from the blissful sensations. There was nothing like this. He moved with drawn-out, hard thrusts.

Their breathing synced as he rocked her, filling her body with intoxicating euphoria.

"I'm so close," he warned.

Remy couldn't bear the thought of him pulling out and missing that connection. She was almost there too. "Come inside me. Come with me," she said.

He grunted as she squeezed him closer with the heels of her feet.

"You're so fucking sexy. So beautiful. Are you ready?"

She moaned in response.

"I'm gonna come inside your tight pussy," he said,

thrusting faster and harder. Incapable of forming words, she dug her nails into the flesh of his back.

His thumb tenderly traced her cheekbone as his movements slowed, elongating the pleasured sensations. He gazed at her lovingly, touching a place she hadn't known existed inside herself—connecting them body and soul as he made love to her. Mikel kissed her, sucking her bottom lip into his mouth and raking his teeth over it.

His actions mixed with his dirty words caused her body to combust. She splintered around him, squeezing her thighs against his hips as he growled his own orgasm, tensing and pulsing inside her.

Panting and breathless, he smiled at her. "I love you, Remy."

"I love you too."

He pulled out of her, slowly. She missed the connection immediately.

Mikel kissed her gently before lying next to her and pulling her against him. She basked in his warmth, her head against the steady thumping of his heartbeat. Reveling in the liquid glow of postcoital bliss, she was filled with gratitude.

What they'd just shared had been indescribable. She was so emotionally stripped bare, tears welled in her eyes. They had evolved throughout the years.

"We better get you cleaned up," he said, sliding out of bed. She lay in her bliss, satiated and boneless, drunk on orgasms.

A few minutes later, Mikel returned, still naked. He slipped one arm under her head, and the other, her knees. After carrying her to the bathroom, he gently eased her into the hot bath he'd prepared.

Candles had been lit around the corners of the room, the shadows dancing on the white tile. Mikel slipped in behind her as they relaxed together. He pulled a silk scarf around her head, securing her hair out of the way. Using a washcloth, he rubbed over her arms and neck, kissing the spot behind her ear. Her heart melted. How did she get so lucky? How was this man hers?

The warm cloth trailed down her breasts and arms before he swirled it across her belly. She sighed as he tenderly cleaned every inch of her body. Tears welled again in her eyes. She loved Mikel, and she wanted to spend the rest of her life with him and share an eternity of moments like this with him.

"Marry me," she said, turning around to face him. Her slick body slid against his. They were chest to chest as she searched his eyes.

Mikel gazed back, as if he too was enchanted by her. "You're asking me?"

"I'm telling you."

"So bossy." He smirked.

"Well?" she asked.

"Come on. I want to show you something," he said, nodding towards the door. She got up, butterflies dancing in her belly as nerves got the better of her. Was this too much for him? Too soon?

He wrapped a towel around her, and then one around his waist before taking her hand. After leading her back to the bedroom, he bent over the duffle bag he had brought earlier, digging around in one of the pockets. She sat on the bed, her legs too weak to stand any longer.

Mikel turned towards her, a smile on his face as he remained kneeling.

"Remy, I've known you were the only woman I could ever love for a long time. I made so many mistakes, but taking a chance on you was never one of them. You taught me that I could be more than I thought possible. You believed in me when I couldn't believe in myself. You gave me the best gift in this world: a daughter."

Remy brushed the tear away that fell down her cheek. Her heart was so full of joy.

Mikel took her left hand, slipping something cold on her ring finger.

"Like most things, you had the courage to do them before me. Marry me, Remy, and let me fill your days with happiness. Let me love you like a husband should. Give me all your tomorrows and I'll make them more special than the last."

"Yes." Remy nodded as she held out her arms for Mikel. He buried his face in her neck.

"I love you so much," she said.

"I love you too. Do you like the ring?" he asked, turning on the bedside lamp.

She gasped. An eight-pointed star of grey diamond glittered back at her, surrounded by inlays of smaller clear stones. The center looked as if it held an entire galaxy. "It's breathtaking."

"I used some of the money that Dre set aside from the business for it. But with what's left, I was thinking we could look at some land and I'd design you your dream house," Mikel said, sitting next to her on the bed.

"It's just so much. I wasn't expecting all of this," Remy said, leaning in to kiss him.

"Sometimes the best things in the world are unexpected," he said.

They lay down, dropping their towels to the floor before they drifted off to sleep, skin against skin, in each other's arms.

Remy awoke to a predawn sky filtering through the blinds. She checked the clock: five a.m. She glanced at her left hand, the ring shining back at her, reliving one of the best nights of her life.

Mikel's snores signaled he was still deep asleep. She'd surprise him with cinnamon rolls for breakfast and maybe they could slip back into the sheets and play with the extra icing. *First, coffee.*

She climbed out of bed before grabbing her bathrobe and tying it around her. Their clothes from last night were still scattered across the floor—small reminders of their time together. Remy smiled before she picked up her dress and panties and grabbed his clothes as well. She would get to do laundry with him for the rest of her life now. As silly as the thought was, it brought a whole list of activities to mind that she would forever share with her fiancé/soon-to-be husband. Butterflies flipped as she hummed on her way to the laundry area in the bathroom.

After dropping all the other items into the washer, she reached into his pants to retrieve his wallet. Remy double-checked all his pockets, her hand freezing when she made contact with something. She held her breath and closed her eyes as her stomach knotted. Gone were the joyous flutters, replaced with nerves.

No.

Remy braced herself as she pulled it out. A plastic bag with two pills. Her heart sank as her eyes burned with tears. A piece of paper was folded inside. She pulled it out and unfolded it with trembling hands and read the feminine script.

Room 305. Friday at three. Bring the cash.

Her ears rang as she stumbled backwards, her stomach churning. She ran to the bathroom and vomited into the toilet. Wiping her mouth as tears poured from her eyes, she quieted a sob. How could she have been so blind . . . again? How could he do this to her?

Remy's whole body shook as her world fell apart. How could he seem so honest and then throw everything away like it was nothing? Like *she* was nothing?

I am done. She couldn't go through it all again. Her heart shredded into a million shards of glass, piercing and slicing her insides into ribbons of regret. The pain was unbearable, every breath a struggle coated in agony.

Her stomach flipped again before expelling every fuck she had left to give for the man who'd taken everything she had and thrown it back in her face.

45
____

MIKEL

ikel reached his hand out, searching for the familiar warm body of his girlfriend.

Fiancée.

He smiled. Rubbing the remaining sleep from his eyes, he sat, searching for his bag. A light drizzle of rain tapped the windowsill. His eyes landed on the worn black fabric, patched in various areas from his travels around the world.

He pulled out a pair of jeans and slipped them on. With bare feet, he made his way to the bathroom. *Still no sign of Remy.*

He brushed his teeth and relieved himself before heading downstairs in search of the woman who had helped him envision a future where he was a father and a husband.

Remy was standing by the sink, staring out the window with her back to him. He slipped behind her, wrapping his arms around her, inhaling her sweet scent in the nape of her neck. She stiffened in his arms.

"Good morning, fiancée."

She turned to face him, her eyes bloodshot. His smile disappeared at the broken expression studying him.

"What's wrong?" Panic kick-started the thudding of his heartbeat. "Is it Lyra?"

She stared at him, her lips trembling as she shook her head.

A part of him relaxed—his daughter was safe. But why was Remy so upset?

"What's goin' on, baby?" He wiped the tears from the corner of her eyes, savoring her soft flesh.

"I just want to know one thing," she said, her chin rising.

"Anything," he promised.

"How long have you been fucking her?" A sob broke her speech.

The floor disappeared, sending him spiraling with confusion and questions. "I haven't been with anyone but you. Who are you talking about? June? I told you I ran into her at the pharmacy and then last night at the bar when she was trying to start something." He wouldn't tell Remy June had also been there to deliver a message from Joe. She'd been through enough.

"And you're using again?" she asked, studying him, clearly scrutinizing his answer.

"I'm not. I swear. Don't you trust me, Remy?" He backed away. "Where is this coming from?"

Remy's trembling hand held out a small plastic bag with a piece of paper and two pills inside. His heart sank. *June's message from Joe.* "It's not what it looks like."

"You're supposed to meet her Friday in room three-oh-five. What about that is unclear? If there is an explanation for this, *please*, tell me." A thread of hope flashed in her eyes.

The confession caught in his throat. How could he tell her Joe got out early, and that she and Lyra were in danger because of him—again? He had the money; he would take care of this once and for all. He'd protect them this time. Once it was done, he'd tell her everything.

"That's what I thought." She shook her head, pulling the ring from her hand and thrusting it into his chest. Her skin against his was electric.

"Baby, I just need you to trust me. I'll tell you everything once I take care of a few things." He grabbed her arms, holding on for dear life. If Remy believed he was capable of cheating on her and using behind her back, then did she really trust him at all?

"I don't know what to believe anymore. But this, this is drugs and a note from a woman you . . . I want you to leave and never come back."

"Remy?" he pleaded.

"Get out!" she yelled.

He dropped her arms and took the ring. He slipped it into his pocket as he forced one foot in front of the other, headed back upstairs where the duffel bag taunted him. *As if you ever had a chance at a happy ending.*

His throat burned as he grabbed his shoes in one hand and grasped the strap of the bag in the other. He glanced at Lyra's room. He'd leave her a note. He scribbled out a letter and drew a heart before setting it on her bed where she'd be sure to find it.

Mikel made his way back to the kitchen, his ribs feeling cracked and broken as he tried to take shallow breaths through the ache in his chest.

Remy hadn't moved.

"I'm gonna go like you asked. Baby, I want you to know everything I have done and kept from you was to keep you safe."

She shook her head and turned from him, her sob

breaking through his remaining walls. Tears pricked his eyes, slipping down his cheeks as he ran out to his truck. The dark grey clouds that hovered above cracked open in a downpour. He was soaked in the few seconds it took for him to manage to climb in the cab.

He slammed his fist against the dashboard. Searing pain shot through his split knuckles. He welcomed the sting. Was he being too prideful, not telling her everything?

No. She would only worry, and perhaps still kick him out knowing that their daughter was in danger because of his past mistakes. If he fixed the problem before he returned and then explained everything, then maybe he would have a fighting chance.

Mikel started the engine, peeling away as he called the only person he knew could help him.

"Joe's back and he's been threatening my family. I need you to help me catch this son of a bitch once and for all."

46

REMY

Days passed, until Friday afternoon hung above Remy like a dark cloud. Mikel hadn't tried to contact her, or his daughter. Lyra carefully picked up the note he'd left for her by her bed and kissed it.

Oh, baby. Her heart ached. She did it several times a day, and it never got easier. "Read Daddy's letter to me one more time, Mommy?" she asked, as they snuggled together.

Remy took the paper and began to read as she fought back tears. "Baby girl, I love you more than all the stars in the sky. You know that's an enormous amount, right? I have to go away for a little while, but I promise I'll be back soon. Be a good girl for Mommy. She'll need extra hugs and kisses. I love you with everything, Lyra. See you soon. Daddy."

Remy swallowed the emotions that burned her throat as Lyra wrapped her small arms around her and squeezed. Remy hugged her daughter back, drawing peace from her little body. At least she had her baby. She'd done it once before without Mikel and she'd do it again.

She glanced at the clock: three p.m. Was Mikel in a hotel

room with June? Was he on a bender? She'd called Bently and Andre to let them know that Mikel might be spiraling. Bently had been vague on the phone but assured her that Mikel was with him and that he'd take care of it.

The washer buzzed to let her know it was time to switch the load of laundry. "I'll be right back, honey." Remy walked to the bathroom as the wind swept the lace curtain, revealing a man walking towards their front door.

Remy's hand flew to her mouth as she gasped and dove out of view. Her back was against the wall. Adrenaline burned her veins. The man approaching her house was a fair bit older now, but she'd recognize that scar and his face anywhere. *Joe Canoby.* What was he doing here? *He's supposed to be in jail.* Was he looking for Mikel? Remy's blood turned to ice.

No.

He was here to finish the job.

Murder.

Remy grabbed her phone from her pocket before dialing emergency services with trembling hands as her doorbell rang.

"Operator, what's your emergency?"

"Th-there's a man at my house. He's going to kill me. My daughter is here." She rattled off the address and shoved the phone in her back pocket, not listening for anything else. She needed to hide her daughter. There was no way she was letting that man anywhere near Lyra. Remy rushed into the little girl's room.

"Mommy? What's wrong?" Lyra asked, tears welling in her eyes.

Remy picked her up off the bed and ran to the only place she thought the deranged man might not look—somewhere her daughter's cries would be muffled. "We have to hide you. I need you to be very quiet. No matter what you hear, promise me you won't make a sound. Stay here until Uncle Bently or Daddy comes to get you."

She opened the dryer and put her inside. It would just be for a short while; help was on the way. She had to hold him off long enough.

"Take my phone. The light and the lady on the phone will keep you company."

The doorbell rang again, followed by loud banging. There was no time to escape.

"I don't want to, Mommy. I'm scared." Lyra clung to her.

"Sshhhh. It's a game. There's a dragon trying to get in the castle, and Daddy is going to come and save you. But right now I'm the only knight to protect you."

Remy kissed her daughter, praying it wouldn't be for the last time, and said the most important words she could think of. "I love you, Lyra, more than all the stars in the universe." Her body screamed at her to comfort her child. The terror in those little brown eyes and the banging on the door tore her in two directions.

Protect her.

Remy shut her daughter in as a loud sound rocked the house. The door must have been nearly off its hinges.

Weapon.

She needed something to defend herself with. The only thing between Lyra and this psychopath was her.

Remy ran to the kitchen and reached for a kitchen knife from the counter at the sound of wood splintering behind her. She gripped the cool metal as she was thrust to the ground, the knife clattering out of her reach.

"Oof!"

A heavy weight pinned her to the ground sideways as pain radiated from her hip. The smell of stale smoke and sweat turned her stomach. His face landed only inches from her arm. She bent her elbow and swung with all her might, hitting him square in the eye.

"You fucking bitch!" he yelled.

She pushed up on her arms and wiggled free, backing into to the other side of the counter. The glint of metal caught her eye under the cabinet, just inches away on the floor. "I've already called the police. They're on the way!" Remy screamed.

Joe jumped on her, pinning her to the ground with his hands around her neck. "Let them come. All that matters is I collect payment for what your boyfriend owes me." He sneered.

"Wh-what do you mean?"

"He stole years away from my family. Now I'm going to take everyone he loves from him."

She winced from his pungent hot breath. "You're wrong. He doesn't love me." She struggled.

"He's across town waiting in an empty motel room thinking he's gonna be a hero. It's too late for cash. I want blood." His hands tightened around her neck.

"No, he's meeting a woman." She defended Mikel—anything to distract him. The longer he talked, the more of a chance she had that the police would show up in time.

He laughed gleefully, shaking. "Nah, darlin'. June is just my errand girl."

The note was from Joe? *I was wrong about everything.*

She struggled under his weight, clawing her fingernails into his arms, scratching at his face. Her attempts only seemed to incite him more. Her throat burned, as he squeezed tighter. She fought to take a breath. Tears pricked her eyes. *Where are the police?*

The room grew darker. It was too late for her—she could accept that as long as her daughter was saved. She stopped fighting. Her hand hit the cold tile, spreading out, searching for her last remaining hope.

Help me.

She touched the cold metal of the knife as her ears rang.

She gripped the handle tightly and swung with all her might. He released his hold on her neck and caught her forearm. She choked on fresh oxygen, her throat burning as if she'd swallowed one thousand tiny shards of glass. He removed the knife from her hand and switched it back and forth in his grasp.

"Well, this just got interesting." He laughed manically. His right arm came up, the knife glinting in the afternoon light. His arm dropped fast as he stabbed her thigh. Pain sliced through her as she gasped, arching off the floor. Black spots covered her vision and Remy screamed. He pinned her back down, eyes trained on her as she tried to gulp in air, fighting to stay awake. The pain was too much.

"When I'm done with you, I'll make sure to take everything else from that bastard, including his daughter," Joe said.

Adrenaline coursed through her as flashes of her little girl's face came to her mind. No one would get there in time. She was the only thing between this monster and Lyra.

Joe's hands wove around her throat again as his devious smile grew. She had lost all hope that anyone would come as darkness began to overtake her. She forced her eyes open, gripping the handle of the knife. Pain sliced through her thigh as she removed the sharp metal from her thigh. With an angry protective roar, she thrust it into his ribs. The evil smile on her attacker's face turned into a grimace as she stabbed him with the weapon over and over. Bile rose in her throat at the sound of flesh and bones breaking beneath the force of her hand.

Warm liquid pooled around her as he staggered off her.

Bang!

Joe's body crumpled to the floor as two hazy figures appeared in her line of vision. Blinking red and blue lights flashed on the walls.

"Remy! Oh my god. I'm so sorry, baby." Mikel's voice pierced through the growing haze as she shivered.

It is so cold down here.

"I love you, Remy. I was trying to stop him before . . . Oh, god." He cried out like a wounded animal.

Relief encompassed her. Her baby was safe.

"Lyra. Dryer," she croaked through the pain.

Take care of my baby. It was her last wish on her fallen star—the only light as the darkness consumed her.

47

MIKEL

Mikel followed the doctor into the recovery room. Remy had so many tubes and wires coming from her body. She was hooked up to a ventilator, the machine breathing for her. Purple handprint bruises showed on her neck. He clenched his fists at his sides. His chest was tight and his lungs burned as the weight of this reality settled on his shoulders.

"We'll move her into the ICU in a few hours once she's cleared," the nurse explained.

He nodded.

"Surgery went well. Luckily the knife missed her artery, but she lost a lot of blood. She had to be resuscitated. We've done all we can do. Now we just need to wait and see."

Wait and see.

What if she didn't make it? He staggered where he stood. The emotional punch of imagining a life without Remy in it stole the breath from his lungs. He'd have a daughter to raise on his own.

The urge to use reared its ugly head as he wished for an

alternate reality where his Dove was safe. What if he never got to see those brown eyes light up, or hear her laugh again? What if he never got the chance to explain and tell her how much he loved her?

"Is she going to make it?" His voice trembled as he used his remaining strength to remain standing.

The doctor's expression was grim as she nodded to a nearby nurse. "She seems like a fighter. I'll check back in a couple of hours. Nurse Dan will see to her care for now. Can you get Mr. Evans a seat?"

Dan moved a chair by Remy's bedside and motioned for him to sit. Mikel did so and reached his hand out to Remy's arm.

"If you need anything, I'll be right around the corner. Just holler," Dan said.

Mikel breathed in, searching for her scent. It was barely there, overpowered by sterile hospital smell. Her flesh was cooler than it usually was. He closed his eyes, no longer able to look at the pain she was enduring, all because of him.

"I'm so sorry, baby." Tears streamed from his eyes. How could he let this happen to her? Why hadn't he just told her everything? "Every time I come into your life, you end up hurt."

Her family were sure to blame him for this, and rightfully so. He'd let them all down. Mikel had promised them he'd take care of her, but he'd failed.

He moved closer, laying his head as close to hers as he could without possibly hurting her. He squeezed her hand. "I wasn't using. I swear, baby. I went to pay him back what I owed him so this could all be over. I should have told you he was out, that he had been sending me messages. I should have told you Bently was going with me to that meeting to catch him extorting me."

He sighed, gently smoothing a few of her dark curls away from her forehead.

"I was doing all of it for us. I just wanted to keep you safe and face my problems instead of running away this time. I should have told you, but I didn't want to see the fear in your eyes. I wanted to protect you, and all I've done is hurt you." He kissed her cheek. His whole body ached as the weight of mortality settled on him. Losing Remy to death was something he'd once thought impossible, but now the tides had changed, bringing reality closer. Maybe the ancient Greeks had it right and the thread between life and death was just that—a simple strand for the fates to decide when to cut.

"Lyra's safe. We kept her from seeing anything. She thought we were playing a game with her, but she keeps asking for you." He sniffled. "You gotta come back to us, baby. We need you to fight a little longer. I can't lose you. I can't—" His voice caught with emotion as his tears soaked the pillow.

Remy didn't respond. The machines hummed and beeped with each rise and fall of her chest.

Mikel kissed her shoulder as the ache in his chest grew, his insides eviscerated with the possibility of having to go on with life without Remy. He closed his eyes, picturing the first time he'd kissed her; the first time they'd made love; the night she'd asked him to marry her, and the moment she'd seen the ring he'd had made especially for her. He held on to every bright and happy memory and hoped with every piece of his heart that for once his wish would come true.

Beep! Beeeeeep!

Alarms and buzzers started going off. Mikel whipped from the bed. The monitor where her heart line should have been peaking and baselining went flat. Unable to draw a breath, his body filled with the weight of dread.

Nurses and doctors rushed in as everything blurred

around him. He was pushed to the side as they tore open her hospital gown and laid her straight. Someone was pulling on his arm, but his feet were lead. He stared at her closed eyes and lifeless body as it was jolted with the paddles only a second after someone called, "Clear!"

Beeeeeeeeep. There was a bump from the electricity and then that flat line.

"No! Baby, no!" The scream that came from him was guttural as he was ripped away from her room by several arms.

Their words were drowned out by the ringing in his ears. His last thread of hope was cut as she flatlined.

EPILOGUE - MIKEL

"Where do people go when they die?" Lyra asked.

Mikel's heart ached—his daughter knew too soon about death. "I like to think that the good ones become stars, watching over us and keeping us safe."

"Like in *The Lion King*?"

"Yeah." He nodded.

"Where is Mommy's star?" Lyra asked.

Mikel moved away so that his daughter could take a turn looking at the star he'd lined up in his telescope from the front porch of his house.

"It's so pretty and bright. Just like Mommy," she said.

His chest tightened. He pulled the blanket around her shoulders more securely and made sure her hat was covering her ears. It was an unusually cold March night, with only a few clouds in the sky. "Sure is."

"Show me mine," she said.

Mikel moved the telescope, searching for the cluster of stars of the constellation his daughter was named after.

"Sorry, baby. Can't see it this time of year."

"Awww," she protested.

"Let's go in. It's past your bedtime."

Mikel picked her up and carried her to her new bedroom that he'd decorated with the solar system. Glowing plastic stars were scattered over the ceiling.

"I love you, Daddy," she said, snuggling into her blankets as he kissed her forehead.

"I love you too, Lyra."

"More than all the stars?" she asked.

"Of course."

He left her door open a crack and walked to the kitchen. As he started clearing away their dinner plates, his phone rang. Mikel wiped his hands before answering it. "Hey, Dre. What's up?"

"Nothing. Gonna go out and have a drink this weekend. You wanna come?" Andre asked.

"Maybe, but I'm sure Bent would be free if I'm not."

"As much as I hate to admit it, your brother is a chick magnet. I've sworn off female company for good."

Mikel frowned. "Is that even possible? Aren't you getting tired of your hand?"

"Fuck you," Dre snapped.

"No, thanks. I'm good."

"Some friend you are," Dre said.

"You want some friendly advice, Dre? Do you really think staying angry at the whole female population is gonna help you move on?"

"Well, it will make sure I don't end up the fool again. Besides, I'm not avoiding every female. Your sister is a woman, my mother—"

Mikel shook his head. "You know what I mean, dickhead."

Andre blew out a puff of air. "You do you, bro. I'll do me."

"Literally."

"You asshole. Couldn't stop yourself, huh?" Andre laughed. "Thanks for the support, *friend*," Andre said, enunciating the last word.

"Anytime."

Dre ended the call and Mikel went back to putting dinner away.

The picture of Remy on the fridge caught his eye. He inhaled long and deep as memories of the attack came flooding over him. There'd been so much blood. His Dove, covered in red. She'd fought with her last breath to keep their daughter safe. He'd never forget the terror that had seized him when June Sampson had come to that hotel room to tell him that Joe wasn't planning on showing but he knew where Remy had lived. Mikel had raced as fast as he could to her. But he'd been too late.

Car lights lit up the driveway as their SUV pulled in. He dried his hands and went to open the door.

Soft brown eyes, shining with adoration, met his. Love and happiness erupted in his chest, overflowing and drowning him in gratitude. The love of his life walked through the door and wrapped her arms around him. He kissed his wife as she relaxed in his arms, a small baby bump growing between them.

"I missed you," she said.

"I missed you too." He kissed her forehead.

"Is Lyra already asleep?" Remy pulled off her coat and hung it by the door.

"Yeah, but she wouldn't go down without me showing her your star."

She nodded. "Ahh, best wedding present ever. She's your daughter, that's for sure."

He chuckled. "How was work?"

"Great. Jasmine's going to have one hell of an opening feast for her bed-and-breakfast. Poor woman looks like she could use a nap. I told her to come over this weekend and I can watch Zoey for her while she gets some rest."

"It will be good practice for when our son is born." He placed his palm gently on her belly.

"Sure will."

He frowned as more memories came back to him.

"Hey." Remy's hands reached to hold his face. "Where'd you go?"

"I was just thinking about you in the hospital."

She kissed his lips, once, twice. "We're all safe. Lyra's doing great with counseling; she didn't see or hear anything. The baby is growing strong." She shuddered. "And *he's* dead, out of our life forever thanks to Bently."

Mikel swallowed. His brother had been by his side, arriving seconds before the paramedics as they rushed to Remy's aid.

"Thanks to you, my babies are safe," he said.

"I'm sorry for doubting you," she apologized again.

"You had every right. And I should have told you everything from the beginning. There are no words for how happy I am to have you in my life." He pulled her close in a hug.

"Well, you can show me. My feet are killing me and I could use a bath." She smiled.

"What my Dove wants, she gets," he said, picking her up and carrying her towards the stairs to their private bath in their new home. He'd remodeled it himself, making sure to add an extra-large tub with jets.

Soon the room was filled with steam, water droplets clinging to their bare flesh as he massaged every last bit of lingering tension from her body. Candles flickered as their shadows danced. Their bodies slipped and slid in their own hypnotic rhythm as they connected as man and wife. Her heavy breathing and quiet cries for more were a private rhapsody as he thrust inside her. She quaked and trembled as water splashed onto the floor. He kissed the pool of liquid that collected in the hollow of her collarbone.

"I love you," she sighed.

"I love you too." He licked around the shell of her ear before sucking the lobe into his mouth, driving deeper as she dug her nails into his flesh. She was close. She was sitting on top of his hips, her nakedness gloriously illuminated in the mixture of moonlight and candles. The small bulge of her pregnant belly rested on his. She had never been more beautiful. He'd missed it all before, this evolution of his goddess. He'd be there this time for everything.

He wouldn't be like those part-time fathers—he was determined to get up in the middle of the night and help Remy. He'd hold Remy's hand as she birthed this new life into the world. He'd wear their little one in one of those wrap thingies Jasmine carried Zoey in. And he'd be there to support his wife in every way.

He moved his hands over her thighs and the scar that was left behind from the day she'd risked everything. He dug his fingers into her hips, lifting her up and then slamming her back down on him. She gripped the edge of the tub to steady herself as her eyes rolled back in her own pleasure.

"Touch yourself," he commanded. Adoration burned him from the inside out. He was still in awe that this woman, this life, was his. She was breathtaking. Gazing upon her was like staring into the sun. So much light, warmth, and love it was blinding.

She didn't hesitate as she dipped her finger to her slit, swirling as he moved her up and down his length, spearing inside her tight warmth. She cried out, coming all over him as he joined her in the heavens of ecstasy.

He fell more in love with her, fell like the stars they wished on.

The End

Thank you! We hope you enjoyed reading *A Fallen Star*.

Now, turn the page for your sneak peek of Chapter One in the next book, ***Glass Secrets*** (Book 2, featuring Andre and Mia's story).

Or visit the website below to order Book 2 in the Shattered Cove series right now.

WWW.AMKUSI.COM/GLASSSECRETS

SNEAK PEEK OF GLASS SECRETS

CHAPTER 1 - MIA

The thud of her shoes hitting the pavement became hypnotic as Mia worked hard to control her breathing. Birds chirped, and the mist began to clear. The rising sun coated her surroundings in an orange glow. This was the best time of day —when everything was mostly quiet, and she could push her body and expel her fears through her sweat.

Her shoulders ached as she pumped her arms a little harder, a little faster. Perhaps she shouldn't have unpacked all those boxes yesterday. But there was no one else to help her do it. After the movers kindly placed her furniture where she needed it, she'd gotten straight to work unpacking. Busyness helped to keep her from thinking too much. *Because thinking leads to remembering.*

Her legs burned as she rounded the corner onto the street where she now lived. Heavy footfalls echoed behind her.

Dios mío. She was alert, as always—every muscle aware that someone was approaching fast from behind. She turned her face quickly, catching a glimpse of a man getting closer. Her shoulders dropped, tension fading. She recognized him.

How could she not? He was at least six feet, and muscled to perfection. She'd watched as he exited his truck all sexy and focused the night before. He'd pulled off his shirt, his rich brown skin glinting from the sun and sweat.

Her handsome new neighbor spoke. "Passing on your right."

"Good morning." She smiled, but he only increased his speed and sprinted ahead of her. Maybe he hadn't heard her? He had earbuds in. Oh well, at least now she had a better view of that tight backside.

Mia pushed herself the remaining several hundred yards to her new home, then trudged up the stairs and into the house, forcing her lead limbs. She grabbed a glass and pushed it into the door of the fridge dispenser. The icy liquid eased down her throat, cooling her body from the inside out. Her muscles were tired, but endorphins were taking over as she gulped fresh oxygen. Time to stretch.

She picked a yoga mat from one of the packing boxes, and opened the French doors leading to the backyard. Whoever had lived here before had kept the landscaping simple. A few flower bushes and trees created a natural line around the bungalow property. A large rectangular pool was the focal point. Maybe she'd go for a swim after her yoga.

Mia started with some simple moves, bending to her knees as she reached her hands out, and stretching her back in extended puppy pose. Breathing deeply, she inhaled light and exhaled her worries. She was intentional, planning her day, giving herself goals and a to-do list.

As she glided through her poses, the hair on the back of her neck stood up. She was being watched. After one more sun salutation, she glanced around, catching a glimpse of *him* on the second-floor balcony of his house.

His lips flattened and his brow furrowed. He seemed

downright angry and snarling. A flurry of confused butterflies swirled in her belly. She waved, breaking their awkward staring contest, hoping her smile would set him at ease.

He turned quickly, entering his house, seemingly ignoring her. Well, okay then. Who pissed in his cornflakes?

"Sometimes it's the people who deserve kindness the least who need it the most." Her mother's words echoed in her mind. Maybe she should properly introduce herself. Her mamá's recipe for polvorones was irresistible, and something told her she could use the sweet gift as the perfect icebreaker for her grumpy new neighbor.

* * *

After a shower and a quick change into some cutoffs and a faded T-shirt, she pulled her dark brown hair into a ponytail. First on her agenda was coffee, and then groceries.

As she drove along the road of the quiet neighborhood, a feeling of calm settled over her. Kids were laughing and throwing Frisbees or playing catch with their dogs. The houses were all well-kept and lawns neatly manicured. How long had she wished she could live in a place like this? Too bad her mother wasn't there to see she'd actually made it happen.

Mia switched on the radio. A few of the latest hits blasted out as she headed towards town. The woods on her right opened up, and the beautiful coastline was breathtaking. Green-blue waves crashed onto the rocky shore. Mia rolled down the window, inhaling in the salty air. The urge to pull over and dip her toes in the cool water was overwhelming. She slowed as she rounded the corner. A blue car was parked at the edge of the road with smoke billowing out of the propped-open hood. A woman with black hair held a baby and staring off towards the waves.

Mia pulled behind the car and parked before getting out. "Are you alright?"

The woman turned, wiping away fresh tears as her cheeks blushed. "Oh, sorry. Uh . . ." The baby she held started to cry. Her mother shifted to bounce and rock the child.

"Are you alright?" Mia repeated, stepping closer.

"No. I'm sorry. I'm not usually a crier. It's just been a really tough . . . year," she said as if she was trying to remember a time when life wasn't hard. Mia could relate. The baby drifted off to sleep, seemingly calmed by her mother's voice.

"We all have bad days. Can I help? I can give you a ride. I was just on my way into town anyways," Mia offered.

A spark of hope lit the woman's angular eyes. "Would you mind? I don't want to sit around waiting for my brother to find a tow. You can drop me off at my sister-in-law's café. It's right on Main Street."

"Absolutely. I needed some coffee anyways. I'm Mia." She reached out her hand.

"Jasmine, and this is Zoey." The woman shook her hand.

"She's beautiful. How old?" Mia asked as they walked towards their vehicles.

"Almost seven months."

Mia helped secure the car seat, following Jasmine's detailed directions. After Jasmine laid the sleeping baby down and buckled her in, they headed towards town.

"Do you live around here?" Jasmine tucked a black tendril of hair behind her ear.

"Yes, just moved in yesterday."

"Oh, where are you from?"

"California. I needed a change of pace but I wanted to be by the ocean, so New Hampshire it was." Mia gave her the carefully practiced answer that stayed as close to the truth as possible while omitting the important details.

"That's a long way from home. What do you do for work?" Jasmine asked.

"I'm opening a yoga studio."

"Yoga? Sounds interesting, but I don't think it's really my thing."

"Well, when the studio opens, you'll have to come check it out. I'd be happy to teach you. I'd love to have company in the meantime. Free sessions until the studio opens. It's a great way to ground yourself. It's helped me deal with stressful life moments." She hoped she wasn't giving too much of herself away, but this was the reason she taught yoga in the first place.

Jasmine seemed thoughtful. "Maybe."

Mia smiled. She felt a pull towards this woman for some reason. Maybe she and Jasmine had something in common.

"Do you have any family in the area?" Jasmine asked.

"No. It's uh . . . just me."

"Mine are gone too," Jasmine said as their gazes met.

"You said you had a brother?" Mia asked, turning onto Main Street.

Jasmine nodded. "Yeah, two actually. Mikel is married to Remy. She owns the Stardust Café—right here on the left. You can park anywhere. And Bently is the oldest."

Mia did as she directed.

"What about you? Any siblings?" Jasmine asked, unbuckling herself and gathering the diaper bag.

"Nope. Just me."

"I don't know what I'd do without my brothers. Especially Bently, the oldest. He basically raised me, and then he jumped in to help me when I found out I was pregnant."

"Oh. Zoey's dad isn't in the picture?" Mia asked.

Jasmine hesitated and drew in a breath. "No."

There was a story there. Mia reached out her hand instinctively to comfort her. "I was raised by a single mom, and though I always missed my dad, she gave me enough love for the both of them." Mia smiled, trying to lighten the mood. "I liked hearing about you and your family. I'd be happy to be a listening ear if you ever need to talk."

"Let's exchange numbers." Jasmine offered, pulling out her phone.

Mia helped Jasmine carry the car seat into the Stardust Café. The smell of fresh coffee and sugary treats instantly enveloped her. A sign in bold lettering made it clear that all of the offerings were gluten-free. She hoped they didn't taste it.

"Hey, Jasmine. What happened?" a beautiful woman in a flowery sundress asked from behind the counter.

Jasmine nodded for Mia to follow her through the back to the kitchen.

"Long story. Mia here was kind enough to be my heroine. Mia, this is Remy, my sister-in-law."

Remy took baby Zoey from Jasmine and gave her cheek a kiss before she reached out to shake Mia's hand. Mia set the car seat on the floor.

"Mia, it's nice to meet you. Are you new in town?" Remy asked as Zoey wrapped her chubby fist around and pulled one of her braids.

"Yes, I just moved from California."

"Wow. That's quite the change of pace, I'm sure. You couldn't have picked a better town. What do you do for work?" Remy asked.

"She's not going to work at your café, Rem. She's a business owner herself," Jasmine interjected, taking a cookie off the cooling rack.

"Oh, you are? What kind of business?" Remy asked, adjusting Zoey on her other hip.

"I'm opening a yoga studio."

"Good. We need more women in business in this town." Remy smiled.

"Are there many?" Mia asked.

"Besides my café, and Jasmine's bed-and-breakfast, there's the book store, but I can't think of any other businesses owned solely by a woman."

"You own a bed-and-breakfast?" Mia asked Jasmine.

"Yes, The Lighthouse Inn. About two miles down the coast from where you found me stranded." Jasmine turned to Remy. "Doesn't Charli own the bar?"

Remy shook her head. "No, her husband's parents still do, but she basically runs the whole place. I never see Zeke or Claire there anymore."

Jasmine nodded.

Zoey reached for the remaining cookie in her mother's hand.

"She's just like her mommy—a sugar addict." Remy smiled.

"Let's hope that's all she gets from me," Jasmine said, seemingly hiding behind a smile as she handed over a large cookie crumb to her daughter.

Remy's expression morphed into concern. "You're doing an amazing job. She's loved and fed and clothed. What more could a baby want?"

"Mia needs some caffeine," Jasmine said, quickly changing the subject, taking Zoey back in her arms.

"What can I get you?" Remy asked.

"Just a black coffee, with one of your lavender scones," Mia answered.

"Coming right up." Remy walked back out into the main part of the café and started making the coffee.

Jasmine spoke. "I just wanted to thank you again for helping me out today and letting me vent. I'd really love to pay you back in some way. I'm having a barbecue at The Lighthouse Inn this evening. Remy will be there, and my brothers—just a few friends and fellow local business owners getting together to have a drink and some great food. Remy is making dinner. I'd love if you came as my guest."

Mia smiled as her chest tightened. She liked Jasmine, and the woman seemed genuine and friendly. She could use a friend right now—hers were thousands of miles away on the other side of the country.

You have to put yourself out there.

"Sure. That sounds fun. Let me know if I can bring anything."

Remy came back into the kitchen, handing her the coffee and a wax paper bag. Mia wrapped her fingers around the warm paper cup, breathing in the delicious aroma. "Thank you. How much do I owe you?"

Remy shook her head, her braids swaying with the motion. "It's on the house."

"I appreciate it."

"Do you have any family out here?" Remy asked.

Mia sipped the coffee before shaking her head. "No. My mother died last year and my father passed when I was a child."

"Oh, I'm sorry," Remy said.

Mia gave her a polite smile.

"I really hope you'll come tonight," Jasmine said.

Remy glanced at her sister-in-law. "Oh, yes! Please come. I'd love to hear more about your plans for the studio."

"I'll text you the address," Jasmine added.

"Alright. Sure." Mia agreed before saying goodbye and thanking Remy one more time for the coffee. She got into her car and took a bite of the lavender scone. An explosion of flavor filled her mouth. The floral essence of lavender mixed with the flaky sweetness of the scone. Seemed like the gluten-free pastries might just be better than she'd thought, much like the locals in this new town. She smiled and headed towards the grocery store.

* * *

Hours later, Mia placed the last polvorones on the plate and licked her finger clean of the powdered sugar. They were still warm—just the way she liked them. She slipped on a pair of flip-flops and walked over to her neighbor's door and knocked. She waited patiently, nerves filling her belly as she carefully balanced the plate of cookies in her hands. It was important to have a good relationship with your new neighbors—and food was the way to everyone's heart.

The pounding of footsteps came closer. A dark shadow passed behind the thick glass of the door just before it flew open. Her neighbor's confused expression quickly morphed into one of anger.

What the fuck is his problem?

"H-hi. I'm Mia, your new neighbor. I thought I'd introduce myself."

He towered over her, jaw clenched. His hands fisted at his sides as his eyes raked over her body. She was sure that was lust in his dark gaze, but the man also seemed livid just with her presence.

"I brought you some polvorones. You might have heard them called Mexican wedding cookies here."

He stared at the plate, his jaw ticcing. More awkward silence.

"Um . . . did I do something to upset you?" she asked, her patience wearing thin.

Something hesitant flashed in his eyes, but then it was gone. "Stay the fuck away from me," he growled just before slamming the door in her face.

She was too stunned to speak. What a complete asshole. The nerve of this guy. She'd tried to be friendly. No one turned down her mother's recipe.

Oh well, at least now she'd have something to bring to the barbecue. She needed a reminder that there were some people in this town who were decent human beings.

One thing was for sure—her neighbor wasn't one of them. And she'd be damned if she ever tried to be nice to him again. She'd just have to avoid him like the plague, neighbor or not.

To continue reading Andre and Mia's story, visit the website below to get your copy of *Glass Secrets* today.

WWW.AMKUSI.COM/GLASSSECRETS

JOIN OUR NEWSLETTER

The best way to get updates about new releases, sneak peeks, pre-orders, giveaways, and more is by joining our newsletter.

You'll also receive a FREE short novel that's not available on any retailer to read.

Visit the website below to join now.

WWW.AMKUSI.COM/NEWSLETTER

THANK YOU

Thank you for reading *A Fallen Star*. We hope you are emotionally satisfied with Remy and Mikel's love story. If you enjoyed this novel, please consider leaving a review on your favorite retailer and sharing it with your friends and family.

Also, you can start reading the other books in *The Shattered Cove Series* right now!

Andre and Mia in ***Glass Secrets (Book 2)***.

Bently and Belle in ***Defying Gravity (Book 3)***.

Atlas and Jasmine in ***The Lighthouse Inn (Book 4)***.

Finn and Charli in ***His True North (Book 5)***.

Thank you again for reading *A Fallen Star!*

Cheers,

Ash & Marcus.

ABOUT A. M KUSI

A. M. Kusi is the pen name of a wife-and-husband author team, Ash and Marcus Kusi. We enjoy writing romance novels that are inspired by our experiences as an interracial/multicultural couple.

Our novels are about strong women and the sexy heroes they fall in love with, are emotionally satisfying, and always have a happy ending.

Discover more about us at:

WWW.AMKUSI.COM

To receive updates about new releases, sneak peeks, preorders, giveaways, and more, visit the website below to join our newsletter today:

WWW.AMKUSI.COM/NEWSLETTER

After you join the newsletter, we will send you a FREE novella to read.

To contact us, use this email address amkusinovels@gmail.com.

Happy reading!

facebook.com/amkusi

instagram.com/amkusinovels

ALSO BY A. M. KUSI

Glass Secrets

(Shattered Cove Series Book 2)

Defying Gravity

(Shattered Cove Series Book 3)

The Lighthouse Inn

(Shattered Cove Series Book 4)

His True North

(Shattered Cove Series Book 5)

The Orchard Inn (FREE on all retailers)

(Book 1 in The Orchard Inn Romance Series)

Conflict of Interest

(Book 2 in The Orchard Inn Romance Series)

Her Perfect Storm

(Book 3 in The Orchard Inn Romance Series)

For a complete list of all our books, visit:

WWW.AMKUSI.COM/BOOKS